Praise for ANTHONY & KEYES

The Trust

"Science fiction at its best: Wonderful three dimensional, complex heroes fighting a battle in a world where it's almost impossible to figure out what's reality and what's a simulation, and who is friend or foe."

—Reviews by Jessewave

Blue Notes

"…insightful and thoughtful and made me smile most of the way through."

—Musings of a Bookworm

"…a pleasure to read, from start to finish."

—Joyfully Reviewed

"I pretty much loved this whole book!"

—Booked Up

The Melody Thief

"It's a beautiful struggling story that I would definitely recommend!"

—Confessions from Romaholics

"A romance with a very realistic approach, and a beautiful introduction to the world of classical music."

—MM Good Book Reviews

By SHIRA ANTHONY & VENONA KEYES

NOVELS
The Trust

THE BLUE NOTES SERIES
Prelude

By SHIRA ANTHONY

NOVELS
Lighting the Way Home (with EM Lynley)

THE BLUE NOTES SERIES
Blue Notes
The Melody Thief
Aria

NOVELLAS
The Dream of a Thousand Nights

Published by DREAMSPINNER PRESS
http://www.dreamspinnerpress.com

PRELUDE

SHIRA ANTHONY
VENONA KEYES

Dreamspinner Press

Published by
Dreamspinner Press
5032 Capital Circle SW
Ste 2, PMB# 279
Tallahassee, FL 32305-7886
USA
http://www.dreamspinnerpress.com/

Prelude

Cover Art by Catt Ford

ISBN: 978-1-62380-596-8
Digital ISBN: 978-1-62380-597-5

Printed in the United States of America
First Edition
May 2013

To the readers of the Blue Notes series, with many thanks for your continued support and encouragement. To Michael Halfhill, for his friendship and his insight, and to Venona Keyes, for suggesting a story about a conductor and a violinist years ago and for opening my eyes to the possibilities.

—Shira Anthony

To beautiful men of music and adventure everywhere, especially FVK, wherever he may be, and to my wonderful friend, cowriter, and co-conspirator, Shira.

—Venona Keyes

Acknowledgments

THANKS to my amazing beta readers for taking the time out of your busy schedules to help us craft a better story. Thanks also to Kate, for her ideas about synesthesia. Special and heartfelt thanks to Rhys, for sharing a bit of herself with me and for helping me understand the healing power of tattoos. You rock, woman!

—Shira Anthony

CHAPTER

Chicago

Seventeen Years Ago

ALEX BISHOP huddled under the stairs that led up to the ancient Chicago graystone as snow danced and drifted about the deserted street. Even in good weather, there were never many people around this neighborhood. That's how he liked it. More people around meant more adults wondering what he was doing by himself, more adults who might ask questions.

He'd been running for weeks, trying to hide from the police who patrolled the streets. He'd done nothing wrong, but he knew that if they found him they'd take him back into protective custody. He wouldn't go back again. He *couldn't* go back—the bruises from the last beating from the older boys at the group home had just begun to fade. He'd always been a strong fighter, with broad shoulders and powerful arms, but he'd been surprised and outnumbered.

"Fag!" one of the kids had called him before the first blow struck him on the chin. Two other kids had grabbed his arms and restrained him as the largest of the gang punched him in the gut. Over and over.

He didn't care what the other kids called him. He was pretty sure they didn't know he really *was* gay. They called all the misfits at the home that. He also didn't care about the bruises. Bruises healed, given time. But the boys had taken his violin from him, and he'd barely gotten it back in one piece. A small crack now ran from the f-hole on the left side of the instrument toward the fingerboard—a constant reminder of the close call. He wouldn't let them take it from him again. He'd rather freeze to death than risk it.

It hadn't been the first time he'd been the subject of other kids' taunts. He'd been moved from his last foster care placement to the home because he'd been jumped by some of his classmates on his way to school. That particular fight had landed him in the hospital with knife wounds to the chest, and he'd nearly died.

"We'll find a placement for you," his social worker, Tori Flynn, told him when he woke up in intensive care a few days later. But he'd seen it in her eyes—she knew it wasn't going to happen. Nobody was interested in taking in a fifteen-year-old boy, especially one who got into fights as often as he did.

Six months later, he was still in the same group home. So with school out for the Christmas holidays, he'd spent most days at the local public library. Nights, however, were far more challenging and a *lot* colder.

Just six more months. That's all he needed before he might be able to qualify to live as an emancipated teen. He could find an apartment, go to school, and nobody would hunt him down.

A strong gust of wind blew, nearly knocking him off-balance. He shivered and looked down at his frozen feet, his threadbare socks visible through the holes in his ancient basketball shoes. Even here, under the relative shelter of the stairs, Alex knew he wouldn't survive the night. He needed to find somewhere warm to sleep.

He peered out into the blizzard, looking for any sign of movement. The streets were too snow-covered for anyone to venture out in cars, and the neighborhood beat cop was nowhere in sight. Alex stepped out from under the stairs and onto the sidewalk and, slipping and sliding on the icy concrete, ran down the street toward the warehouses that lined the train yard. It would be safe inside one of the vacant warehouses.

Ten minutes later, he was dizzy and frozen to the bone, his torn sweatshirt nearly soaked. Still, he kept going. It wasn't much farther now. Crates lined the sidewalks near the abandoned storage buildings, and he hopped up onto one of the smaller ones, ignoring his numb feet. He reached for the ledge underneath the cracked window.

I have to get inside, he thought with growing desperation as he pushed on the window. It was frozen shut. His head felt thick. His brain refused to cooperate. *I have to get inside.*

With renewed determination, he reached once more for the window and set his foot against the edge of the crate. There were no treads left on his soles; his foot slipped. As he fell, he clutched his backpack in an effort to keep it from flying out of his hands. He landed on his side in the snow. Sharp pain lanced his head as he hit the unyielding metal of a fire hydrant.

The world went dark.

"HEY, wake up!"

Alex looked up into a pair of deep blue eyes and blinked. The girl was tiny, but he guessed she was about his own age. Instinct took over, and he reached for his backpack. It was gone.

"Where is it?" he demanded. His head spun and his hands felt clammy as he began to panic. That backpack was everything—the *only* thing he had left of his mom. He grabbed the girl by the shoulders and shook her in desperation. She pushed him away with surprising strength. Weak from the cold and unprepared, he fell backward onto the hard concrete floor. "What the hell did you do that for?"

Her eyes narrowed. She was pointing a small knife at him. "I don't like being touched. Besides, *you're* the one who grabbed me, remember?" She brushed shoulder-length black hair from her face and he saw something familiar in her expression: fear. He knew only too well what that looked like. She was obviously used to defending herself.

"I… I'm sorry. I don't want to touch you… I mean, I didn't mean to. It's just that…." He saw it now—the ratty backpack sitting just behind her. *Thank God.* He started to shiver.

She eyed him warily, then, apparently deciding he meant her no harm, set the knife down next to her. "Put this on." She handed him a ragged sweatshirt and helped him pull off his soaked one. He did as he was told, although he was uncomfortable with her seeing his bare chest. He'd never gotten used to the lack of privacy at the home.

"Thanks." He hesitated a moment before adding, "Can I have the backpack, please?"

"Sure. No problem." She reached behind her and retrieved the pack, all the while watching him as if she still worried he might hurt her. He couldn't blame her. He was at least twice as large as and stronger than she. He did his best not to look threatening.

"How did you get me inside?" he asked as he rummaged through the backpack. Not that he thought she'd taken anything, but he needed the reassurance that nothing was broken.

"Rolled you onto a piece of cardboard. It slides pretty good on the snow." She looked quite pleased with herself.

"Oh. Thanks. For bringing me in, I mean. I'd probably have frozen out there."

She shrugged.

His stomach growled and his cheeks warmed with embarrassment.

Great.

"When's the last time you ate anything?" She appeared only mildly amused by his reaction, her expression maternal.

He looked away from her—he was damned if he was going to let some girl pretend she was his mother. He'd rather starve.

"Suit yourself," she said with an offended huff. She pulled a stale piece of bread from a paper bag and began to devour it. "I have more," she added, her words just barely comprehensible now that her mouth was full of food. "The clerk at the corner grocery lets me have the bread when it's too old to sell. I have some cheese too. It's a little hard, but...."

He glanced around, trying to ignore the smell of the bread and the queasy feeling in his belly. Through the single high window above them, he could see that the snow was still falling in heavy flakes. They were inside one of the empty warehouses, in a small room that looked as though it had been used as an office years ago. It was lit by a single bare bulb that hung from the ceiling. In the corner was a small pile of blankets and an old milk crate with a tattered photograph on it. The photograph was of a woman who looked very much like his companion—her mother, perhaps?

"You have electricity?"

"Yep. Connected it myself." She flashed him a proud grin. "And I found a heater." She gestured to a battered and rusted space heater in the corner of the room.

His stomach protested once more, louder this time. Without a word, she reached into the bag, pulled out a piece of bread, and offered it to him. This time, he took it and nearly swallowed it whole.

"Hey! Don't eat it too fast," she warned, "or you'll puke your guts all over the floor." He nodded, then slowed down and began to chew more deliberately. "I'm Rachel, by the way." Her eyes shone with bright confidence.

"Alex," he replied, his mouth still full.

"What's in the backpack?" She handed him another piece of bread.

"Nothing." Well, nothing of any real value, or at least nothing of value to anyone but him: a baseball, a threadbare sweater, an extra pair of shoes (nearly as worn as the pair on his feet), a photograph of his mother, and his most prized possession—a battered violin that had once been hers.

He took the second piece of bread from her and chewed it slowly this time. It had been days since he'd eaten anything this substantial, and he wanted it to last. She was right—he felt the familiar nausea that came when food found its way to an empty stomach. He ignored it; it would pass. It always did.

"Are you hiding something in it?"

"No. But there's something important to me in there."

"What?" Her mouth was once again full of bread.

"Nothing."

"Come on. You can tell me. What's inside?"

He took a deep breath. That she hadn't already inspected the contents of the backpack impressed him—most of the other kids he'd met on the street hadn't respected his belongings. It was another thing he hated about living in the home. "A violin," he said at last. "My mother gave it to me before she died. She was a music teacher." He didn't care if she laughed at him.

"A violin? Really? Can you play it?"

"Yeah." He wiped his mouth on the back of his sleeve. She was surprising, this girl. She didn't think his violin was stupid or gay. At least, she didn't seem to.

"Will you play something for me?"

He stared at her, trying to decide if she was serious. Her face was lit with eager interest that seemed genuine. Although it *was* a little strange that she'd asked him to play his violin when she'd just met him. *You'd think she'd want to know more about me first.*

"If you play something for me, I promise I won't tell Family Services you're here," she said. He swallowed hard; the last thing he wanted was for the Department of Children and Family Services to catch up with him. "I'm just kidding," she quickly added, perhaps realizing her mistake. "I won't tell anyone you're here. Besides, Family Services will want to take me back too. No way am I going back to foster care."

His heart still pounding in his chest, he studied her face to see if she was telling the truth. "If I play for you, can I stay here a few days, until the weather is better?"

She smiled. "Deal."

He breathed a sigh of relief, pulled his backpack onto his lap, and unzipped it. He opened the clasps on the battered violin case, then reached inside and withdrew the bow. An audible sigh escaped his lips as he picked up a tiny amber stone and ran it over the hairs spanning the wood. The hairs had once been thick, but years of playing and no money to have the bow rehaired had taken their toll.

"What's that?"

"Rosin," he explained, feeling once more in control of the situation. This was something he knew about. He put the rosin back into the case. "It makes the horsehair sticky so the strings vibrate better."

"*Real* horse hair?" Her eyes were wide.

"Uh-huh."

"That's what they use?"

"Yep."

Her mouth shaped the word "oh" and she watched him with rapt attention as he picked the violin up and held it in his hands, drumming his fingers on the fingerboard to warm them. After a minute or so, he began to tune the strings, two at a time. Finally, he settled the chinrest under his jaw and put bow to string.

And as the snow continued to fall outside, the sounds of Bach and Mozart echoed through the empty warehouse. That night, and every night for the next three years, he played for her before they went to sleep.

CHAPTER  2

Chicago

Present Day

DAVID SOMERS had a headache. He'd hoped it would pass, but it had only gotten worse in the past fifteen minutes. He waited stage left as the orchestra finished tuning.

Deep breath. Focus.

The concertmaster sat back down—the signal for David to walk onto the stage of Orchestra Hall. *His* hall. *His* orchestra. He breathed in slowly before schooling his expression and walking onto the stage, utterly focused. He knew he looked the part of the confident performer: his Armani tux was perfectly pressed, his posture faultless, and his stride confident. The orchestra stood as he entered. The hall, filled to capacity, rang with polite applause.

But David's disinterested poise was merely a sham. He was irritated to the extreme. Only his strong sense of duty had brought him back to the stage tonight for the second half of the program. That, and his modern music series's potential sponsors, who he knew sat in the center box seats—the box that had been owned by Somers Investments for more than sixty years.

He glanced stage left to where the soloist waited to make his entrance. David had seen him for the first time only moments before, and he'd been left with the distinct impression of a street thug. The man was tattooed, for heaven's sake. There was no place for such a thing in the refined world of classical music. True, the soloist wore the traditional tails of an artist making a solo appearance with the Chicago Symphony, one of the finest symphony orchestras in the world. But that was *de rigueur*, expected of him, regardless of his personal tastes. No, it was the telltale ink visible at the other man's throat as he buttoned up his shirt that had taken David by surprise.

"Lastislav Voitavich is ill," his personal assistant, James Roland, had told him as he arrived at the back entrance to Symphony Center that afternoon, "but we've managed to find a replacement."

David hadn't been concerned. Such last-minute substitutions were rare but not unheard of. He knew there were plenty of violinists who would give their eyeteeth to take the stage under his baton and with such a prestigious orchestra. There were few conductors on the classical music scene with his reputation, let alone as young as he.

"Has the replacement performed the piece before?"

"Of course, Maestro," James assured him. "Several times, I'm told."

"That will be sufficient." It would be just that—sufficient—nothing more and nothing less. That was the way with all last-minute substitutions. The evening would not be a memorable one, but David would make sure his audience did not leave disappointed. The orchestra's performance would be outstanding.

"There is one thing you should know, though," James added in a quavering voice. They'd worked together for nearly five years, but David knew he'd never been an easy man to please. Then again, one didn't get a reputation like his by having lax standards.

He glared at James. He didn't appreciate being troubled with such nonsense before a performance—he needed time to prepare, to focus on the music and review the score. "What do you wish to tell me?"

"Th-the... the soloist... he... ah—"

"I don't care *who* he is as long as he can play the Sibelius." David ran a hand through his hair in frustration.

"He… he can, of course." Beads of sweat appeared on James's forehead.

Five minutes before he took the stage for the second half of the concert, when he read through the bio James had handed him, David realized what a mistake he'd made by not pressing the issue further.

It's a concert. Nothing more. There will be time to kowtow in apology to the symphony association tomorrow, if need be. He detested kowtowing, but he also knew he did it well.

David rarely made any sort of public speech, let alone an announcement in the middle of a concert. He despised public speaking, but there was nothing for it—the substitution had been too eleventh hour to print something to add into the programs.

"Good evening," he began with a practiced smile. "There has been a slight change in tonight's program. Our featured soloist, Lastislav Voitavich, has taken ill." There were murmurs from the audience, so David waited until the hall was silent before continuing, "Alexander Bishop has graciously agreed to perform the Sibelius." Instead of voicing their disappointment, the audience applauded with surprising enthusiasm. "Thank you." David was unsure what to make of the response. He nodded stage right. There was renewed applause as the violinist took to the stage.

Alex Bishop. A rock star masquerading as a classical violinist. Tattoos and groupies. David didn't doubt Bishop was *competent*—his assistant was young, not stupid. Still, David loathed this "new breed" of musician who all too often graced the covers of magazines like *Time* and, more recently, *Rolling Stone. Tattoos, indeed.* The term "crossover artist" was a mere marketing tool intended to exploit an artist's good looks and increase sales. He'd heard so-called crossover artists perform before, and he hadn't been impressed.

He signaled for the concertmaster to provide the soloist with an opportunity to tune before turning to face the orchestra, his back to the audience. The Sibelius Violin Concerto was a challenging but not overly taxing piece, and he'd rehearsed his orchestra well. *The orchestra will shine, despite any deficit in the quality of the fiddle playing.* He raised his baton and did his best to ignore the auburn hair tied at the nape of the soloist's neck.

Alex Bishop was attractive enough. Tall and muscular—taller than David himself. David was surprised he noticed, but there was something about Bishop that commanded attention. Still, in spite of his apparent ease in front of the large crowd and his undeniable stage presence, Bishop was no more than a pretender to the world of classical music. *All hype and no substance—a creation of Hollywood agents and a second-rate player, no doubt.*

Bishop glanced over to David, his instrument tucked under his chin. Their eyes met for a brief moment. Bishop's dark-brown eyes simmered with passion and focus. David raised his baton higher, the signal to the orchestra for the downbeat. One deft flick of the baton later, the orchestra began the first measures of the Sibelius Violin Concerto in D Minor.

As a conductor, David had always preferred the less emotional modern repertoire to the sweeping romanticism of Brahms, Mahler, or Sibelius. Tonight's program—and the Sibelius concerto in particular—was a nod to the wealthy patrons who kept the orchestra's finances in the black. Its soaring and plaintive melodies failed to move him, although he knew his audience would respond with enthusiasm. It was a tedious thing, to be required to accommodate the common musical tastes of his benefactors, but David tolerated it, since he'd included a less tonal, more challenging piece later in the symphony's performance schedule.

David glanced over at Bishop. Their eyes met again as Bishop began the first few notes of the solo line and the heady tones of his violin filled the concert hall. With effort, David returned his focus to the score that sat on the podium in front of him. He didn't need to read the music to conduct the piece—he had committed every measure to memory—but he sought the distraction.

He's better than I expected. Far better, really, although David would hardly admit it to himself.

Bishop finished the opening phrase of the movement with obvious ease. David found himself taken aback by the intensity of the other man's playing, as well as the natural musicality and the warm tone he coaxed from the fiddle. The violin Bishop played was serviceable. It was no Stradivarius or Guarneri, but the instrument sounded nearly as resonant as the finest instruments he had heard through the years. "A good instrument can make the performer," his old friend and predecessor, John Fuchs, had once told him. "But without talent, it is only an instrument."

As the evening progressed, Bishop began the second movement: a slow and sensual adagio. Once more, David found himself transported by the artistry with which Bishop conveyed the depth of the composition, and again David found himself struggling to maintain his focus and not lose himself in the music. After the third and final movement, the crowd jumped to its feet. Amidst the enthusiastic applause were resounding calls of "Bravo!" from some of the patrons, including, David noted with pleasure, the two men and one woman seated in the Somers's box.

The audience was satisfied with no fewer than four bows, each time calling back both soloist and conductor to the stage with more cheers and applause. As they walked back and forth across the stage for each bow, David watched with interest, half expecting Bishop to react as a rock star might and toss an article of clothing to his adoring fans. He did nothing of the sort, but bowed with surprising grace and maintained the decorum expected from a soloist performing with a world-renowned symphony orchestra. Rather than basking in the glow of the audience's response, Bishop appeared slightly ill at ease with the adulation, although he smiled personably.

After the final bow, David followed Bishop offstage. He had intended to retreat to his dressing room, but several fans already crowded the wings, blocking the way. Irritated by the lack of security, David attempted to walk around the gathering crowd by taking a path through the wings instead of directly out to the corridor. Several orchestra members milled about, clearly anxious to congratulate Bishop on his performance. Seeing David, they nodded in a formal manner—they had long since learned that he did not wish to be disturbed after a performance. David returned each gesture with a curt nod, sidestepping the approaching fans before slipping out the door and into the hallway.

He closed the door behind him and looked up into a pair of dark eyes. Bishop, it appeared, had also sought to avoid the backstage chaos. He smiled at David. "Maestro," he said. After transferring his violin and bow to his left hand, he offered his right hand to David. The casual warmth of the gesture took David aback—he was used to being the one to initiate such contact with the orchestra's guest artists.

They shook hands in silence. David hesitated a moment before withdrawing his hand and saying, "We appreciate your willingness to fill in at the last minute."

"It was my pleasure," the violinist murmured. He watched David as if unsure what to make of him. "I've played the concerto a few times, although never with such a skillful conductor."

Accustomed to compliments, David was unmoved. "Thank you."

Bishop shifted inelegantly on his feet. "Listen," he said, "we're having a little party at my place. Just a few friends, a couple of beers, that sort of thing. Nothin' fancy. Would you like to join us?"

"I appreciate the invitation, but I'm expected at a donors' party in a few minutes."

"No problem." Bishop smiled and nodded. "I understand."

Was that disappointment David saw in the other man's face? *Unlikely. He's relieved. Besides, can you see yourself at a party with a few friends and a "couple of beers"? He's just trying to be kind.* Then, realizing that his response had been rude, David said, "Perhaps another ti—"

His words were cut short by shouts and giggles as two teenage girls launched themselves at Bishop, nearly knocking his violin from his hand.

David stepped backward to avoid the onslaught and almost collided with a woman with long blond hair who swooped in to protect Bishop from the girls. *The girlfriend, no doubt. Time to leave.* He turned and strode quickly down the hallway to his dressing room, closed the door, and took a deep breath on the other side.

ALEX bent down and caught his instrument before it hit the ground, but when he stood up again, David had vanished. Alex managed a self-conscious smile as another woman planted a wet kiss on his cheek, missing his lips by a hair's breadth.

That was strange. He was sorry to see that David had disappeared. There was something appealing about David Somers, not the least of which was his command of the orchestra and his unique musical voice. Alex had heard David conduct before, of course, but performing under his baton had been a refreshing experience.

"Thanks for the rescue, Mar," he said after he'd signed the girls' programs.

"You looked like you needed it." Marla laughed as the girls headed off toward the exit.

He took his roommate's arm and led her down the hallway to the green room, where he'd left his coat and case. Marla waited as he wiped the rosin from the strings, fingerboard, and bridge of his violin with a small white cloth. Satisfied with his handiwork, he gently laid the instrument in its case, loosened the hair of his bow, and locked it into place in the lid. He clicked the case closed and picked up his coat without a word.

"You're quiet tonight." Marla watched him with obvious interest. "Disappointed with the performance?"

"Nah. It was one of the best concerts I've played."

"Sounded pretty good to me too, but then I'm no musician." She pressed a pensive finger to her lips and, cocking her head to the side, asked, "So, how was he?"

"He?"

"The *maestro*." She laughed. "David Somers. You said it yourself, he's probably the best young conductor on the classical music scene. Did he live up to his reputation?"

"He...." Alex hesitated. He wasn't sure how to describe David. "He's certainly a difficult man to approach. Still...."

Marla's musical laughter filled the room. "I wasn't talking about his *personality*, silly boy, I was talking about his musical ability." She eyed him with suspicion before adding, "But it seems as though he might have made more than just a musical impression on you."

Despite Alex's best efforts, his jaw tightened. "You're playing matchmaker again."

"Can't blame a girl for wanting a Michigan Avenue apartment of her own, can you?"

"You couldn't afford it without a roommate."

She sighed and shook her head. "No, probably not." Alex paid the mortgage and utilities on the condo they shared—he insisted on it now that he was making good money performing. The advance on his last recording hadn't hurt, either.

"Besides," he added with a smile, "I've got a least a few more years' rent to pay you back before we're even."

"Eh, you're right." She waved her hand in the air as she often did when he let her win. "I figure I've got about a year left before I'm out on the street. So how about the maestro?"

"Don't think he's my *type*." Alex emphasized the word and glared at her, shaking his head.

"You never know."

Her expression held an open challenge he chose to ignore. Instead, he opened the door to the green room and picked up the violin case. With her arm firmly wrapped around his waist, they walked back into the crowded hallway. He signed a few more autographs until Marla began to push through the crowd, leading him to the stage door. The fans, assuming Marla was his girlfriend, looked irritated, some openly hostile. He ignored this. He was used to it. Besides, Marla was adept at fending off the women she affectionately called "simpering spineless sluts."

As they walked out of the Adams Street entrance, Alex spotted a limousine waiting a few yards away. The driver held the door open and a lone figure walked quickly over, avoiding any contact with the public. David Somers, dressed in a dark coat with a white scarf flung about his neck, ducked into the limo. As he sat down, he glanced back to where

Alex stood. Their eyes met for an instant before the driver closed the door.

Marla eyed Alex with suspicion.

"What?" He shot her a look of mock irritation.

"Nothing." She grinned at him. "Nothing at all."

They crossed the street and headed the half block to Michigan Avenue for the shortcut through Millennium Park to their apartment.

CHAPTER 3

DAVID stepped out of the limousine and strode up the stairs of the Gold Coast home of Doris Pinchley-Bates, one of the symphony's most generous benefactors. He handed his long coat to the maid, leaving his silk scarf hanging loosely about his neck. Doris met him without delay, wearing a dress far too short for a woman of her age, her platinum-blonde hair trailing down her back. She wore heels so high that she stood nearly as tall as David, who was just shy of six feet, and expensive jewelry adorned her ears, fingers, and wrists. Doris, as John Fuchs wryly noted upon his retirement from the CSO, was a "cross between a whirling dervish and an aging pinup model."

In spite of this (for he agreed with John, at least in principle), David had to admit that Doris was rather pleasant to chat with if one was forced to chat at all. Her knowledge of music was above average, and she openly challenged his programming choices, listening to his opinions with eager enthusiasm even when she disagreed. She had also been instrumental in keeping the CSO in the black, even in times of economic difficulty when other symphonies had struggled to keep their doors open.

"My, my," Doris murmured, taking David's arm as she always did, "but that *was* a delicious concert." She drew out the word "delicious" for effect and flashed him a hungry smile. "Bishop is quite the fiddle player. Attractive too. Speaking of which, where *is* your lovely violinist? I assumed you'd bring him along."

"I honestly hadn't thought of it." Well, he was a conductor, after all. Since when was *he* responsible for guest lists at social functions? If she'd wanted Bishop to attend the party, she could have said something sooner.

"I do hope he'll consider a return engagement, in spite of your poor manners."

"We have no need for another violinist this season," he answered in an attempt to foreclose the discussion, although he doubted this would placate her. When Doris had an idea, it was difficult to dissuade her. Then again, David had to admit Bishop was talented.

"Perhaps *your* needs are different than *ours*," she purred as she shot him an overly bleached smile.

David was used to her open flirtation, and he ignored it with casual aplomb. *Cougar* in any sense of the word was far too tame for Doris. David considered himself fortunate that she'd long since given up on him, although in the ten years following the death of his wife, Doris had attempted to seduce him on at least seven separate occasions. Perhaps she'd finally caught on that he wasn't interested, or perhaps she had decided he wasn't worth the effort. Either way, he'd been relieved to have overcome that particular obstacle to their working relationship.

"I have the name of his agent," she continued when he didn't take the bait.

Agent, indeed. Bishop worked with someone out of Los Angeles. David knew their type: far more interested in image than in real talent. "How fascinating," he said as he snagged a glass of champagne from one of the passing servers.

Doris laughed and guided him over to a cluster of concertgoers from whom she was working to solicit donations for the symphony. David took a deep breath and willed away the tension in his neck. Why were these social functions still such anathema to him?

The well-dressed group consisted of five women who insisted upon kissing David on the cheeks in the manner of the French, and one bored-looking middle-aged man. As expected, the women gushed about the concert and David's conducting before launching into enthusiastic praise of Bishop's performance. From the ravenous looks on the women's faces, David guessed the adulation had less to do with Bishop's musical prowess than his taut body.

"You really *must* bring him back, Maestro," one of the women said with a casual touch to David's arm. "I have never been so moved by a performance before. He literally *oozes* sensuality."

David nodded politely, catching Doris's canny grin and doing his best to ignore it. "I will consider it." For the sake of the symphony's coffers, he might well be persuaded to overlook his personal contempt for all Alex Bishop represented, but he could hardly be expected to do so with enthusiasm.

The party dragged on. He progressed from group to group and conversation to conversation, still sipping his champagne. He'd learned long ago not to drink much in public—it was far easier to handle interactions with other people with a clear head. His late wife had encouraged him to try drinking a bit so he'd "loosen up," as she put it, but it didn't tend to sit well with an anxious, roiling stomach. Helena had been the only person who understood how truly uncomfortable he felt around other people. When he thought of her, the music in his head was both sweet and haunting—a familiar melody that wound itself around his mind and tugged relentlessly at his heart, coaxing him onward and inviting him to open himself to the possibilities.

"Imagine you're in a movie," Helena had told him after one particularly harrowing evening spent hosting Somers Investments clients at his family's estate. "They're the oddball characters and you're the star." She continued to knead away the tension in his neck, the sweet smell of her perfume lulling him into something like a trance. "You don't care what they think, and they think you're the hottest thing since the pet rock."

"Pet rock? What's a pet rock?"

"Or—" She giggled, ignoring him and wrapping her arms around his chest. "—imagine them as one of the characters in *Rocky Horror*."

He'd laughed in spite of himself. She'd once forced him to watch *The Rocky Horror Picture Show*, and although he'd never have admitted it to anyone, he'd found it entertaining.

"More fun than the old underwear trick."

He'd loved that about her, her sense of humor and confidence. She'd become his strength, his "seeing eye dog," as he'd once called her (to more giggles, of course). His guide and confidante. In the end, he'd done a damn good job at fooling everyone but Helena. Even his grandfather hadn't noticed the pathetic, quivering mess of nerves that lurked beneath his confident façade.

As he worked the room, David almost regretted turning down Bishop's invitation to join him and his friends for a few beers. Almost regretted it, for the thought of an informal get-together with friends was terrifying. He'd become adept at persuading prospective donors to part with large sums of money, but in his private life, he was far less successful. The thought of navigating an informal party at Alex Bishop's apartment made him slightly ill.

"Just be yourself," his wife told him, "and you'll be fine." Helena had always been the one to attend to their social calendar, arranging weekends at their lake house with friends and planning vacations in the Caribbean when his busy schedule permitted. After her death, he'd preferred his seclusion and failed to keep up with their friends. He found it far easier to be alone than to be constantly reminded of her absence or his lack of social skills. He couldn't remember the last time he'd gone to a party that was unrelated to his work.

He wished he'd had the presence of mind to invite Bishop to attend the donors' party, as Doris had hoped he might. It would have been a livelier affair with Bishop in attendance, although the outcome would have been the same: his assistant would be contacting Alex Bishop's agent in the morning to arrange for an encore appearance. David knew better than to bite the hands of the people who kept his orchestra solvent, and he knew which battles were not worth fighting.

David's next stop was the cluster of the three VIPs for whom he had arranged seats. Old friends of his grandparents, they had convinced James and Lillian to purchase the Somers Investments box at the CSO more than four decades before. The irony that although James Somers had found it quite appropriate to support the symphony financially, he had never approved of David's career choice, was not lost on David.

"Quite beautifully played, David," Charles Madison said as he shook David's hand. "Your mother would have appreciated the performance."

"I'm sure she would have," Charles's wife, Adele, added sadly.

David wouldn't have known. His mother and father had both died when he was just four years old. He barely remembered either of them.

"You're very kind," David murmured reverently. He offered them a wistful smile, an expression he had mastered through years of his grandfather's tutelage. James Addison Somers IV had been a consummate businessman and patron of the arts, well respected in both.

"Everyone you meet is a potential client," the old man would say. "Every impression you make reflects upon the family name." The prestigious Wall Street investment firm David's great-grandfather had built from the ground up had been everything to James Somers. And when David's parents had died on holiday in Italy, James had just assumed David would take the reins when he grew up.

"Do you want to tell him?" Adele asked her husband. Her excitement was obvious.

"You go ahead, sweetheart. This was your idea." Charles stood a bit straighter and the corners of his mouth edged upward.

"David," Adele said as she took David's right hand in both of hers and looked directly into David's eyes, "Charles and I have decided to sponsor the modern music series next season in your grandfather's memory."

"I'm sure he would have appreciated that, Adele." It was a lie; James Somers had detested modern music. David, however, was more than pleased. This was exactly what he'd hoped for. He wondered whether his grandfather would have appreciated how masterfully he'd played his hand.

BACK in his apartment in the early hours of the next morning, David lay in bed, gazing out the window of his penthouse. The late-autumn sky was dark and lit with stars. As the first hint of sunrise added a touch of pink on the horizon, he finally closed his eyes and fell asleep.

He awoke some time later with a start, covered in sweat, the ache of arousal making his groin pulse. He had a dim recollection of a dream—an image of Alex Bishop. The sound of unfamiliar music faded as his eyes adjusted to the bright morning light. The music was melodic and urgent in its complexity—a counterpoint of bright inquisitiveness woven with a heady romantic tone. Something new and appealing and unlike anything David had ever imagined before.

He took a few deep breaths before glancing at the clock. It was late—after ten o'clock—and he'd been asleep only three hours, but he knew he would not sleep again. Instead, he got out of bed and headed for the shower, unwilling to dignify his physical need with the attention it craved. Once finished with his morning ablutions, he tossed a silk bathrobe over his shoulders and made his way to the kitchen. He would need strong coffee to get through the day's rehearsal schedule without yawning.

He poured hot water over the grounds at the bottom of the french press and set it to steep before retrieving the newspaper from the front door. After tossing the paper onto the counter, he turned to the fine arts section to see if there was a review of the prior evening's concert.

What was that music? He tried to recall the dream as he watched the coffee swirl about, but could remember only bits and pieces of it—random phrases, nothing more.

He wasn't disturbed to imagine music when he thought of Alex Bishop. In David's experience, nearly everything in his life had a certain melody to it, whether it was the memory of an evening spent with Helena at the estate or the view of Lake Michigan from his penthouse apartment. Conflict with his grandfather was as much characterized by music as it was by shouting and pain. Music was part of his life, a sense to be experienced just as the more pedestrian senses of sight and smell. And yet this music was different, somehow. He just couldn't figure out why.

He pushed the plunger to the bottom of the press and poured his coffee. Black was the only way he would drink it today. He needed the clarity of the jolt of caffeine. As he brought the steaming hot liquid to his lips, the phone rang.

"Good morning."

"Doris—" David sighed and looked longingly at his soon-to-be-cold cup of coffee. "—how good to hear your voice."

She laughed. "No doubt you'd been expecting my call. I suppose you also won't be surprised to hear that I've had my people trying to book Alex Bishop for a return engagement."

"Is that so?" He'd figured as much. He cradled the phone against his ear and walked over to the refrigerator to scare up something for breakfast.

"I've gotten nowhere." Her sigh was audible through the speaker. "You can't imagine how disappointed I am."

"Of course," he told her. "But you know how difficult it can be to—"

"Robert and I have left half a dozen messages with Bishop's booking agent and still no return call."

David was tempted to point out that it had been less than twelve hours since Alex Bishop played the last note of the Sibelius the night before, but he held his tongue. "It sounds as though you've done your best, Doris. Perhaps you should wait until tomorrow to try again."

"Seriously, David. You know how difficult it is to book some of these artists. Surely you can appreciate that each day that goes by means we're less likely to get the booking. Why, only last year we lost the opportunity to bring Raimondo Pelli back again."

David managed a quick sip of coffee as she rambled on.

"…and the symphony association just about had a fit."

"Hmm."

"You're not listening, are you? Did you even hear what I said?"

"Yes, Doris, I'm still listening." He swirled the half-empty cup around, barely listening. "Of course, I understand. But there are other violinists who—"

"We can't risk losing Alex Bishop the way we lost signore Pelli."

David repressed a sigh and put his cup of coffee down. On the telephone, Doris was far more exasperating than in person, and lack of sleep was doing nothing to improve his mood.

"David, I need your help with this," she said, sounding nearly as irritated as he felt. "Will you call him? The agent?"

"Doris, you know I don't usually contact agents directly." His stomach lurched. He needed to get her off the phone before the lack of food and caffeine took its toll.

"Just this once. I promise I won't ask you to do this again. But Alex Bishop is—"

This time, it was he who interrupted her. "Doris," he said, "I'll call the agent, if that will satisfy you. But just this once."

Five minutes later, after writing down Kenneth Sykes's name and phone number, he hung up with a sigh. *Damned rock star musicians. Anyone with a modicum of intelligence would jump at a chance to play with the Chicago Symphony—even change his schedule, if need be.* Bishop, apparently, was not just anyone.

David drank the remainder of his coffee and finished the croissant, fruit, and cheese on his plate with resignation. The croissant, which he'd microwaved to warm, was now slightly hard from sitting, the coffee was cold, and the cheese a bit dry. Begrudgingly, he picked up the phone once more and dialed.

"Good morning! Sykes Agency, Tiffany speaking."

"Good morning, Tiffany. This is David Somers. I would like to speak to Kenneth Sykes."

"Kenny's not here," said the girlish voice on the other end of the phone. "I don't expect him in at all today. You see"—she half whispered this as if it were a secret for David's ears alone—"there was this *big* party over at...."

David frowned as the woman droned on. After a full minute had passed, he took a deep breath and interrupted, "Excuse me, *miss*...."

The girl giggled. "Tiffany."

"Tiffany, this is *Maestro* David Somers, Music Director of the Chicago Symphony Orchestra."

"Oh, I'm so sorry. I do go on sometimes, don't I?"

David was tempted to tell her that yes, indeed she *did* go on, but instead said in his commanding professional voice, "I'm trying to reach Mr. Kenneth Sykes. Is this his office?"

"Of course! I'm his assistant, Tiffany" was her gleeful response.

"Tiffany. It's a pleasure to speak with you. Can you please have Mr. Sykes call me back later this morning?"

"Oh, you wouldn't want to talk to him this morning, Mr. Somers." Her voice was suddenly serious. David imagined Sykes was probably sleeping off the big party, and his upper lip curled in disgust. "Can I have him return your call later? Maybe tomorrow?"

David realized he was gripping the phone so tightly that his knuckles had turned white. He took a deep, cleansing breath and in his most patient voice said, "Please tell him that I'd like to speak with him about Alex Bishop."

"Of course, sir." She took his number.

"Thank you, Tiffany."

"You're welcome. Stay warm, Mr. Somers."

Did everyone think Chicago in winter was the Arctic? "I will," he replied, at a loss to come up with any other response.

"Ciao!"

"Good-bye, Tiffany."

David set the phone down with a sigh. There was a reason he had hired a booking agent. No matter. He'd done what he'd promised. And if Alex Bishop never played with the CSO again, that'd be just fine with him.

CHAPTER 4

ALEX glanced over at the clock. It was 5:00 a.m. The autumn sun was still several hours away from making an appearance. The impromptu get-together to celebrate his CSO debut had ended two hours before, after which he and Marla had worked until nearly four o'clock just cleaning up the apartment. He lay in bed for almost an hour more, but in spite of his utter exhaustion, sleep was elusive. He wondered vaguely what the donors' party David mentioned had been like and whether the conductor was long asleep.

Marla's right, you are interested in more than just his music. Face it.

He padded out of his room, snagged the *Chicago Tribune* from outside the front door, then walked to the living room. He opened the paper to the arts section, hoping there would be a review. He was not disappointed. "Hometown Violinist's Last-Minute Engagement a Gem," read the article on the first page of the section.

> *The latest installment of the CSO's "Winter Romance" subscription series, featuring works by Mahler and Sibelius under the masterful leadership of conductor David Somers, was outstanding. In spite of the flawless execution of the Mahler Symphony No. 4 in the first half of the program, it was the surprising performance of renowned crossover violinist Alex Bishop during the*

second half that brought the crowd to its feet. The normally staid audience was wide-awake and entranced by the spell Bishop wove with his technically flawless and sensual execution of the Sibelius Violin Concerto in D Minor. While the orchestra kept up with Bishop technically, they were quickly outplayed, lacking the fire of the multigenre violinist.

He smiled. It had been a memorable evening in more ways than one. He'd been hoping for an opportunity to play with the CSO since he'd heard David Somers conduct several years earlier, but his agent had never been able to manage it. He'd heard that Somers was a bit of a classical purist, and he guessed his forays into jazz and rock hadn't impressed the conductor.

The sun had just begun to rise over Lake Michigan. He looked out the windows to the lake beyond and smiled. He loved this place, with its amazing view.

The battered violin case on the fireplace mantle caught his eye. He walked over and picked it up, then placed it on the glass coffee table by the couch before unfastening the latches and pulling out his old violin. He ran loving fingers over the large crack near the f-hole and thought of Rachel.

They'd lost touch nearly fourteen years before, right after he'd graduated from high school in Chicago and begun his undergraduate work at the New England Conservatory of Music. Last he heard, she'd been adopted by a wealthy New England family and had moved to the Northeast. He'd tried without success to find her on the Internet—he'd never learned the last name of her adoptive family. Eventually, he'd just given up.

He put the violin under his chin. He doubted it could be played anymore, but he hadn't wanted to fix it. It just hadn't seemed right.

Fifteen years before:

"GET up, you big lug!"

"Damn, Rachel! Do you have to be so loud in the morning?" Alex put the pillow over his head and tried to go back to sleep, but she turned him over and shook him.

He rubbed his eyes and scowled at her. Bright morning light poured in through the window of the loft where there were no blinds to contain it. He hated mornings, especially when he'd been up late the night before playing on the busy "L" platform downtown. He'd made about a hundred dollars. Not a bad haul for a Friday night.

"Get your ass out of bed or you're going to be late! Mr. Nelson's waiting, remember? No, of course you don't remember. You never check the calendar, do you?"

"Shit!" Alex shouted when he saw the time on the bedside clock. He bolted out of bed and grabbed a shirt from off a nearby chair with no thought as to how clean it might be. How could he have overslept on such an important day, when his violin teacher had arranged for him to play for some as-yet-unnamed conductor friend of his?

"Take this." She offered him a Pop-Tart. The tempting smell of coffee wafted in from the small kitchen, but he knew he had no time for it this morning. Instead, he grabbed his violin and headed for the door, the pastry in his other hand.

"Thanks!" He stuffed the food in his mouth and scrambled out of the apartment. His breakfast left a trail of crumbs out the doorway. "I'll be back around dinner—I'm working the afternoon shift at the bookstore!"

"Good luck!" she shouted down the hallway after him. "Call me and let me know how it goes!"

He took the steps leading down to the street three at a time. Roger Nelson's studio in Oak Park, on the outskirts of Chicago, was nearly an hour by public transportation. Alex full-out ran the last ten blocks, pushed open the door, and stood in the studio waiting room, panting and covered in sweat.

"You're late," a familiar voice chastised as the studio door opened.

"I... I...," Alex panted, doing his best to catch his breath. "I... overslept. Sorry!"

"The maestro's been waiting for nearly an hour." Roger shook his head and clicked his tongue.

"Sorry," Alex apologized again. "I... was... out late... last night. Forgot... to set... the alarm."

"Playing on the platform again?"

Alex nodded, bent over, beads of sweat dripping from his brow.

"You really need to get some sleep, Alex. One of these days you're going to sleep right through a performance."

"It's all right, Roger," said a voice from inside the large studio room. "Give the kid a break."

Roger shook his head, then gestured Alex inside. "You still awake, old man?"

"I may be looking at retiring in a few years—" The silver-haired man coughed and waved his hand dismissively. "—but I'm not dead."

"Right." Roger Nelson's eyes narrowed as he handed the other man a bottle of water. "You've been smoking again, haven't you?"

"Without your sunny disposition to brighten my days, I need at least one vice to keep me going."

Roger's expression darkened, and Alex wondered whether the two men might be more than just "friends." Not that he and Roger had ever talked about relationships, especially their own, but Alex had always suspected Roger might be gay. He wondered if his teacher suspected the same about him.

"So this is your student, then?" the other man asked.

"Alex Bishop, meet John Fuchs."

Alex's eyes widened with recognition as he reached out to shake John's hand. "It's an honor, Maestro. I apologize for being so late, I—"

"Don't sweat it, son," the conductor of the Chicago Symphony interrupted with a warm smile. "I'm guessing Roger made you wait on at least a few occasions. He's certainly kept me waiting a few times."

This time it was Roger who coughed.

"So I'm told you're interested in NEC." John gestured for Alex to sit down next to him, then motioned for Roger to bring Alex a bottle of water.

"I've always dreamed about going to New England Conservatory." Alex winced inwardly at how young and overly eager he must sound. "I'm just not sure I can afford—"

"If you've got the talent, there are scholarships available." John's expression was both understanding and kind.

Alex accepted a bottle of water from Roger and guzzled nearly half of it. His heart was still racing, but it wasn't from exertion anymore. Talking to John Fuchs made him incredibly nervous. "I… I'm not sure I'm that good."

He silently hoped he could manage to play in front of Fuchs without falling on his face—the man was a legend! He'd listened to the conductor's recordings when his mother was still alive. How old would he be now? Late forties? Fifties? Like most teens, Alex wasn't very good at judging age, and in spite of the white hair, John's face was full of youth. Expressive. Attractive too.

"That's not what I've heard." John shot a wink in Roger's direction. "Your teacher seems to think I'm not wasting my time."

"Maestro Nelson is very kind." Alex's cheeks heated as he gazed with genuine admiration at the man who had guided him for such a long time. Even now, he wasn't very comfortable with compliments, although over the years he'd learned to respond to them with something other than stuttered embarrassment. "He's been teaching me for nearly seven years. He's never charged me for lessons."

"True." Nelson rubbed a hand through his salt-and-pepper hair. "But you've paid your bill by helping me teach the younger students." He turned and winked at Fuchs. "Alex here's quite the charmer. The female students especially enjoy his work."

Alex squirmed in his seat. In all honesty, he loved working with the younger students, but he was more uncomfortable with starry-eyed girls than he was with his teacher's praise.

Perhaps sensing Alex's continued embarrassment, John changed the subject. "So what are you going to play for me today, Alex?"

"The first movement of the Wieniawski violin concerto." Alex was relieved to be moving on from the uncomfortable conversation— playing his fiddle was familiar territory and something he wasn't self-conscious about.

Roger nodded in tacit approval, then walked over to the upright piano pushed up against the studio wall and pulled a piece of dog-eared music from the substantial pile on the piano's stand. The piano bench creaked as he sat down.

"Excellent!" John took a swig of his water and sat at attention. "Although I suppose I'll also have to put up with Roger's less than stellar piano playing, won't I?"

Roger scowled good-naturedly at John as Alex pulled his battered instrument from its case. "Dear, dear," Roger tutted with a quick glance at John. "We really must do something about getting you a new instrument, Alex."

"This one's fine, Maestro." Alex tightened his bow and tucked the violin under his chin.

"No. I really don't think so. The sound has only deteriorated over the years. It's really not suitable for someone the likes of Maestro Fuchs."

Alex stared at Roger in stunned silence. He had no other violin, and he had no money to repair the crack on the top of the old fiddle, let alone buy another instrument. *Why would he bring this up now?* "But, Maestro, I… I…," he stammered, his face hot with shame. He knew the violin was woefully lacking, even though he loved it dearly. He'd asked his social worker about whether there might be money available to buy a new one, but she'd just sighed. He was lucky the state paid for his rent.

John shook his head. "Really, Roger, do you have to be so cruel?"

Alex fought the urge to sink into the floorboards and disappear.

"Put the instrument away, Alex," Roger said.

For a moment, Alex hoped his teacher was joking. But Roger's tone was serious, firm. He took a deep breath and began to pack the violin away. He felt miserable—he'd wanted nothing more than to play for Fuchs. He'd already sent his college application to NEC, and he'd been wondering how he'd come up with the money to fly to Boston or even make an audition tape. "I'm very sorry, Maestro Fuchs. I hope that when I get a better instrument, you'll still be willing to hear me play."

"Roger...." John blew out a breath that sounded like air being released from a steam pipe.

"Oh... all right," snapped Roger. "But I couldn't help it, could I?"

John scowled and shook his head again.

Roger shrugged, then got up from the piano and walked over to the wooden armoire on the opposite side of the room. Without a word, he opened the large doors and pulled something out, then walked silently back over to where Alex was still packing up his ancient violin. "There's no need to postpone the audition, Alex."

"What? Why not? But you said—"

"You have a far more suitable violin to play." Roger pulled a brand-new violin case from behind his back and held it out to Alex.

Alex stared at the case, then back up at Roger, uncomprehending.

"Well? Don't you want to see what's inside?"

"S-sure." Alex gingerly laid the case on the table and popped open the latches to reveal a green crushed velvet lining. Inside were a beautiful violin and not one but two bows. Alex's jaw dropped. One of the bows alone was probably worth more than he earned in an entire year playing for tips.

"My gift to you, Alex Bishop." Roger glanced over to John, the wrinkles around his eyes more pronounced with his broad smile.

"But really, I can't—" Alex could never pay his teacher back for this. It was a gorgeous instrument. Italian, probably nineteenth century.

Alex guessed it sounded as magnificent as it looked. It must have cost a fortune. *Thousands* of dollars. Tens of thousands, even.

"Yes." Roger cut across Alex. "You *can* and you will. But you must promise me one thing first."

"Yes. Of course." Alex was more out of breath at that moment than when he had first arrived at the studio. "Anything."

"Promise me that you'll send me tickets to your Boston Symphony debut," Roger said, deadpan.

"My...?" Alex started. Then his cheeks grew warm. "Sure. You got it."

John smiled. "Perhaps I'll be fortunate enough to conduct."

"Thank you, Maestro Nelson. I... I can't tell you how much this means to me. I've never...." Alex's eyes burned with unshed tears, and he fought back sudden dizziness. It was all so unreal. He tightened his left hand around the neck of the violin to reassure himself that he hadn't imagined the entire thing.

My violin? Alex wanted to tell his teacher he didn't deserve a gift like this. But the call of the instrument—the need to feel it against his neck and under his fingers—was too powerful. He *had* to hear it, to play it, to feel the vibrations against his jaw.

"We're keeping Maestro Fuchs waiting, Alex." Roger appeared a bit uncomfortable with Alex's emotional response. He took his seat once more on the bench, then asked, "Shall we?"

Alex nodded and Roger depressed the A key several times, using the pedal to sustain the pitch as Alex tuned his new violin. Even just tuning the instrument, Alex could feel its warmth. Once more, tears threatened, and Alex struggled to focus and not give in to the strange mixture of excitement and fear. He knew it was insane to play such an important audition on an unfamiliar instrument, and yet he understood that this challenge was somehow part of the audition itself. He wasn't sure he was up to it. But when the piano intoned the opening phrase of the concerto, Alex put bow to string and completely lost himself in the music.

What Alex didn't know then was that John Fuchs had heard him play before. "Roger told me you played on the corner of Congress and Michigan for tips," John told Alex years later. "I didn't believe him when he said you were as good as some of my CSO violinists, so I decided to stop by after a rehearsal. He was right."

Alex made his professional debut under John's baton.

The Present

"UP ALREADY?" Marla yawned and pulled her bathrobe around her as she walked into the living room. She was not an early riser, and she gazed at Alex with a mixture of concern and irritation. Her hair was tied in a ragged ponytail, her face clean of makeup.

Alex thought she looked far more beautiful without what she affectionately referred to as her diva face. He knew better than to tell her that, though. Years of friendship had taught him it was a mistake to challenge her fashion choices. And as she so often pointed out, he'd never looked twice at a woman or taken any interest in women's fashion trends. He, in return, had just joked that he was "a disgrace to stereotypical gay men everywhere," having relied upon her to help him choose nearly every item in his wardrobe, even his tuxes.

"Never went to sleep. Sorry if I woke you." Alex closed the tattered violin case and replaced it on the shelf. She eyed him with suspicion, then shot him a meaningful smirk. "Don't start," he said as he sat down on the leather couch and put his feet on the coffee table.

"I *know* you, Alexander James Bishop." Her eyes twinkled with mischief. "I haven't seen you this distracted since you met Yoshi." The mention of Yoshi's name took him by surprise. He hadn't thought about Yoshi in years. "Yep," she said triumphantly. "Yoshi."

"Not the same." His gaze drifted from the living room to the lake. An airplane was visible on the horizon, but he barely registered it—he was still remembering the warmth of David's hand in his own and the other man's trim body. *A tux never looked so good.*

She plunked herself down next to him on the couch. "I know you, Alex."

He ignored the jab. "I wonder what Yoshi's up to these days."

Yoshi Takamoto. The first man he'd ever loved. *Loved and lost.* They'd spent most of undergraduate and graduate school as a couple, sharing a small two-bedroom apartment off-campus with Marla.

"Last I heard, he was sous chef at a three-star restaurant in Italy." Marla leaned into him so their shoulders touched. "You really should look him up the next time you're playing over there."

"Yeah." But Alex's thoughts had already strayed back to David Somers.

"You're headed to France in a few days, you know. You should look Yoshi up."

He tried to remember the French gig. He knew he was supposed to be playing the Berg this month. Was that in Paris?

"You wouldn't be so shocked about your concert schedule if you actually *looked* at it from time to time."

He laughed and leaned back against the cushions. "That's why I pay you the big bucks. Just tell me what I'm supposed to play and I don't care whether I'm on the L platform or in Timbuktu."

"You really *don't* care, do you?" She poked him with her big toe.

"Nope. I don't care where. I just *play*. You should know that by now. At least I know what I'm playing."

"Well I, for one, enjoy the hotels and the shopping." She pulled her knees up to her chest and hugged them. "So don't go getting any ideas about only playing in the States. I'm looking forward to Paris and Milan."

"As if I'd interfere with your shopping obsession!" He put his arm around her and kissed her cheek.

"A girl's gotta do what a girl's gotta do." She leaned her head on his shoulder and yawned. "Oh, and by the way, Kenny texted me a few minutes ago."

"Yeah? And what does Mr. Personality want?"

"Alex, *stop*." She elbowed him and snorted. "He *is* your agent, you know."

"Must be some lucrative gig, or he wouldn't be texting you at the crack of dawn. What time is it in LA, anyhow? Six in the morning?"

"He probably hasn't gone to bed yet. Sometimes I think I should leave all this"—she gestured around the apartment—"behind and move in with him. At least *he* wouldn't complain about my playing matchmaker."

"Yeah. He'd just try to get you into bed," he said. She glared at him, but he ignored her and continued, "So, what did he want?"

"The Chicago Symphony wants you back again. I guess David Somers was impressed." She watched him for his reaction.

"Like hell. I'm sure it's only the symphony association that's interested in having me back. He didn't look all that impressed."

"What difference does it make?" Her expression was solemn, but he knew she was baiting him.

"None," he lied, knowing she could see right through him. The thought that David Somers might be interested in asking him back was far more important than he was willing to admit.

"Well, it doesn't really matter, anyhow."

"Why's that?"

"Because you're completely booked. That's why."

He did his best not to let his disappointment show. He'd had enough of her teasing for one day. "Have you told Kenny?"

"Yep. Texted him back. I'm sure he'll be getting a call in a few hours, though. I've heard the CSO's booking agent can be quite persistent."

"Let me have that," he said, pulling the phone out of her hand.

Her eyes narrowed and she frowned at him with obvious suspicion. "What are you up to?"

He grinned and said, "You'll see."

Get yr lazy ass out of bed & call CSO back or I'm never going on a date with you, he typed.

Marla grabbed the phone out of his hands just as he pressed the Send key. "Oh!" She grabbed a pillow off the sofa and hit him over the head with it repeatedly. "You are *so* going to pay for that one!"

CHAPTER 5

"MAESTRO Somers," Paulette Pyée said as she leaned forward to kiss David on both cheeks. "I'm so glad you could make it tonight."

"The pleasure is mine, *ma chère*." David handed her his coat, which one of the servers took with a nod. "And I can't thank you enough for offering the studio up as a symphony benefit."

"You know I'd do anything for you, David," she replied. "Besides, I have ulterior motives. I thought I might be able to interest you in another piece for your apartment."

"Perhaps a small painting for the hallway. It's been looking a bit bare." In truth, he wasn't particularly interested in purchasing more art for the penthouse, but Paulette had graciously offered to donate 10 percent of the profits from the open house to the CSO, and he could well afford to purchase something himself.

"We have some fabulous artists showcased," she cooed as she led him over to the bar. "I'm sure we'll find something perfect for you."

"Sazerac," she told the bartender.

"You remembered." David touched her lightly on the forearm and smiled.

"Of course." Slipping into French, she continued, "A good host always remembers a favorite guest's preferences."

"You're too kind."

"For you," she said as she took his arm, "I'd do just about anything. You know how I adored Helena. Now if I could only find you someone who could take care of you as well as she did—"

"Mademoiselle Pyée," one of the gallery assistants interrupted, "I need you to make sure the canapés are all right. They mixed up the order, and it seems they're shrimp instead of scallops."

Paulette shook her head and gave David an apologetic smile. "We'll speak later, David," she told him. "In the meantime, I suggest you start with the red room. There are a few pieces there that might suit your tastes. I'll find you later."

"Of course," David said, silently relieved not to be forced to discuss his personal life. She smiled once more before she left the room.

David sipped his drink. It was quite good, with just a hint of licorice from the absinthe. Leave it to Paulette to make sure the caterer had Sazerac whiskey on hand, with its whisper notes of cinnamon, vanilla, and honey. No doubt she had ordered it with him in mind. He'd make a point to thank her again later.

The gallery was beginning to fill with people. Built on the upper floor of a reclaimed warehouse, it was divided into spacious rooms by walls that reached only to about two-thirds of the way to the high ceilings. The original wooden floors had been sanded but retained their mottled, worn quality, and the outer walls of the freestanding rooms were painted in vibrant hues, in sharp contrast to the ecru walls where the artwork was hung. Benches of brushed aluminum covered in sleek leather were scattered in the middle of the rooms, leaving plenty of space for patrons to mill about.

The red room toward the back of the gallery housed the more unusual pieces, as well as the most expensive. On the way, David greeted a number of symphony benefactors, as well as local celebrities and politicians. Paulette's openings, especially those held in early winter, were always well attended. David had come here first with his wife long before he moved to the area to take the job with the CSO. After her death, he'd tried to avoid the gallery, but he knew he could not: Paulette's regulars were also symphony patrons.

"You will attend the party," he could almost hear his grandfather say when, at fifteen, he'd asked if he could go to the movies with friends instead of yet another party. He had despised the large gatherings held at his grandparents' estate—they were more business than social occasions.

Strange, how he still remembered his mother tucking him into bed on the night of just such a party. He'd been three or four at the time, and he'd wanted to go downstairs to meet the guests. "You really aren't missing anything," Caroline Hayden Somers had told him as she pulled the covers over his shoulders and kissed him on the forehead. "Someday, you'll long for the days when you could run around the gardens or go swimming in the lake." He could still imagine her scent—freesia and lilies—and the softness of her lips pressed to his forehead.

"But I want to go with you," he'd protested.

She'd been right. When he finally was old enough to attend the gala celebrations, he'd quickly realized they were less than satisfying. She, too, disliked parties and was happier to spend time in the tiny rose garden behind the guesthouse. Her sanctuary. Sometimes he wished he had a place he could go where he could just be himself. The closest thing to that garden he'd ever known was the studio in his apartment. Lately, however, he felt none of the peace there that his mother had found among the flowers and trees.

A hand brushed his arm and he pushed the memory away, greeting a symphony patron with his usual polite charm. He stopped several more times to chat with other guests, finally reaching the red room half an hour later.

The room was crowded. Servers circulated with champagne and hors d'oeuvres on silver trays, the scent of expensive perfume mingling with the smell of the food. One of the paintings by the back corner caught his eye, and he moved through the room, making sure to greet some of the guests on his way and thank them for coming out to support the symphony. The painting was rectangular, modern, done in pastels. The description of the piece said it was a depiction of Lake Michigan, although there was little recognizable other than the multicolored hues of the Chicago sunrise. It was more a blur of color, a hint of the original. He stood, staring at it, for several uninterrupted minutes. He decided he would buy it, but not for the hallway, for his practice studio—the place in his home in which he spent most of his waking hours. Inspiration, perhaps, for an as-yet-unwritten composition.

As if. How many times had he hoped for that elusive inspiration? And yet each piece he'd written had been as flat and unremarkable as all the rest. No, his grandfather had been right. Conducting was a far more appropriate career. His overwhelming success was proof enough and his abysmal failures as a composer more so. Still, he'd purchase the painting. It would look lovely hanging over the table near the piano.

Determined to let Paulette know of his interest, he turned to leave the room and nearly walked headlong into another guest.

"Maestro Somers?"

"Mr. Bishop." Alex Bishop was the last person he'd expected to see. He'd spent the better part of three days trying to contact the man's agent and had been left utterly frustrated by the effort.

"Please," Bishop said, offering his hand, "call me Alex."

"Alex."

"May I call you David?" Bishop gripped his hand and flashed him a warm smile.

"Of course." Alex's comfortable familiarity rattled him. Seeing him here, in such an intimate venue, caught David off guard. Not that he'd show it. He was far too well trained in handling just such awkward situations. He'd be pleasant, polite, and then he'd excuse himself to find Paulette.

Alex gestured to the painting David had been admiring. "It's beautiful," he said, turning to face it. David couldn't help but notice that Alex was dressed quite well in a fitted button-down shirt with narrow stripes, a pair of well-tailored wool trousers, and a slim tie. As before, David could see a hint of ink at the other man's throat. For a moment, he found himself wondering what the tattoos looked like without the shirt.

"I'm considering purchasing it." David hadn't intended to admit this.

Alex shifted slightly on his feet and gestured to the small piece of paper that described the painting. "I'm afraid you're too late."

David hadn't seen the silver mark at the bottom. "It's sold," he said, doing his best to mask a frown.

Alex appeared to have guessed at David's disappointment. "Selena has several other pieces in the show. Similar. You should check them out." When David said nothing, Alex continued, "She's a good friend of mine. Just sold several of her paintings to a collector who's commissioned three more. She'll be having her own show here in a few months. Paulette can't stop gushing about her."

Alex knew Paulette? And he knew the artist? "I'll take a look." Then, deciding he was already irritated and had nothing to lose, David added, "And perhaps when you have a chance, you can speak to your"—he tried not to grit his teeth—"agent. Mr. Sykes doesn't appear to be interested in giving me the courtesy of returning my calls." If it had been up to *him*, David wouldn't have called after the first fiasco, but several other association members had called to ask about Alex making a return appearance, and he'd finally given in.

Alex looked genuinely mortified. "I… I'm really sorry about that. Ken is—well, I'm not sure how to put it—a handful? I'll make sure he calls you."

"I'd appreciate that."

"No problem." Alex snagged a champagne flute from a passing server and took a hasty drink. "And if there's anything I can do to accommodate the CSO's schedule, I'd be happy to. I really enjoyed the other night."

David looked down at his drink, then swallowed the remainder faster than he'd meant to. The tension in his neck abated with the alcohol. He couldn't help but think he should leave, maybe find Paulette—anything but stand here trying to converse with Alex. Instead, he did something he hadn't intended. "How was your get-together after the concert?"

Alex appeared buoyed by David's question. "It was great. Low-key. Just a few friends. I'm sure your donors' party was far more interesting. Someone from the symphony association—Doris Pinkley-something, was it?—called my agent to invite me. I didn't get the message until the next day. I'm sorry I missed it."

"Doris Pinchley-Bates. And don't think twice about it. I'm sure if you do perform with the symphony again, she'll make sure you know about her shindig well in advance." Why was he trying to assuage Alex's guilt? Surely he didn't really care that he'd missed the party. And yet there was something about Alex Bishop that made David wonder if he'd underestimated the man yet again.

"Thanks. I try to go to those things." Alex ran a hand through his hair and the corners of his mouth edged upward. "Not that I like them all that much," he added. "But I understand how important they are. I promise I'll make it up to you."

David felt his cheeks warm, but passed it off as just the alcohol and the crowded room. For the first time, he realized Alex was wearing his hair down. Long enough that it skirted his upper back, it fell over his shoulders in a cascade, layers curling just slightly at the ends. A hint of a melody flickered through David's mind, then fled. "I really should be going," he said, deciding it was time to move on, perhaps get another drink.

"I'm sorry." Alex offered him a charming smile. "I've been monopolizing you. This is your fundraiser, after all."

"I don't mind." It was the truth. In fact, he realized he minded Alex's company far less than any of the other guests'. He had almost enjoyed it.

He's right, though. You need to be circulating. He nodded at Alex, who smiled again and turned to leave.

"Mr. Bishop... Alex?"

"Yes?"

David reached into his pocket and handed Alex a business card. "If you don't mind, would you ask Mr. Sykes to call me? It'd go a long way to placating the symphony association if we could schedule you for next season. This is my home number."

Alex took the card and their fingers brushed. "I'll make sure he calls you. And I apologize again for any inconvenience."

"It's not a problem," David heard himself say. What was it about this man that had him forgetting the wasted time spent on the phone? "Enjoy your evening, Alex."

"You too."

"DAVID."

He glanced around the practice studio, his fingers resting lightly on the piano keyboard. He'd been reading through some music for the modern series, trying to decide which piece he'd need to cut to keep the program under two hours, but he'd heard the voice and stopped playing.

"Who's there?" he asked, seeing no one and wondering if his housekeeper had let a guest in without warning him.

"David." The voice was familiar, although for the life of him, he couldn't place it.

He stood up and walked to the door, ready to give Sarah a piece of his mind, but as he reached for the handle, he heard footsteps behind him. Soft. The sound of bare feet on the thick oriental carpet. He turned around.

"What are you doing here?" he demanded, wondering how Alex Bishop had gotten inside without his noticing.

"You wanted me to come." Alex's voice held no anger or surprise, only an enticing warmth that made David struggle to contain his anger at the interruption. Alex was too confident, too friendly.

"I wanted nothing of the sort, Bishop. I'm trying to get some work done. Please leave." He moved toward the piano, but Alex stood directly between him and the instrument.

For the first time, David noticed that it was not just Alex's feet that were bare. He wasn't wearing a shirt. Black ink danced on the smooth skin and muscle, begging to be touched. David's self-control was woefully lacking. He heard the faint sound of music from somewhere nearby as he reached out to touch the satiny skin....

"Mr. Somers? Sir?" Sarah, the housekeeper, stood in the doorway of the rehearsal studio. "I'm so sorry. I didn't mean to wake you."

Damn. He'd been daydreaming. "Please don't apologize." David struggled to hide his discomfort at his obvious lack of self-discipline before raising his eyebrows in a silent question.

"I'm heading out to do some shopping. Is there anything you'd like me to pick up for you?"

"Not that I can think of," he answered. "But thank you for asking."

She nodded, then closed the door, leaving him alone once more.

What on earth was he doing, thinking about Alex? Daydreaming about him, no less? Certainly, the man was attractive enough. Charming, as well.

Exactly what you don't need.

Dating was not only a waste of time, it was an unwelcome distraction from his music. And how long would it take Alex to figure out that David was nothing like his public self?

CHAPTER 6

ALEX looked down at the card in his hand. He'd been sitting on the couch, staring at the damn thing for nearly ten minutes and holding his cell phone in the other hand. He'd even keyed in the number.

What the hell was wrong with him? He'd never hesitated to ask another man out before. He'd done his homework. David Somers had been married, years ago, but Paulette insisted he was gay. Single and gay.

He took a deep breath and tapped the Send button.

"Hello?"

"David? This is Alex Bishop. I hope I'm not catching you at a bad time."

There was a hint of a pause before David spoke. "No. Not at all. What can I do for you, Alex?"

"I thought I'd check to see if Kenny ever got back to your booking folks."

"He did. Thank you. Mr. Sykes said he'd need to check with your manager first. He says she has your calendar."

Alex laughed. "That's a good thing. I have the hardest time keeping up with it. Fortunately, my manager is also my roommate."

"Oh." Alex thought he heard a note of disappointment in David's voice.

"Marla's a smart woman. She knew she couldn't afford a view of Lake Michigan on her own. We share the place."

"I see. I just assumed you were seeing each other when I met her after the concert." David's voice was brighter now. Alex was sure of it. "So do you live near the park?"

"Harbor Point Tower."

"We're neighbors. I'm just down on Lake Shore Drive at Oak Street Beach."

"Really? That's great." Alex leaned back on the couch.

David paused as if unsure how to respond. "I do appreciate your calling," David said, breaking the silence. "I'm glad I was able to make contact with your agent."

"I am too. Listen, David"—Alex hoped he didn't sound as nervous as he felt—"if I'm out of line here, just tell me. I know you gave me your number so I could follow up about the gig. But I was thinking maybe you and I might get together sometime."

"You want to go on a date with me?"

The way David put it so bluntly reminded Alex of how totally unprofessional he had been to ask David out at all. "I... well... yes."

Another pause, this time longer than the last. "That's very kind of you." Another pause. "I don't mean to be rude, but I generally don't date."

Not an out-and-out rejection. Alex heard hesitation in David's voice, but there was something else that convinced Alex David wasn't an entirely lost cause.

"We could just have lunch downtown. Nothing fancy. Just talk." He almost said, *We can hang out*, then thought better of it.

"All right." David still sounded tentative, and Alex hoped he hadn't forced his affirmative. The man was always so polite. "Where were you thinking?"

Alex hadn't thought that far ahead—he'd stalled out at the "do I ask him or not?" part of the equation. "A friend of mine has a new place I've heard is good. Tapas."

"Tapas sounds lovely. We have a guest conductor this weekend, so I have no other engagements on my calendar."

Alex repressed a chuckle, imagining a servant standing at attention as David spoke on the phone, ready to update his busy social calendar. "Let's make it Saturday, then." Saturday was sooner than Sunday.

"Saturday it is. Why don't we meet at Symphony Hall? I have a few administrative matters I need to take care of in the morning. Say, eleven?"

"Eleven would be great."

"See you then."

Alex tapped the phone, leaned back on the sofa and ran a hand through his hair. Something about David made him nervous—something he couldn't quite fathom. Something under the calm and composed exterior. Alex had never met anyone quite like David Somers.

Saturday couldn't come too soon.

CHAPTER 7

ALEX leaned against the doorframe of David's Orchestra Hall office, leather jacket unzipped, a knitted scarf hanging loosely around his neck. "Am I interrupting?"

"Not at all." David looked up at Alex, then back down at the papers spread out in front of him. "Please, come in." He'd just about given up on his work, anyhow. He'd gotten nowhere, mostly because he'd been nervous.

Why had he agreed to see Alex at all? He was baffled that he'd given in so easily when Alex had pressed him about lunch. *No. That's not fair. He just didn't give up as easily as you thought he might.*

Alex settled into one of the chairs in front of David's desk. "Work a lot of weekends?"

"A few." David signed a piece of paper and set it aside. "But I'm finished for the day." He inhaled slowly, doing his best not to reveal his unease. He'd been thinking about Alex since the concert. Dreaming about him.

"Great," Alex said as he popped up from the chair.

The sudden move nearly made David jump. *Where does the man get so much energy?* He covered his reaction by standing up and pulling his jacket and scarf from off the coat-tree. Somehow, it didn't surprise David that Alex was out the door before he'd managed to wrap the scarf around his neck. Rather than irritating, he found Alex's enthusiasm quite charming.

"Where to?" he asked as he caught up with Alex, who was holding the elevator doors open.

"Is Tapas still okay with you?"

"Perfectly all right."

They made their way down Michigan Avenue. The wind was biting, but it didn't deter a group of women from running toward them, laughing and chattering away as they blocked Alex's path. "Are you Alex Bishop?" one of them asked. Her compatriots had pushed her to the front of the group, and her cheeks were bright pink. David suspected it had little to do with the cold weather.

"That's me." Alex offered them a warm smile. This was followed by a round of giggles before one of the women dug what appeared to be a map of downtown Chicago out of her purse and shoved it at Alex.

"Can I have your autograph?" she asked. "Please?" She fished out a pen and handed it to him without waiting for his response.

"Sure. Who would you like me to make it out to?"

David noticed that Alex didn't hesitate as he pulled off his gloves and exposed his fingers to the frigid air. David's hands felt cold in his cashmere-lined gloves, and yet Alex, a man who made his living with his hands, didn't seem to mind.

"Teri," the young woman said with a shy smile.

"Teri," Alex repeated. "With a *y*?"

"No, one *r* and an *i*." She nodded as Alex met her eyes before writing on the map.

One by one, he signed autographs for each of the young women, and with each signature, David admired Alex's comfortable demeanor. With every woman he took the time to ask questions, listen to her answers, and respond. When they left, they were clearly enthralled. Not that David was ever approached by a fan on a Chicago street—he was more than content with his anonymity—but he could not imagine handling such a situation as gracefully.

"Occupational hazard," Alex said as they walked the three more blocks to the restaurant uninterrupted. "Sorry about that." This time,

Alex's smile was for David. David wanted to believe it was warmer, more genuine. Not that he'd ever been a great judge of emotion.

"Not at all," David replied, relieved that with his scarf wrapped about his chin, Alex could not see him swallow hard. What was it about this man that left him feeling so awkward? Certainly he'd met men like Alex before. And yet, as they ducked into the restaurant, David knew he was lying to himself. He had never met anyone like Alex Bishop in his life.

The restaurant was yet another surprise. David had heard of it— trendy and nearly impossible to get a reservation at, even for someone with David's connections. The small table at the back was intimate and out of view of most of the patrons. Given Alex's reception as they walked the scant blocks from Michigan Avenue, David could understand why.

"I'm really sorry about all of that," Alex said after the waitress brought them their drinks and took their orders. He appeared genuinely contrite.

"No need to apologize. Your public truly does seem to adore you."

There was a blush on Alex's cheeks, and David thought he looked supremely uncomfortable with the compliment. "I know you probably won't believe it," Alex said after he'd taken a sip of his beer, "but I hate the attention."

David considered Alex's statement. Normally he wouldn't have believed a word of it, not coming from someone who was so obviously at ease in the limelight. But there was something genuine about Alex. Unpretentious. How had he missed it before? *You missed it because you assumed he's something he's not.* He wondered what else about Alex he'd overlooked.

For the first time that day, David noticed Alex's shirt was unbuttoned to reveal more of the tantalizing ink on his chest. David had always found tattoos base and unappealing. But Alex's fascinated him, much like the plumage of some exotic bird. David was the bird with the dull feathers, watching, transfixed, wanting to touch the tattoos. Wanting to touch Alex….

To his great consternation, David realized he'd been staring. He lifted his drink to cover his slip. Alex, perhaps noticing David's gaze, brushed the open skin at his neck with his fingers.

"So I hear you know my former teacher, Roger Nelson."

David relaxed a bit with the familiar territory. "Roger's an old friend. He and John Fuchs contacted me about moving to Chicago and applying for the music director position when John decided to retire."

"I remember John mentioning it. Said you were living in Milan. 'Hiding out', I think he called it."

"Indeed." David realized he was smiling at the memory. "He and Roger showed up at the villa, bags in hand, and refused to leave until I had submitted my letter of interest to the symphony association."

"Sounds like it worked," Alex replied with a chuckle.

"Not immediately. Roger and John spent several weeks creating mayhem for the staff. Nearly drank half of the wine cellar in the process." David smiled once more and leaned back slightly in his chair. "My housekeeper threatened to quit if they didn't leave. Told me she wasn't cut out for cleaning up after 'rowdy Americans'."

"Rowdy?"

"Have you ever seen John and Roger after a few bottles of wine?" Alex shook his head. "Let's just say that they can be a bit boisterous and leave it at that."

"Are you kidding? Now that you've piqued my curiosity?" Alex leaned forward with one elbow on the table, his chin in his hand. "Do tell."

David laughed outright this time. "The last game of truth or dare they played—mind you, I had gone to bed long before this, but Gianetta told me about it the next morning—John ran across the formal gardens in just his underwear."

"Could have been worse," Alex pointed out.

"Indeed."

"Have you heard from them lately?"

David nodded. "A few months ago, when I was traveling to South America. They've bought a lovely house together in Costa Rica. I spent several nights there. Seems John's finally decided it's time to settle down."

"I'm glad to hear it. I'd always wondered about them."

"John's always been prone to wanderlust," David said as the waitress arrived with a slew of small dishes and set them out on the table. "As Roger explains it, it took nearly two decades for them to admit they had feelings for each other, and another decade for them to act on those feelings."

"I guess some things are just worth the wait." Alex's gaze settled on David, and David schooled his expression to hide his discomfort. For the past half hour, he'd been caught up in their conversation and he hadn't thought much about the effect Alex had on him. Now, however, he was once again self-conscious.

Perhaps sensing this, Alex began to talk about the different dishes, suggesting David start with the spicy *patatas bravas*, then a bit of the *paella risotto* to cool off. Together, they worked through the nine dishes, tasting each and comparing flavors. With each round of tasting, David relaxed a bit more. The wine helped.

After about an hour of comfortable conversation, David finally got up the nerve to bring up the topic that had lingered at the back of his mind since they'd arrived. "Please tell me if it's too personal a topic," he began with some hesitation, "but I have to admit I'm curious. I've never seen tattoos quite like that. What is their origin?"

Perfectly rude, thought David, *and none of your business.* He couldn't believe he'd asked the question. He also couldn't quite fathom Alex's expression—not that he'd ever been very good at reading complicated emotions—but Alex didn't seem angry or disturbed.

"A friend did them for me. His family was Samoan. The style is based on the traditional Pe'a, but it's similar to Hawaiian tattoos."

"I've heard a bit about the Hawaiian tradition," David said.

"They're usually done from the waist down. A rite of passage. I suppose it was for me too." Something in Alex's voice told David there was more to the story, but he knew better than to press the issue. He knew enough Hawaiian culture to understand that each and every mark was literally pounded into the skin of the man receiving them. The pain of the practice was part of the rite, and the tattoo a mark of strength. He wondered if Alex had experienced something similar.

"It's quite mesmerizing." David's face warmed at the admission. "The pattern, I mean." He knew the slip was at least as obvious to Alex, but Alex appeared unfazed.

"Thank you." The corners of Alex's mouth turned upward as he reached for his beer.

A few minutes later, the waitress brought the check, which Alex paid over David's protests. "I was the one who invited you. Remember? Besides, I was thinking of a change in plans. Are you up for a little exploring?"

"I certainly don't mind. Where to?"

"There's an outdoor circus in Millennium Park. I saw a write-up in the paper. We could walk around a bit. There are some Christmas vendors too, so we might even find some gifts while we're at it. Sound all right?"

"Of course." The sun was out and David liked the idea of being outside for a change.

It was a short walk from the restaurant to the park. With the sun, more people had ventured out, and the place bustled with families, children, and couples. Small booths—vendors selling handcrafted gifts and ornaments; food carts; and variations of carnival midway games—lined the walkways of the park. Actors costumed as elves interacted with children, and reindeer roamed about in a pen at one end.

Alex led David down the long walkway past a fire-breather, a sword-swallower, a man dressed as Santa Claus who rode a monocycle, and various other performers. They finally stopped in front of a woman juggling large candy canes. For a few minutes, they simply watched as she threw them up and caught them behind her back, under her knee, and between her legs. Then Alex reached out a hand.

She grinned at him, then tossed him one cane. He tossed it back to her in perfect rhythm with the others, and she continued to toss him one after another as he returned each one. Then she threw him another one, so that he had two canes that he fed into the loop. Finally, she relinquished all of the canes so that Alex juggled all four.

"Very nice." The juggler watched Alex with obvious admiration. "Need a job?"

David stared as Alex tossed the canes back to her. "I'm a little overwhelmed with work as it is." Alex looked over at David and winked.

"Impressive. Where did you learn to juggle?" David asked as they walked on toward the Pritzker Pavilion.

"I had a gym teacher in middle school who taught me the basics. Roger said it was good for my violin playing. Honestly, I don't know if it helped."

"It certainly hasn't hurt." David smiled at Alex as they walked past booths of vendors selling food and crafts.

"Hot dog?" Alex pointed to a cart to their right.

David couldn't remember the last time he'd eaten a hot dog, but after wandering around for the past hour or two, he was hungry again. "Why not?"

David followed Alex's lead as he piled onions, relish, sauerkraut, and mustard on the hot dog. His attempt to eat it without getting it all over himself was only partly successful—he ended up using half a dozen napkins to clean up the mess on his face and hands. Somehow, seeing Alex in the same predicament made him less self-conscious, and he found himself laughing as Alex reached over with another napkin to get a spot he had missed.

"Hot chocolate to wash it down?" Alex gestured to the skating rink entrance. "There's a little concession inside. It's pretty good."

"Sounds wonderful." David meant it too. He was pretty sure the last time he'd had hot chocolate was when he'd gone skiing with Helena, years before.

A few minutes later, they were standing outside the rink, sipping steamy cocoa.

"Hits the spot, doesn't it?" Alex asked. David nodded. "I used to come here to skate, years ago."

David took note of the wistful expression on Alex's face. "When's the last time you skated?"

"I honestly can't remember. Might have been before I left for college."

"Then we should skate." He hadn't meant to offer, but it was obvious to David that Alex wanted to.

"Really?" Alex's eyes were bright with pleasure.

"Really." David repressed a chuckle. There was something endearing, almost childlike, about Alex's response.

"Then let's get some skates." They finished their drinks before heading back inside the rink.

"Skates?" David was momentarily confused.

Alex chuckled. "Yes. They rent skates by the entrance. It's a lot harder to skate in shoes."

David managed a tight smile, realizing how painfully obvious it was that he had never skated in his life. Alex, however, took him by the hand and led him over to the skate rental kiosk. "Two pair. Size ten and half and…."

"Size nine and a half," David finished. Much to his own surprise, he was almost looking forward to trying. Alex's enthusiasm was contagious. "But this one's my treat."

"You got it."

"So how does this work?" David asked after they'd laced up their skates.

"Ever skied?"

"A bit." He had learned to ski as a young boy, and his grandfather had encouraged him even when he grew older. Skiing, James Somers had reasoned, was an activity worthy of the man who would ultimately inherit the Somers family fortune. David always found it ironic that he had met Helena on the ski slope. In this case, as in many others when it came to David, the old man had miscalculated. He hadn't considered that someone he deemed unworthy of his grandson's affections might also ski.

"Same general idea. A lot more slippery."

Alex stood up and offered David his hand. Determined to do this himself, David stood up without Alex's help. He wobbled wildly on the blades of his skates until he reached out and steadied himself on Alex's arm. "I didn't realize how much work it is just to stand in skates."

"You get used to it. Try to balance on the blade so that your ankles don't do all the work for you." David nodded and allowed Alex to help him over to the ice. At the edge, Alex stepped onto the smooth surface and held out his hands. "Ready?"

David took a deep breath. "I'm ready." He took Alex's hands, and Alex pulled him gingerly onto the ice. As Alex moved backward, David followed, doing his best to keep his feet parallel.

"Everything okay?"

David nodded once more, feeling a bit more confident than he had. Not that having his hands in Alex's was particularly good for his concentration. He found it difficult not to watch Alex's fluid movements as he traveled across the rink. *Backward.* He chuckled.

"Something funny?"

"I was reminded of the quote about how Ginger Rogers did everything Fred Astaire did, but backward and in heels." David realized how absurd it was the moment he said it. He was about to apologize, to tell Alex he was far from reminiscent of a Hollywood starlet, but Alex laughed, a deep belly laugh that sent David wobbling. Instinctively, David held Alex's hands tighter.

"I'm flattered," Alex said as he steadied David. "My manager would be thrilled if I paid more attention to her shoes. She tells me I'm a fashion dud."

David's cheeks warmed in spite of the cool air circulating around the rink. "I don't think you'd do well in drag," he heard himself say as he contemplated Alex's broad shoulders. They were a far cry from any woman's.

"Glad to hear it. I'm not sure they make shoes in my size, anyhow." They reached the far side of the rink and Alex asked, "Ready to try a bit on your own?"

David felt more confident than he should, and he answered, "I'm ready."

Alex gave David a quick lesson on skating, including how to stop. "Although sitting down isn't a bad way to stop," he added with a smirk, "if it looks like you're about to collide with something solid."

"Thanks for the encouragement." He could do this. How difficult could it be? With this thought, he released his grip on Alex.

David was a far cry from graceful as he began to move on his own over the slippery ice. Still, mimicking the other skaters' movements and remembering what Alex said about skating being a lot like skiing, David made slow and steady progress around the rink. The muscles in his legs protested until he began to balance on the blades. With each stroke, his confidence grew, and for just a moment, he felt the rush of air by his ears. Then a muscle in his foot cramped, and he winced.

"Take a break?" Alex suggested, no doubt taking pity on David.

David nodded and wobbled over to the wall, then inched his way along it until he reached the exit. A moment later he was seated on a bench, unlacing one skate and flexing his toes to try to work through the cramp.

"Here, let me." There was no time to protest as Alex took David's foot in his hand and massaged it with powerful fingers.

It felt so good that David pretended to watch the skaters behind Alex, afraid Alex would notice his body's visceral reaction to the sensual touch. David fought the urge to close his eyes and moan. "It's better now," he said quickly as he pulled his foot away. "Thank you."

Alex smiled and waited for David to pull the skate back on and lace it. David made a point to avoid Alex's gaze, although he was uncomfortably aware of it nonetheless.

"Good to go?" Alex offered David his arm.

David nodded and leaned on Alex, telling himself that he needed the assistance but knowing what he really needed was to touch Alex again. He forced himself to let go of Alex once he began to glide. Alex skated off a ways, then made a large circle around the rink, stopping to check on David as he flew by.

After a few minutes, David relaxed and ventured a bit farther from the wall. It really was a bit like skiing. Not so difficult. With practice, he might even enjoy skating. Buoyed by his success, he glanced over his shoulder to find Alex. Alex smiled reassuringly at him.

When David focused once more in front of him, a young boy charged by him, less than a foot away. In an effort to avoid a collision, David tried to stop. Which would have been fine, except he hadn't quite regained his balance. Before Alex could reach him, David began a spectacular and thoroughly awkward spin. He teetered on his blades, then promptly fell. On his ass.

"Shit!" David didn't mean to swear. He honestly couldn't remember the last time he'd sworn in public.

Alex was now standing beside him. At least he wasn't laughing. Instead, he offered David a hand up. David noticed that the kid he'd nearly collided with had rejoined several friends. They were watching him.

"I can do it," David said. It was bad enough he'd landed so impressively on his behind. He wasn't going to admit to anyone that he needed help. Eschewing Alex's offer of assistance, he put his hands on the cold ice and tried to get back to his feet. This attempt ended with his falling backward again.

The boys on the other side of the rink laughed and pointed at him. David's gut clenched with a fierce wave of anger and frustration. He grabbed Alex's still waiting hand and, with all the grace of a duck on land, managed to struggle back to standing.

"You okay?" Alex asked after David had regained his balance.

"Fine" was David's terse response. Why on earth had he ever believed this was an acceptable way to pass the afternoon?

"Here, let me help you off the ice." Alex's expression was one of concern and regret.

Rid of his skates a few minutes later, David considered the most polite way to say it was time to go home.

CHAPTER  8

DAVID arrived back at his penthouse apartment around seven. Alone. He wasn't worried that Alex would call him again; he was convinced he'd frightened the man off. *A good thing too. You and he are completely incompatible.*

Sarah offered him some dinner about an hour later. He told her in no uncertain terms that he wasn't interested. Instead, he sat in silence, watching the city lights reflected over the lake.

The date had been an unmitigated disaster. He didn't need anyone to tell him that. His ass still hurt—he was sure the bruises were already blossoming there, rainbow colored. Not to mention his sore ankles and the nasty skate-shaped mark on his thigh from when he'd fallen the second time. He'd draw himself a hot bath, then retreat to his bedroom to lick his wounds.

"YOU'RE back already?" Marla asked as she walked into their apartment, arms full of shopping bags.

"Yes. I'm back already." Alex was in no mood for her teasing tonight, not after blowing things so impressively with David Somers.

"That good, huh?" She dropped the bags by the door and joined him at the kitchen counter.

"It was. Until we went ice-skating."

Her laughter filled the room. "You took David Somers—David la-di-da Somers—*skating*?"

"It was the Millennium Rink. He suggested it. We had a good time at lunch; then we went to the outdoor circus—"

"You went to the circus?"

"Yes, but—"

"And then you went skating? You've really lost your mind." She pulled two bottles of beer from the fridge and gave him one, which he took without protest. "What were you thinking?"

"I obviously wasn't thinking. Go ahead, rub it in."

"I'm sorry, sweetie." She stood behind him and massaged his tense shoulders.

"It was my fault. All of it. But shit, Mar, it was going really well until he slipped and fell on the ice."

"Not the icebreaker you were expecting?"

"Shut up," he grumbled as he took his beer and sucked half of it down without a breath. "I thought it'd be fun. He's a little uptight, and—"

"Just a little?" She laughed again and rubbed his shoulders some more.

"All right. So he's *really* uptight. But lunch at Janey's place was great, and Christmas shopping just seemed so… predictable."

"Predictable and safe."

"Yeah. I know. I was an idiot."

"It's okay," she told him. "There are plenty of other men out there."

"Right." *Just none quite like David Somers.* How could he have fucked things up so royally?

She kissed him on the cheek, then sat down beside him on the other stool. She was waiting for him to say something; he knew her too well. When he didn't immediately offer more, she prodded, "So?"

"So maybe I'll give him a call tomorrow. Apologize. See if he wants to try again. I could offer to take him to brunch."

"Sounds like a great plan. Except that we leave for Paris tomorrow."

"And you were going to tell me when?" He glared at her, even though he knew it was his fault he hadn't bothered to check the calendar.

Marla sighed. "Right about now. I was going to remind you to pack. The dry cleaners delivered your tuxes and a couple of your suits while you were out. I left the itinerary on your dresser. You do know that iPhone of yours is good for more than just listening to music, right? There's a calendar app. Actually, there are about a thousand calendar apps if you don't like the one that comes with the phone. They even remind you when you have an appointment."

"At least I know what I'm playing." Alex finished his beer and stood up.

"The car to O'Hare is coming by just after two thirty to pick us up. And don't forget you go to Milan after that, so be sure to bring both tuxes. You might not have a chance to get them cleaned in between gigs."

"Got it." He waved at her as he headed for his bedroom. He'd pack tomorrow. Tonight, he decided, he'd let himself mope. Of course he'd known David was a long shot. Still, as he lay on his bed and watched the stars come out through his window, he wished he could see David again. He made a mental note to call David before he headed to the airport.

CHAPTER

DAVID closed his eyes and let the hot water run down his face. Steam curled around the room in wisps, fogging up the shower enclosure like a cloud. The rich scent of bergamot soap filled his nostrils and eased the tension in his muscles. He barely registered the classical music over the radio, interspersed with traffic and weather updates. He hadn't slept well the night before; Alex Bishop had haunted his dreams. He couldn't remember anything but that he'd dreamed of him. That, and the vague recollection of the music that seemed to accompany any thought of the man.

It took David several minutes to realize that the music on the shower radio had changed. It was no longer Beethoven filtering through the speaker but an achingly familiar melody. The same melody that had been taunting him—always lingering at the periphery of his senses: the melody from his dreams. Frustrated by the static that obscured the melody, he reached over to turn up the volume.

That's when he caught a whiff of citrus and musk on the moist air. He paused, inhaling deeply, seeking to take in the intoxicating essence that both excited and relaxed him.

"David."

The static began to fade with the voice. David tried to turn around, but two powerful arms encircled his waist, preventing him. His body responded to the contact, his cock beginning to fill.

"What are you doing here?" he demanded.

"Do you hear it, David?" Alex whispered into his ear, ignoring the question.

"Hear it?" David could barely think with Alex's wet skin pressed against his own. Alex was naked too, his erection pressed against David's back. David gasped as Alex's fingers lingered on his nipples, teasing them. He knew he should feel self-conscious—he always did— but he didn't want Alex to stop.

"The music," Alex said. "Don't you remember it?"

"No." He wanted to remember, though. With every fiber of his being, he wanted to hear the music.

"Maybe this will help." Alex rubbed soapy hands in gentle circles over his neck and shoulders, traveling slowly, sensually, down his back, scraping his nails against David's skin. Alex slid his hands past David's waist and onto his buttocks, then caressed his thighs with the same circular pattern.

David keened, as if something deep in his soul were about to ignite. He craved Alex's body as much as he needed to hear the music that was connected to his presence.

"Just let yourself feel, David, and you will understand," Alex coaxed in a deep, throaty voice. That voice was like a siren call— irresistible. David couldn't think.

Alex ghosted a finger down David's spine, then slipped it between the firm globes of his buttocks, pausing for a moment at the sensitive flesh hidden there. The heat of David's arousal was almost more than he could bear. He felt compelled to turn around, to feel Alex's wet skin, to taste the lips he'd dreamed of. His heart beat riotously against his chest, his body defying its master, seeking closer contact with the man whose hands now skated up the sides of his thighs. The music was louder, more insistent than ever, ringing in David's ears.

"Do you understand yet?" Alex dragged wet lips across David's neck, nipping at the skin, licking, sucking. "Do you hear it, David?"

David reached out to touch Alex's skin, wanting to feel the hard muscle beneath, wanting Alex, needing to possess him. "Please," he moaned. "Let me hear it."

David awoke in his bed, alone as always. Nearly morning, judging by the slight hint of pink on the horizon. A vague snippet of music floated through his thoughts: the same music he'd heard in his dreams. He got up and went to his practice studio, knowing he wouldn't sleep until he'd at least attempted to put the music down on paper.

Two hours later he was still seated at the piano, surrounded by small piles of wadded-up, discarded staff paper that littered the floor. For all the mess, he only had ten measures to show for his efforts. He felt the familiar frustration and insecurity threaten. Would he ever be able to compose something as beautiful as the melody he'd heard in the dream?

What melody? It doesn't exist.

Twenty-two years before:

"GRANDFATHER, I took second place in the composition competition at school!"

David had been waiting for his grandfather's return to give him the news, keeping an eager eye out the bay window at the front of the Somers's Connecticut estate for nearly an hour. He'd worked for months to compose the delicate rondo for the contest, never expecting it might be good enough to place—he was a first-year student at the prestigious Fiorello H. LaGuardia High School of Music & Art in Manhattan and one of only two freshmen to enter the competition.

James Somers set down his polished briefcase and contemplated his grandson through heavily lidded eyes. "Second place?"

David's heart sank when he saw the look of disappointment on the old man's features. "The judges said I was the most promising composition student they'd seen in years."

"Then you will just have to prove them correct by taking first place next year, won't you?"

James handed his jacket to the butler without further comment as David, barely fifteen, fought back tears. He knew better than to show his grandfather any weakness; since he'd come to live with his grandfather, he'd been taught not to bring dishonor to the Somers family name. Mastering his emotions, he said, "Yes, sir. I will, sir."

"Good." James began to ascend the marble staircase, his heavy footfalls resonating in the grand foyer.

David waited until his grandfather disappeared upstairs. Head hung low, he walked back to the music room on the far side of the mansion. Determined not to disappoint his grandfather again, he sharpened a few pencils, then sat down at the grand piano and shuffled papers about. He would win next time; he would make *damn* sure of it.

Present Day:

A MUSCLE in David's cheek twitched as he tried to concentrate on the staff paper in front of him. But try as he might, he could not remember the music that had been so vivid in his dream. His housekeeper knocked on the studio door and entered with a tray of food. Silently, she laid it on the table, then smiled at him and left him to his work.

The music seemed so real. If I could only remember….

His phone vibrated in his pocket. He pulled it out and absentmindedly tapped the screen, still thinking about the music.

"Yes?"

"David? Are you all right?" He heard concern in the familiar voice.

"Yes, Rachel. I'm fine."

"You sound terrible."

"It must be the connection" was his terse reply.

"If I'm interrupting, I can call you back later." Rachel sounded disappointed.

"No. I'm sorry. I was working on something and got a bit carried away." He got up from the piano and picked up a half a sandwich, considering whether he really wanted to eat it. "How are you?" He hadn't seen or spoken to her since Thanksgiving at the villa in Milan.

"I've been trying to reach you," she said. "Your housekeeper says she's been giving you my messages. Someone asked me how my brother was the other day, and I realized it had been almost two weeks since I'd heard from you. I finally gave up and called your cell." She sighed audibly. "I'm fine, though. Thanks for asking."

"I'm sorry. I've been a bit... distracted lately." *Had* he been avoiding her calls? There just never seemed to be enough time.

"Distracted? You? About what?"

"Nothing." His answer was too fast, almost defensive. He was certainly not going to tell her about his ill-fated date with Alex. "What's new with you? How's work?"

"Fine. Not much new. But there was something I've been dying to tell you. Terrific news, really."

"News?" With disgust, he looked down at the piles of crumpled music paper on the floor.

"David," she chastised, "you aren't listening to me."

"Sorry." She was right—his mind was not focused on their conversation.

"It's fine. You don't need to apologize. It's just that I saw the review of the Sibelius online, and I tried to call you."

"While the orchestra kept up with Bishop technically, they were quickly outplayed, lacking the fire of the multigenre violinist." He recited the critic's words verbatim—it was times like these that he rued his photographic memory. "I was not entirely pleased with the review."

"No. Knowing you, I'm guessing not."

"So what is this news?" he pressed, annoyed to be reminded yet again of the concert and the young violinist he could not seem to banish from his thoughts.

"The soloist. I *know* him!"

"You...." David's voice trailed off and he rubbed his jaw.

"Alex Bishop." David could hear the excitement in her voice through the phone. "I *know* him. We went to high school together."

David was speechless. His sister *knew* Alex?

"David? Are you still there?"

"Yes," he replied, making sure his tone betrayed no emotion. "I'm still here."

"Well... what did you think of him?"

What did I think of him? An interesting question. He imagined his fingers on Alex's taut skin. His jaw tightened and his face felt hot with embarrassment. *Thank goodness she can't see you.* "He's a fine fiddle player" was his honest if less than forthcoming reply.

"I'm *so* glad. I always thought he was an amazing musician. I've seen his picture a few times in magazines, but I put off trying to contact him. I'm not sure why I hesit—"

"Is there something else you wish to discuss?" he interrupted, ill at ease with the direction the conversation had taken. The last thing he needed was another reason to think about Alex Bishop.

He heard her audible intake of breath and realized he had once again been rude. How was it that he could direct an entire orchestra of musicians and fail so miserably at a simple conversation with his sister?

"No. Nothing else," she said before he could apologize. She paused, then added as if she'd just remembered, "Oh, except that I'm going to be in Europe for work while you're there. Can we meet in Paris?"

"I'd love to see you. I'm staying at the Hotel de Sers."

"Great," she answered, her voice perking up once more. "As soon as I have some definite dates, I'll e-mail you my itinerary."

In spite of himself, he almost smiled. He enjoyed her company— it would do him good to think about something other than his work for a change. Or Alex Bishop, for that matter.

"Take care of yourself. Don't work too hard, okay?"

"I won't." He stared down at his food without seeing it.

"Talk to you later."

"Good-bye, Rachel."

David took a bite of the sandwich he'd been holding, then replaced it on the table. This connection to Alex through his sister felt strange, almost ominous.

He frowned and turned back to his composition. He would not compose any more music tonight, nor any more this week—he was traveling to France in the morning for a stint as guest conductor with the Orchestre de Paris. Inwardly, he knew it was just an excuse. He wouldn't compose anymore not because of his schedule, but because every time he tried, the image of Alex resurfaced and left him more unsettled. The memories of his past failures still seemed so fresh. Alex was simply one more failure to add to David's extensive list.

Abandoning the rest of his food on the table, he stood up and walked over to the window. The sky over the lake was a cold gray and the clouds almost silver. The dissonance of the traffic from North Lake Shore Drive quickly faded, replaced by the faint counterpoint of music. The music in David's mind shimmered much like the waves that danced over the water. Alex's music. Ever beyond his reach.

CHAPTER 10

SALLE PLEYEL, one of Paris's most famous concert halls, was filled with a standing-room-only audience. Pleyel was one of David's favorites for its excellent acoustics as well as its understated modern design. Tonight, less than a week after leaving Chicago, David was not a performer—he had come to hear the final performance of Damien Guest's conducting engagement. Tomorrow, David would conduct the Orchestre de Paris in the first of a week of concerts saluting the great composers of the twentieth century.

David sat by himself in the orchestra section. He glanced down at his program as the lights began to dim. He knew only that the concert was dedicated to his preferred modern music: Symphony No. 5 by Dmitri Shostakovich and Alban Berg's Violin Concerto, a technically challenging piece he hoped to bring to the CSO in a future season.

He closed his program and looked up to see Guest enter stage right to enthusiastic applause. After the orchestra finished tuning, Guest looked to the wings for the soloist who would perform the Berg. David, who had paid little attention to the details of the program, felt a strange mix of excitement and apprehension as he saw Alex take the stage.

The applause crested and died. Alex nodded to Guest, tuned his instrument, and for the next hour held the audience, including David, in rapt attention. The piece was demanding, featuring Berg's signature twelve-tone chromatic scale, but with the more familiar sonata and dance forms. At times, the music was tonal, with a sweet, rising melodic line in the violin, and at others, strange and difficult to grasp. There was no mistaking the technical prowess and fiery musicality of

Alex Bishop's Berg, nor the beauty of his tone, and when the orchestra played the last note of the last movement, the entire audience, including David himself, rose to its feet to applaud. Although the Shostakovich on the second half of the program was superb, it could not top Alex's performance.

David hadn't planned on lingering after the concert, but by the end of the evening, he felt compelled to go backstage and congratulate both men on an outstanding performance. He gave his name to the security guard and strode down the length of the auditorium to the green room, where he shook Guest's hand.

"Good to see you, David. I heard you were in town. What did you think of the concert?" Guest looked genuinely pleased to see him and interested in his response.

"It was impressive. I'm glad I was able to make it."

"It means a lot to hear that, coming from you. But I can't take the credit for the first half of the performance. That would go entirely to Mr. Bishop here." Alex, who had been standing with his back to them, chatting with a few concertgoers, turned around as Guest said, "Alex Bishop, I'd like you to meet my good friend, David Somers."

Alex's face registered momentary surprise as he reached out his hand in greeting. "Maestro Somers and I have met," he said as a hint of a smile played on his lips. "I had the pleasure of filling in on a CSO program recently. It's good to see you again, David."

David found himself hard-pressed to hold their ill-fated date against the man. Alex was, as always, both friendly and warm. David took Alex's hand and shook it firmly.

"That's right," Guest said. "Sibelius, if I'm not mistaken, wasn't it?"

Alex nodded. "So did you enjoy the concert tonight?" Alex asked with an impish grin.

"Yes," David replied, vaguely aware that his hand and Alex's were still touching, "very much so."

Alex seemed to bask in the glow of David's response.

For a moment they just stood there. Then Alex withdrew his hand and smiled again. "It's the first time I've performed the Berg. Been playin' it for years in the studio, but I never felt ready to play it in public. It was always Roger's favorite."

"For good reason, apparently," David replied. "It's almost as though it was written for you."

David was sure he didn't imagine the hint of blush on Alex's cheeks.

"I saw that you're conducting tomorrow night. Shoenberg's Five Pieces for Orchestra. Interesting choice."

"I find it quite thought-provoking. The French are far more receptive to the modern repertoire than the symphony association. Of course, twelve-tone music has been around for more than half a century, so in truth, it's not all that modern anymore."

"It seems to me you've made some progress at the CSO on that score. I saw you've commissioned a few of the works on the schedule this season."

"I didn't realize you were aware of the CSO's schedule."

"Are you kidding?" Alex laughed. "I always know what's happening in my hometown. When I'm not performing, I'm usually in the audience. At least when I'm not holed up in the studio practicing."

David hesitated for a moment, then said, "Thanks for calling. After the ice skating." He didn't add that he'd considered calling Alex back but had lost his nerve.

Alex didn't press him about it but offered him a warm smile that made it clear he wasn't angry David hadn't returned the call.

They continued to talk about the CSO's upcoming season and about Alex's performance schedule, which would take him to Milan in two days. The green room, which had been abuzz with activity, was now quiet but for the two men conversing.

"Monsieur Bishop," a French security guard interrupted in passable English as he peered into the room, "I am sorry to bother you, but we must to lock the hall."

David looked around. The room was completely empty and he hadn't even noticed.

"Not a problem," Alex answered in unaccented French. "Just five more minutes. Sorry for the inconvenience."

The man nodded, and Alex turned his attention back to David.

"You speak French?" David asked. Yet another surprise.

"Yeah," Alex answered with a self-deprecating laugh. He shifted on his feet, appearing a bit uncomfortable. "I found out a few years ago that these ears were good for more than just music. I learn pretty quickly. My Italian's better. My German, not so much."

There was another awkward silence as David tried to decide if he should invite Alex out for drinks. Finally he asked, "Would you like to get a drink? There's a nice bar a few blocks over."

Alex hesitated, and David wondered if he'd misread the other man's interest. "I'm afraid I have plans tonight."

"Oh," David responded, doing his best to mask his disappointment. He hadn't expected Alex to accept—he'd assumed Alex would want nothing to do with him after their disastrous date, anyhow.

"But you could join me," Alex put in. "I mean, it's not a date or anything. I'm just heading over to my hotel to change, then I'm meeting an old friend at a club in the sixteenth arrondissement. It's called Club Jazz. Food's pretty good."

"Thanks for the invitation. I… I'll consider it." David wasn't sure what to make of the invitation. He thought Alex sounded reluctant.

"No problem. I'll be there most of the night. Feel free to stop by."

"Thank you. I may take you up on it." David managed an awkward smile.

Alex gathered his things before they walked out of the green room, past the security guard, and onto the busy rue du Faubourg Saint-Honoré. "It was great seeing you again," Alex said blithely as David hailed a cab. "I hope I'll see you at the club."

TWO hours later, David stood in the doorway of Club Jazz, a large and dimly lit nightclub hidden on a tiny Paris side street. The place was packed, but there was a small unoccupied table in the corner at the far back, away from the stage. He looked around for Alex, but he couldn't make him out in the crowd.

This was a mistake. He sat down and ordered a glass of red wine. He'd never been comfortable in places like this, even less so when he was alone, although he loved the music. He'd loved listening to live music when Helena had been alive. She, as always, had made it easier for him. By her side, he'd felt stronger, more self-assured.

On the small stage, a jazz combo played an eclectic mix of standards and newer music. David sipped his wine, letting it linger on his tongue to get the full measure of it. It was surprisingly high quality for a house wine. The music was even more so. As the sounds of a jazz violin rose over the din of clanking glasses, David's eyes were drawn back to the stage. Alex, dressed in a faded pair of jeans and a dark-blue T-shirt, had joined the trio.

He plays jazz as well? David shouldn't have been surprised, but he'd assumed Alex only played rock.

The crowd applauded at the end of the piece, and someone shouted, "Play some Jean-Luc Ponty!"

Alex said something to the other musicians, then began to play "Enigmatic Ocean," one of the venerable jazz violinist's most popular jazz-rock crossover pieces. Ponty's version was clearly recognizable in Alex's rendition, but Alex's embellishments called to mind the concerto he'd performed only hours before. David couldn't help but smile at the clever reference to Alban Berg in his improvisation.

After Alex had played several more Ponty pieces, someone else shouted, "The Rolling Stones, 'Satisfaction'!" Alex flashed a devilish grin as he launched into a jazzy version of the rock song, replete with complicated riffs and string plucks for effect. David's respect for Alex grew by leaps and bounds as he took in Alex's performance. Alex Bishop was undoubtedly the most natural musician David had ever met.

ALEX scanned the room as he played, looking over to where David sat with a nearly empty glass. Their eyes met for a split second, and he shot David a lopsided smile.

He hadn't expected David would come tonight; he'd assumed his friendly demeanor backstage was offered in politeness. Had Alex done the right thing by inviting David? He hadn't spoken to Yoshi before he'd started playing, and he'd been looking forward to catching up on the years since they'd lost touch. He didn't want to be rude to either man. He should have thought things through, but he'd been too surprised by the realization that David might be willing to take another chance on their relationship to think clearly.

Someone in the crowd shouted, "'Devil Went Down to Georgia', Charlie Daniels Band!" and Alex focused once more on the music. He'd play one more, he decided, before joining David at his table. He'd explain the situation to Yoshi and arrange some time for them to talk before he left for Milan the next day.

"You sure?" he asked in French to the crowd's deafening cheers. "Okay." He winked at one of the band members, who shook his head and laughed. A moment later they were playing the popular country music song as easily as they had played the Rolling Stones.

At the end, the club erupted into cheers and whistles. Alex bowed with a flourish, his face flushed from the effort. Someone shouted, "Encore!" but Alex shook his head.

"Nah," he said in French as he laughed. "Time for me to take a break. I get to have a beer too, you know!" He laid his violin in the case at the back of the stage and latched it shut, then looked up and met David's eyes again. David was smiling.

Alex's heart beat hard against his ribs as he descended the steps from the stage. His excitement had nothing to do with performing and everything to do with David. One of the waitresses walked by and Alex grabbed her arm, whispered something in her ear, and looked over at David. She nodded, and he continued to make his way through the crowd, stopping from time to time as someone slapped him on the back or tapped his shoulder to get his attention.

He was only a few tables away from where David sat when someone shouted, "Alex!" from behind him. He turned around to face a handsome, slightly built Asian man with a small gold hoop in his left ear.

"Yoshi!" Alex exclaimed.

Yoshi threw his arms around Alex, embracing him with enthusiasm and planting kisses on his cheeks.

"Damn, Alex, it's *so* good to see you! I'm glad you tracked me down—it's been way too long."

"Thank Marla. I was still thinking you were in Italy."

"Logan's been on my case to move back to Paris for years," Yoshi explained. "It was his idea to open the club."

"So, where is the love of your life?" Alex asked. "I need to be sure you're not still pining away after losing me."

"Losing you? Yeah. As if. We all know *I* dumped *you*." Yoshi clapped Alex on the back.

"In your dreams, Takamoto."

"Logan!" Yoshi yelled across the room. "Get your designer ass over here!"

Over by the bar, a man with shoulder-length dark hair, dressed in a black skinny suit, looked in their direction. He shook his head, then sauntered over, eyes narrowed. "Not funny," he said as he put his hands on his hips and glared at Yoshi. "I am *not* the kitchen help."

"No, you're certainly *not*, sweetheart." Yoshi encircled his arm around the newcomer's waist. Logan looked at Alex and pursed his lips in tacit approval. "Logan Moore, meet Alex Bishop. Alex, this is my partner, Logan."

Alex thrust his hand out and Logan took it. "So you're Alex?" he said as he batted his eyes to reveal a hint of purple shadow on his lids. Turning back to Yoshi, he added with a leer, "You lied to me, Yoshi.

You're most definitely in the doghouse. He is more than just attractive."

"But not nearly as beautiful as you, Lo," drawled Yoshi before kissing Logan. For his part, Logan flashed Alex a look as if to say, *He hasn't changed at all, has he?*

"Looks like you do a good business," Alex said.

"Better than expected." Yoshi beamed. "It doesn't hurt that word got around that you might be playing here, either."

Alex snorted. "I wonder how they found out." When Yoshi just shrugged, Alex added, "So does this mean you're going to pay me for the gig?"

"Nah. You're too expensive. Besides, why should I pay if I can guilt you into performing?"

"You've done a great job with the place," Alex said as he gestured around them.

"Lo decorated the club. He says he's no good at interior decorating, that he's an 'haute couturier'"—he parodied a French accent—"but I think he's got a pretty good sense of style, don't you?"

"I love it." The place had an exotic, Far Eastern feel to it. Silk tapestries in varying shades of blue and turquoise hung from the walls. The wooden tables and chairs were hand-carved and much like those Alex remembered seeing on a trip to Bali a few years before. "You've got talent, Logan."

Logan's cheeks pinked at the compliment.

"So," Yoshi asked, "where's this friend you mentioned over the phone?"

"Let me get him," Alex replied, realizing he'd nearly forgotten about David in his excitement at seeing Yoshi again. *Hopefully the wine will make up for my lack of manners*, he thought as he turned around to David's table. It was empty.

The waitress came over to the men, carrying a tray with a bottle of 2006 Château Margaux and two glasses. "The man who was sitting there," Alex said in French, pointing to the table, "do you know where he went?"

"He left a few minutes ago, monsieur," she replied.

Alex thanked her, then turned back to Yoshi.

"Everything all right?" Yoshi asked.

"Guys," Alex said, feeling like a jerk but knowing Yoshi would forgive him, "I'm so sorry. Do you mind if we meet tomorrow for lunch instead? There's something I need to do. I promise I'll explain later. It's kind of important."

"Don't sweat it," Yoshi replied. "The club's open for brunch. If you can locate your mystery man, why don't you bring him too? Lo doesn't work weekends, and I'm pretty much done overseeing the kitchen by noon, so you could come by around one if you'd like."

"Thanks, Yosh, I appreciate it. It was great meeting you, Logan. Sorry to beg out so quickly."

"Love doesn't wait," Logan put in as he pulled Yoshi tighter against him.

"Good luck," Yoshi called after Alex. "See you tomorrow."

Alex ran back up the stage steps and grabbed his violin. He reached into his pocket as he walked out of the club, then pulled out his cell phone and tapped one of the presets.

"This better be important, Alex" came Marla's voice through the receiver a few seconds later. "I'm having dinner with Jean-Philippe."

"Jean-Philippe? Who's Jean-Philippe?" Alex strode over to the avenue and flagged down a taxi.

"You don't need to know anything about him." Alex heard the sound of clinking glasses in the background and Marla's throaty giggle. "Just tell me what you want."

"I need to know where David Somers is staying," he said, as if it were the most innocuous thing imaginable.

This time the laughter on the other end of the line was directly into the receiver. "David Somers? What—"

"Don't even go there, Marla," Alex interrupted.

"And how should I know where he is?"

"Because the CSO's been after Kenny for the past few weeks," Alex said, at the end of his patience, "and because David's booking agent sent Kenny his contact information. I know he'd have forwarded it to you."

She huffed into the phone. "Okay, okay." He heard some muffled noises and guessed she was typing something into her iPhone.

"He's at the Hotel de Sers, near the Champs-Elysées," she replied after a moment's pause. "Very nice. Intimate. Perfect rendezvous for—"

"Thanks." He hung up before she could begin another round of questions. She'd be angry with him, but she'd get over it quickly enough. Maybe he'd even throw her a tidbit or two about having spoken to David in the green room after the concert. Or maybe not.

CHAPTER 11

DAVID lay back on the couch in his hotel room, legs stretched out on the cushions, his feet bare. In one hand he swirled a glass half filled with amber liquid—cognac he'd ordered from room service. The small carafe on the table was nearly empty. Even now, he regretted leaving the club without speaking to Alex.

He'd tried to be patient and not give in to the overwhelming urge to leave. For the first time in years, he'd enjoyed being at a club and listening to music. He'd also been looking forward to drinks with Alex after he'd finished performing. But then he'd seen Alex with the man he guessed was the old friend he'd spoken of, and he'd realized he'd imposed on Alex's kindness.

You have no one to blame but yourself. You forced him into a situation where he felt compelled to invite you. The memory of the increasingly vivid dreams in which Alex played a part had somehow emboldened him. He'd given in to his longing to see Alex again and the low-thrumming physical desire that surfaced regularly in his dreams. He'd been selfish. It had been a mistake to take Alex up on his offer.

As the alcohol dulled his sense of guilt, David wondered vaguely what his late wife would have thought of the powerful sexual need he'd repressed for so many years. She'd known he was gay—he'd never hidden that from her. But had she known how much he'd struggled not to give in to the temptations around him even before they married? He was sure she'd guessed at it.

Helena had been an insightful woman. She'd married him knowing that theirs was a marriage of convenience. A marriage that had developed into a deep friendship but nothing more. They'd met as little older than teenagers and she'd agreed to marry him three years later, knowing his sexual orientation. He realized now just how generous she had been, marrying him to protect him from his grandfather.

"I love you," she'd reassured him when he'd ask her why she married him. "Love is about far more than just sex. It's about security, friendship, and happiness. You've given me all of those things, David. I want you to have those things too."

He'd been afraid to love then. And although he knew it was far too soon to call his feelings for Alex Bishop anything approaching love, he was afraid.

He closed his eyes, trying to imagine the music in his dream. Why was it so elusive, like Alex's lips?

ALEX climbed the stairs to the second floor of the hotel, carrying his violin case in his right hand. He took the steps two at a time until he realized he'd look like a complete idiot if he showed up at David's room covered in sweat and gasping for breath.

You're going to look like an idiot anyhow. What had he been thinking? *You weren't thinking at all.*

It had taken a little sweet-talking, but the clerk had recognized him and had traded David's room number for Alex's autograph. Alex reached the door and knocked. He heard soft footfalls and the sound of the latch turning.

"Alex?" David answered the door wearing a pair of black silk pajama pants and a matching bathrobe that hung open to reveal his hard chest and flat abdomen. In the dim light of the hotel room, David Somers looked even more attractive than he had at Salle Pleyel, and Alex's breath caught in his throat. David's dark hair was tousled, and his expression was softer, more inviting. *Sexier than fuck.*

Alex swallowed hard and did his best to maintain his composure. "David. I hope I didn't wake you. I realize it's getting late...." He gripped the handle of his violin case so tightly he was sure his knuckles were turning white.

"Not at all. Please, come in." David motioned him into the sitting room and closed the door behind him.

The faint smell of alcohol hung on the air, mingling with the scent of David's aftershave. Alex felt the heat of his arousal and shifted the violin case in front of him to cover it, trying not to stare at David's enticing chest.

"So, Alex. What can I do for you?" David closed the bathrobe and tied it shut.

Alex breathed an inner sigh of relief—it was hard to think clearly with that smooth skin within his reach. "I hope I didn't wake you." He'd said that before, hadn't he? He'd never been insecure, but around David he felt like a geeky kid. "I saw you at the club tonight. You left before I had a chance to offer you a drink." He searched David's face for an inkling of understanding but found nothing in the controlled expression there.

Why did I come here again? As usual, he hadn't thought it through. But there'd been something in David's face, back at the club, that left Alex feeling as though he *needed* to come.

"Look," Alex said when David didn't speak, "I can see you're ready for bed. I should probably get going." He turned back toward the door.

"Stay."

Alex turned and stared at David, unsure how to respond. It had sounded almost like a command.

"Please," David added with a gesture to the sofa and something approximating a smile. "Would you like some cognac?"

"That would be great." Alex put the violin down and took a seat. *Is he just as nervous as I am?* Alex hadn't considered the possibility before. David always seemed so confident and in control. Had he missed something?

David raised the carafe, filled one of the empty glasses, and handed it to Alex. The silence weighed heavily between them.

"You left before I could introduce you to my friends."

"To be honest, I was tired. You seemed preoccupied, and I needed to get back." David took a seat in the chair across from the couch, the coffee table between them.

"About that," Alex said. "I'm sorry. It wasn't fair of me to invite you, knowing that I couldn't devote my full attention to you. I'm sor—"

"You needn't apologize. I simply did not want to be in your way."

Alex laughed softly and shook his head. "You wouldn't have been. Yoshi and I've known each other since college." He wasn't sure why he felt compelled to explain. "He opened the club last year. He always wanted a place where he could show off his culinary skills and feed his need for music." Alex chuckled.

"What's so funny?"

"Yoshi couldn't carry a tune in a bucket, if he could find a tune to carry. And I can't be trusted with anything more than boiling water. I guess things haven't changed all that much."

"Cooking is a little like music." David gazed down at his glass. "It takes talent and a great deal of practice."

"Do you cook?"

"A bit."

Alex guessed David was downplaying his ability, and made a mental note to himself to finagle a dinner invitation to David's.

"More cognac?" David lifted the bottle and smiled.

"Sure. It's very good. Thanks."

"It's one of the reasons I like this hotel. They keep a bottle or two of my favorites on hand."

"I'd never tasted cognac until I started performing in Europe." Alex brought the refilled glass to his nose, swirled it about, and inhaled. "My manager, Marla, gave me a crash course on wine and liquor. I think I'm spoiled for life." He thought wistfully of the expensive bottle of Margaux he had left with Yoshi and Logan back at the club. *Some other time, maybe.*

This time, the silence was more companionable. Alex finished his drink and set his glass on the table. "So when do you head back to the States?"

"In eight days. Before Christmas."

"I hope we can see each other then." He wanted to invite David to brunch the next day, but he knew it would be a mistake, just as tonight had been. They needed time alone, not with Yoshi and Logan. He wouldn't rush things, and he wouldn't screw things up again. Not if he could help it. He smiled before adding, "And I promise no ice-skating this time."

"Perhaps" was all David said.

Alex knew better than to push the issue—whatever David Somers was, he was not someone who acted on impulse.

Alex stood up and retrieved his violin. "Thanks for the drink. I really should be going, and I'm sure you need your rest before the concert."

David stood politely and followed Alex, as if unsure of what to say. "I…," David began as Alex reached to open the door.

Their faces were inches away from each other. Alex saw obvious hunger in David's dark-blue eyes, a hunger that mirrored his own. He wanted to kiss David, to touch his face and claim his lips. And for just a moment, he was sure David wanted it too. But then the moment passed. "Good night, David."

"Good night."

DAVID watched Alex walk briskly down the hallway toward the stairs. He shut the door, picked up his half-empty glass, and brought it to his lips. For a moment, he had thought—no, he had *hoped*—Alex was going to kiss him.

There was nothing stopping you from taking the lead, was there? He took a deep breath and finished the rest of the alcohol with a quick glance at the place where Alex had sat.

Yes, he thought with determination, Alex Bishop was a man with whom he wanted to get better acquainted. *Much better.*

CHAPTER *12*

DAVID slept fitfully that night, and if he dreamed, he didn't remember it when he awoke. By ten o'clock, he was seated behind a piano in one of the practice rooms at the Salle Pleyel. Playing through music on the day of a performance helped keep his instincts sharp. Today, he had chosen to play through some of the pieces that made up Chopin's Opus 25 Études—romantic, heady music better suited to a temperament such as Alex's than his more self-possessed nature.

Alex. It was impossible to deny that the choice of Chopin was related to the brief dreamlike encounter of the previous evening and the near kiss that had left David craving satisfaction. It irked him that anyone could throw him so out of kilter, let alone a former street kid with shocking tattoos. And still he wanted to see Alex again. He was at a loss to explain it.

"Am I interrupting?" said a voice from the doorway to the practice room.

"Rachel?" David stood, dumbfounded to see his sister leaning on the doorjamb. "I didn't expect to see you in Paris."

She sighed melodramatically. "You really don't remember, do you?" When he looked at her in confusion, she said, "I told you I was going to be in Europe. That I was going to meet you in Paris, remember?"

David had a vague recollection of the conversation. "Right. Sorry."

"Still happy to see me?" She walked inside and stood on tiptoes to kiss him on his cheek.

"Always." He'd missed her. *It's been far too long.* "How long are you staying?"

"I'm headed to Milan in three days, but I took a few personal days so I could spend some time with you."

"I'll call ahead and let the staff at the villa know you're coming."

"I've got a hotel in the city this time, so don't bother. I'm meeting an old friend. I've also got dinner plans at Antonio's. He was the one who told me you were performing in Paris."

"No attorney-client confidentiality?" David laughed and shook his head in mock irritation. Antonio Bianchi was a good friend and the lawyer who represented David in negotiations of his European contracts.

"If I didn't know better, I'd think you were trying to hide from me, David," she teased.

David chuckled. "I have been a bit busier lately than usual."

"'Distracted', I think you called it."

She was right. He had called it that, and he knew the reason for it, although he wasn't going to share that with her. "So how are Antonio and his son?" he asked, changing the topic.

She cocked her head and narrowed her eyes. "I know you're changing the subject. You know I won't let go of it that easily," she warned. "But for now, I'll let it slide.

"They're fine. Tonino says Massi's talking up a storm and getting into everything. Apparently, that's what two-year-olds do."

"A two-year-old is a good distraction for him," David said.

Rachel's eyes widened in obvious surprise.

"I may know nothing about children, but it hasn't been that long since Helena died that I can't remember the need to focus on something other than the loss."

Rachel's eyes filled with tears as she laid her hand on his arm. "I know. I miss her too."

"So how about some lunch?" David again steered the conversation away from a difficult topic. "I have nearly four hours before I need to be back for the performance this afternoon."

"That would be great," she said as he gathered his music and tucked it back into his portfolio.

David allowed Rachel to lead him out of the building and onto the Paris street. For a moment, he imagined the hotheaded teenager she'd been when Helena first brought her to live with them at the estate. Bright, full of energy and promise. He still remembered Helena and Rachel giving Cook the night off and making chocolate chip pancakes for dinner, or the time he'd watched Helena paint Rachel's toenails bright blue.

At first, David thought taking Rachel in was a bad idea, not only because his grandfather objected to treating a former street kid as one of the family, but also because he himself had been jealous of Helena's attachment to Rachel. His fear that Rachel would interfere with his marriage was more quickly put to rest than the old man's ambivalence—David realized almost immediately that there was enough room in Helena's heart for them both. His grandfather never understood how fortunate they were.

David wondered if Helena hadn't deliberately brought Rachel into their lives because she realized she might not always be at his side. Helena's health had never been good. She'd suffered from bouts of unexplained illness for years, and the doctors had been unable to determine the cause. Chronic fatigue, they'd said with that look David knew meant they believed it was all in Helena's mind. And yet only a few years later, she was dead of cancer. He wasn't sure what he would have done without Rachel to help him through it. Helena would be proud to see the successful and loving young woman Rachel had become. Prouder still to know that at her core, Rachel hadn't changed.

The honk of a taxi brought David back to himself. "I really am glad to see you," he told her as they walked side by side.

She smiled and took his arm, then hugged him without missing a step. "I know, David," she said. "I know."

CHAPTER 13

FOUR days after leaving Paris, Alex walked off the stage at the Teatro alla Scala, his violin safely tucked under his right arm. It felt good to perform again. The three days of rehearsals had done much to improve his mood after David's lukewarm good-bye in Paris. *At least he didn't brush you off outright*, he thought as he greeted some of the orchestra members who stopped to congratulate him. He'd call David when he returned home. He wasn't sure what to make of David's mixed signals, but he wasn't about to write him off either.

Never one to sulk, Alex had taken to walking the city, sometimes accompanied by Marla. She dragged him shopping and forced him to buy several new suits and a tuxedo for afternoon concerts. If she suspected anything of what had happened with David, she kept it to herself.

"Great job, as always," she told him when she met him in the hallway behind the stage. She had, as she often did, watched the performance from the wings. He knew it made her too nervous to sit out in the audience. He didn't care where she was; he was just happy to have her there.

"Thanks, Mar."

"I've got a surprise for you." She took him by the arm and led him toward the green room.

"More clothing? I can't wait."

"Nope," she replied as she licked her lips. "Something even better than Dolce & Gabbana."

"I didn't think that was possible."

"There *are* a few things better than designer clothing. Not many, but a few." She winked at him and bit her lower lip suggestively.

"Are you trying to make me blush? Because you know it won't work."

"I can try, can't I?"

She opened the door to the green room and his jaw dropped.

"R-Rachel?" he stammered as he saw the tiny brunette standing in the room. She was very much as he remembered her, although she wore her hair in a short pixie cut and sported just a hint of makeup. She wore a deep-blue vintage dress of airy chiffon—it reminded Alex of some of the photographs he had seen of Jackie Kennedy.

Her eyes lit up when she saw him. "Alex!" she exclaimed as she ran into his arms. He swung her about like a child; he couldn't remember having ever been so happy to see someone in his life.

"*You're* the surprise?"

She smiled as he put her down. "I was in town on a buying trip. Marla told me you were playing here. I'm staying at your hotel."

"I didn't know you two knew each other." Alex looked to Marla for an explanation.

"We didn't know each other until Rachel called me a few weeks ago, looking for *you*. Seems she keeps up with her brother's reviews and saw your name."

"Your brother?" Alex looked to Rachel, not quite following what Marla had just said.

"Yes. My brother. Adopted brother, really. David Somers." Rachel smiled.

"You're *David's* sister? No shit." He put his hand on a nearby chair to steady himself. "Damn, Rachel. I tried to track you down a few times, but I didn't know your new name."

Rachel looked embarrassed. "I have to admit I followed your career. I kept thinking I should get in touch with you, but I worried you might not want to revisit you childhood. I was an idiot. It never even occurred to me that you might know David until I saw the *Chicago Tribune* review of your CSO concert."

"No worries. I'm just glad you found me. We have a lot of catching up to do." *And then some.*

There was a knock on the green room door, and several admirers entered to congratulate Alex on his performance.

"I've made us reservations at one of my favorite restaurants." Marla glanced like a mother hen from Rachel to Alex. "We'll go on ahead. You can meet us there when you're done greeting your fans." She handed Alex a card with the name and address of the restaurant.

"Sounds great." He wanted nothing more than to leave with them, but he wouldn't be rude to the newcomers—this, too, was part of his job.

Marla put her arm around Rachel as they walked over to the door. Rachel turned back and smiled at Alex again. "It's really good to see you again, Alex," she said. "I've missed you. I can't wait to catch up."

"I'll see you soon."

AN HOUR later, Marla and Rachel were seated at a table near the fireplace in the small restaurant, already on their second glasses of Chianti.

"I can't tell you how glad I am you were able to make it to Milan on such short notice," Marla said. She'd been about to burst with excitement since Rachel had e-mailed to say she could extend her business trip to coincide with Alex's La Scala gig.

"Honestly, I was happy to stay away from New York. I'm having some work done on my loft, and without a kitchen, I'm better off on the road."

"You're always welcome in my kitchen." Marla shook her head. "It's not like Alex or I use it all that much."

"Would you believe Alex taught me to cook?"

"Are you kidding me?" Marla stared openly at Rachel and laughed. "Alex actually did the *cooking* when you two lived together?"

"Well, it was more like he taught me how to boil water. He used to say he was the king of macaroni and cheese." Rachel's eyes seemed to warm with the memory. "He never progressed past the boxed food stage. I ended up taking cooking lessons one summer when I was in college."

"Well *that* makes a lot more sense. At least I know he wasn't faking it when he burned the soup last week. If we eat together, he does the dishes and I order takeout. It's a lot safer that way." Marla snorted as she topped off their wineglasses.

"So tell me about the violin," she prodded after a pause. "He still has it, you know."

"It was one of the only things he had left of his mother. Even after Maestro Nelson gave him a new instrument, he still played it sometimes. He said it reminded him of her. His father was a violinist. He died when Alex was a baby, but when Alex was old enough, his mother gave him the violin."

"What happened to her? I've always wanted to know, but I didn't want to pry."

"From what he told me, she got a bad flu or something. She taught piano and gave voice lessons and it paid the bills. They did all right, but they didn't have insurance, and she made too much for Medicaid. Alex told me she finally went to the hospital, but she died the next day. He thinks it probably had turned into pneumonia, but he was never sure. The Family Services ladies never really explained it to him—I guess they thought he was too young to understand. You get a lot of that crap, growing up in the system."

"That's horrible." Marla blinked back tears. "You'd never know how much he's been through. He never talks about it."

"He told me he got into a lot of fights at school. They moved him to a bunch of different foster homes and finally stuck him in a group home when they couldn't find him a placement. The day I met him, he was running away. Some of the other boys took his violin. That's how it got cracked. I guess they were jealous—he played for tips on the street and he did pretty well for himself. He told me he was tired of being a punching bag. I think he was afraid he'd hurt one of them if he defended himself."

"He used to joke that his music kept him out of jail. Sounds like it really did."

"I always knew he'd be a success." Rachel sipped her wine. "He had so much passion for music. It didn't really matter if it was rock or classical—he loved it all."

"He's a passionate man. I should know."

"Oh." Rachel's eyes widened. "Are you two together? I mean, I thought…."

Marla laughed. "Oh, no! I didn't mean it *that* way. We're just roommates. He's never questioned his sexual orientation, at least as far as I know. Not that it stops women from drooling all over him." She made a face and shook her head in mock disgust.

"We never really talked about it as kids, but I always suspected he was gay," Rachel said. "Is he seeing anyone?"

Marla brightened. She'd been waiting for this moment but had held back in part because she wanted to be sure Alex's sexuality wouldn't present a problem for Rachel. It hadn't been easy; she was tired of seeing Alex mope around when she knew she might have it within her power to do something about it.

"Now *that's* an interesting question." She swirled her wine around in the glass and leaned across the table to share her precious secret. "There *is* someone that I think he's fallen pretty hard for, but the two of them seem to be a little stuck. Or maybe just stubborn." She took a sip of her wine. "You know, I think men are even worse at this sort of stuff than women. Alex won't talk about it, even when I push the issue."

"Strange. Alex doesn't seem the hesitating type."

Marla leaned in toward Rachel. "He's not. Although it's not as though he has to work very hard to find men to date."

"I can imagine. Good-looking, successful, great personality. So is this someone a musician as well?"

Marla nodded and tried to hide her delight. "Actually, he's a pretty well-known musician."

"Really?"

Barely able to contain herself, Marla said, "Yep. In fact, I'm pretty sure you've heard of him." She didn't try to disguise her pleasure—she loved juicy stories, and she loved sharing them even more. And *this* story was one of the best ever.

"You're killing me, Marla," Rachel groaned. "Who is he?"

Marla hesitated for just a moment, then said, "David Somers."

"My brother?" Rachel's eyes grew wider. "You're kidding me!"

"Nope. Alex's got it *really* bad for that dark and mysterious brother of yours, although he won't admit it."

"*David?*"

"I don't really know if he *does* like Alex, to be honest. I've never met the man, except just to shake his hand after a concert. I didn't realize he was gay. Or bi, I guess." Marla leaned back in her chair and took another sip of her wine.

"Gay," Rachel confirmed. "David's marriage to Helena was strictly platonic, from what he's told me. But seriously... *Alex?* He doesn't seem David's type. David usually goes for subdued, silent men. You know—just like him. Uptight."

"They went on a date about two weeks ago. Alex was totally dejected afterward. Said he'd made a big mistake, taking David skating."

"Skating? My brother went *skating?*" Rachel shook her head in obvious disbelief. "I don't think there's any doubt he's interested in Alex. I've been pushing him to try skating for years."

"It gets better," Marla put in with glee. "Alex asked me to get him David's contact information when he was in Paris last week. He wanted to know where David was staying."

"And?"

"And nothing. He was back at our hotel again that night." She didn't mention her own date hadn't gone anywhere either. "We left the next afternoon. I've tried to find out what happened, but he wouldn't talk about it. The most I've gotten out of him is that he's supposed to call David when we get home and that maybe they'll go out again."

Rachel pushed a stray lock of hair from her eyes. "Alex would be good for David," she said with a sly smile.

"Speaking of Alex," Marla said as she looked up from the table and waved.

ALEX grinned and planted a kiss on Marla's cheek, then did the same for Rachel. It had taken him longer than expected to wrap up at the concert hall, and he was a little concerned the two women might be irritated with the delay. One look at them, however, told him they were having a perfectly wonderful time without him. The realization pleased him to no end—there were few people he loved as much as Marla and Rachel.

"Did I miss anything?" he asked.

"Only about two glasses of my favorite Chianti *riserva*." Marla poured the last of the wine for Alex, waved to the waitress, and ordered another bottle.

"You two look like the cats who swallowed the cream," Alex said as he took them in. *Thick as thieves, as my mother used to say.*

"We do?" Rachel asked with an innocent expression.

Marla handed him the glass of wine. "I was just telling Rachel about this *wonderful* little lingerie boutique I found downtown. If you'd like, you can come with us tomorrow."

Alex screwed up his face in mock disgust. "I'm done with shopping," he said before he took a long drink of the wine and settled into his seat. "And I don't think I need any new lingerie." Marla snorted and shook her head. "I was thinking a few hours in the gym and then a late lunch with my old roommate. If she'll have me, that is."

"That sounds great, Alex," Rachel replied. "I can meet you after Marla and I finish."

Alex filled Rachel in on his career over a saffron risotto. As they moved on to the next course, a traditional winter pot roast, Alex asked Rachel about her work for Sotheby's, which she explained had her traveling most of the year.

"So, tell me about the Somerses." Alex couldn't contain himself any longer. "How did you end up getting adopted?"

"I met Helena after you left for school, through a program that helped foster kids go to college. She told me I should apply to Yale and a few other Ivy League schools. When I got accepted to Yale, Helena made sure I had everything I needed—school supplies, those sorts of things—and she invited me to stay at the Somers's estate during breaks. She made me feel like I was part of a family."

Rachel pressed her lips together and took a deep breath. "Helena was diagnosed with breast cancer about a year and a half later. She was only twenty-five." As she spoke the words, her eyes wandered to the fire. "Helena wanted to make sure I'd be taken care of, no matter what happened to her. She and David decided to adopt me." She laughed. "Technically, I guess you could say David's my father."

Alex leaned back in his chair. He had no idea what to say. He was still trying to square Rachel's story with the man he knew.

"David's grandfather was still alive when the adoption was finalized. I don't think it was easy for David." Rachel took a sip of wine and shook her head.

"David's grandfather didn't approve of the adoption?" Marla asked as she dabbed her eyes with her napkin.

"James didn't want anything to do with me. I understand why. I really do. I don't think he ever understood how devoted David was to Helena and how much he wanted her to be happy."

"You think he knew David was gay?" Marla asked.

"No," Rachel replied. "At least if he did, he was in denial. He just didn't like Helena, at least to begin with. She was also a foster kid, so he just assumed she was after the Somers's money. Later, I think he realized she was good for David. David says she was a wonderful hostess for the parties at the estate. There were a lot of newspaper articles about them. You know, in the society pages."

"What was James Somers like?" Alex had completely forgotten about his food by now and was entirely caught up in Rachel's story.

Rachel sighed openly. "On the surface, a lot like David. Cool. In control. But inside… he was just bitter. Angry. He lost his temper a lot, especially at home. I can't even imagine what it must have been like for David, growing up with that. But in public, he was always charming. The perfect philanthropist. David would never say it, but I think the car accident that killed his parents killed James a little too." She smiled as if she'd realized how morose her words had sounded, and was attempting to lighten the mood. "Still, you have to admit it *is* a little unusual to adopt a twenty-one-year-old. I'm not surprised James had a cow."

"So David stood up to the old man?" Alex asked.

"He did," Rachel answered, "although it cost him. His grandfather was always so hard on him; it must have been terrible. Not that David ever complained to me about James's treatment. He loved his grandfather. I think he spent his entire life trying to live up to that man's expectations. It's like James pinned all his hopes and dreams on David, since he was the last of the Somerses."

Alex had begun to suspect David's cold exterior was just a cover for something else, something David did not want to share with anyone, even his sister. *He's insecure.* The realization struck Alex with particular force. One of the most in-demand conductors of his generation—a man who could handle temperamental artists as easily as his demanding donors—was unsure of himself.

"Earth to Alex." Marla studied him over her wineglass. "Something on your mind?"

"Hmm? Nah. Not really. It's nothing important." Alex was sure Marla knew him well enough to know *who* was on his mind, but after the Paris fiasco, he'd resolved not to give her the satisfaction of confirming her suspicions.

THREE hours later, having overindulged on food and drink, they shared a taxi back to the hotel. Alex, exhausted from both the concert and the conversation, collapsed fully dressed on the bed and slept until well past noon, waking with just enough time to meet Rachel for lunch, as promised.

The rest of the week flew by. Performances kept Alex busy in the evenings, and when he was not playing, he spent time with Rachel and caught up on the intervening lost years. In spite of the good company and the warm reception he received from the Milan critics, Alex couldn't help but think of David.

Had David known of his connection to his sister? Why didn't he say something? It made no sense. But then so much about David still puzzled him.

CHAPTER 14

THE hotel phone rang and Alex sat bolt upright in bed. "Pronto." His voice came out as a sleep-deprived croak, and he coughed a few times.

"Alex?"

"Marla. I was trying to get some sleep."

"You're supposed to be here, sitting next to me... on the *plane*, Alex!"

"Damn! You're shitting me."

Marla's laughter came through the handset.

"It's not funny." Alex rubbed his eyes. "Why didn't you wake me up?"

"Rachel and I stayed at the villa last night, remember? I told you yesterday—girl time. And I told you last week that I rebooked us on an earlier flight, remember?"

He vaguely remembered the conversation about the villa, although he couldn't remember a conversation about changing flights. Not that he'd have paid much attention to it anyhow. He never did. That was Marla's job.

"When does the flight leave?" His head pounded like a set of timpani. He'd spent most of the night before at a jazz club, and he'd had too much to drink. He figured he'd gotten about three hours' sleep, tops.

"In about ten minutes. Don't even try to make it—it won't happen."

"Shit. I'm really sorry. Can you get me on the next flight?"

"Already tried that," she replied. "There's nothing available nonstop to O'Hare. Even in first class."

"Damn."

"Don't worry. It's not like you're stuck in Milan forever, although that prospect doesn't sound so bad to me." More laughter. He smiled at her lack of concern—he loved that about her. Give Marla lemons, and she'd make lemon chiffon pie. "I've rebooked you on a flight from Paris to Chicago. You'll still have to hurry, though, if you want to catch the flight from Milan to Paris. It leaves in two hours."

"You're the best, Marla." He meant it too. "I'll see you back in Chicago tonight. I promise I'll do better at checking my schedule next time. I owe you one."

"You better believe it. Now get your lazy ass in gear and get to the airport!"

THREE hours later, Alex ran through Charles de Gaulle airport, clutching his violin and wishing he hadn't decided to wear the expensive Italian shoes Marla picked out for him two days before. Cross-trainers would have been a far better choice, he lamented as the leather cut into the backs of his heels.

Anything for beauty. He wondered if he could get away with hiding them at the back of his closet. *Yeah, right. She'll be digging them out from behind all the others and waving them in your face.* He laughed and wiped his forehead with the back of his hand.

The flight from Milan had arrived late, and getting through security cost him precious time. When he arrived at the gate for the flight to Chicago, the boarding area was empty. He shoved his documents at the gate attendant, who waved him down the Jetway and shut the door behind him. He glanced at his ticket as he boarded through the open cabin door. First class.

Apparently there had been no business class seats available. He didn't want to think about what the seat had cost. Marla's reminder that all of his travel expenses were deductible hadn't made him worry less about the extra cost of business class. But first class? *You know you can afford it. Just take a deep breath and enjoy it for a change.*

The flight attendant smiled at him as he walked onto the plane, still wondering if he should have asked for a seat in coach. "Can I put that up front for you?" She gestured to his violin.

"Thanks," he said. "I'll put it in the overhead. I get a little antsy when it's more than a few feet from me."

The woman glanced at his boarding pass. "Seat 3B is yours," she said. "On the aisle. We'll be leaving in about five minutes. Can I get you something to drink when we're airborne?"

"Thanks. I'll take a beer. German Weiss, if you have any."

She nodded and opened the overhead bin. He laid his violin and his jacket inside before looking down to note that the window seat was occupied. At the sight of the passenger seated there, he gasped.

"*David?*" He'd never been so surprised to see anyone in his life. Except maybe David's sister, six days before.

"Alex?" David was obviously just as surprised. "I thought you were in Milan."

"I was." Alex buckled his seat belt as the attendant closed the cabin door and began her spiel over the PA. "I missed my flight and…." He trailed off in stunned realization. He'd been too tired to put all the pieces together before, at the hotel. "I didn't oversleep. She changed the itinerary and didn't tell me about it." He began to laugh.

"I'm sorry." David's brow furrowed. "I have no idea what you're talking about. No doubt it's a coincidence that we ended up sitting together—"

Alex shook his head. "This *isn't* a coincidence at all. We've been set up."

"Set up? By whom?"

The plane taxied down the runway, and Alex realized David probably thought he'd lost his mind. "We were set up by my manager, Marla, and your sister."

"My sister? Why would she and your manager want to arrange our meeting?" His expression turned to one of barely hidden indignation as he continued, "Surely this isn't still about the booking with the CSO next season."

"I don't think this has anything to do with my performing with the CSO."

"Then by all means, please enlighten me."

Alex took a deep breath, admiring the extent of Marla's subterfuge and debating how to explain the entire thing to David. The plane leveled off and the flight attendant arrived and gave them their drinks.

Time for a little honesty, Alex thought as he took a long swallow of beer. He figured it couldn't hurt at this point. "After our date," he explained, "I told Marla I wanted to see you again, but we were leaving for Paris the next day."

"You wanted to see me again?" David appeared pleased to hear this.

"Yeah." Alex was surprised David hadn't understood that he'd called to ask him out again. Not that he'd specifically said that in the message. He made a mental note to be more direct in the future.

They flew through a bank of thick clouds. Little pinpoints of sun began to reveal themselves as they continued to climb.

"The night I showed up at your hotel—Marla was the one who told me where you were."

"Indeed." The edges of David's mouth quirked upward. It was the first time that day Alex had seen David relax.

"She and Rachel know each other. They must have put their heads together and changed my flight to match yours."

David chuckled. "Are you disappointed?"

"Are you kidding? If I hadn't had to leave for Milan, I would have asked you out again." Alex hoped the heat in his cheeks wasn't visible. He quickly finished his beer, noting that David had also finished his drink.

"I'm sorry," David said with obvious regret. "I didn't mean to put you on the spot. After my performance in the hotel room, I'd certainly have understood if you didn't want to see me again. It was a mistake," he added, "not being honest with you."

"About what?"

"I also wanted to see you again."

Alex smiled his relief.

"So where do we go from here?"

David's eyes caught the sunlight from outside as the plane pierced the cloud cover. Alex couldn't resist staring—the light made the dark blue appear almost silver.

"Chicago?" Alex quipped. God, but the man was good looking. Better looking, even, than he'd realized before. And when he smiled, revealing the tiny lines around his mouth and eyes....

David raised a sardonic eyebrow in response. "Join me for dinner at my place tonight," he offered, for once taking the lead. "I'll ask my housekeeper to prepare something for us."

"I'd like that very much," Alex replied as he motioned for the flight attendant to bring them a few more drinks.

"DAVID." Alex was, as always, accompanied by the familiar music that seemed to waft in on the warm breeze through the screen door.

David knew this place—his family's summer home on Nantucket. Outside, the sound of waves crashing on the beach mingled with the music and became a tantalizing crescendo of sound. The smell of salt tickled his nostrils. He closed his eyes, straining to hear the melody over the rumbling water. The sound was closer this time but still just beyond his reach.

"Please." David was too far gone now, any sense of dignity lost with the overwhelming need to hear the music and understand it. He knew Alex was standing behind him, but he didn't turn around. "Please," he repeated. "I have to hear it."

"There's nothing stopping you from hearing it but you, David."

Alex lifted the hair at the back of David's neck and began to lick and suck the sensitive skin there. David rose to meet Alex's mouth, pressing into the touch, craving more. Alex's arms encircled his chest and pulled him closer, the tantalizing feel of skin against skin making him dizzy, weak. He couldn't smell the ocean anymore, only Alex's clean, crisp fragrance and the telltale masculine musk.

"I don't understand." It was a plea, an admission that he was entirely inadequate, that he didn't deserve the music. "Please. I have to know. What must I do to hear it?"

"Surrender...."

"Alex."

"Huh?" Startled out of his slumber, Alex glanced over at his companion. David was sound asleep, though Alex was sure he'd heard him speak his name. He yawned and checked the monitor screen; they would land in Chicago in less than an hour. Unable to resist, he watched David as he slept. Even in sleep, his presence was palpable, commanding. And yet there was something in David's face that also appeared vulnerable, almost childlike.

What secrets do you hold, David? He wondered what he was getting himself into, and yet he knew full well he wanted David regardless. He didn't care what danger lurked beneath that perfect face; he wanted David more than he'd ever wanted anything. Pain and loss were part of life—shrinking away from something so alluring, so exciting, was not an option. *Damned if you do....*

CHAPTER 15

AS THE plane taxied to the terminal, Alex sent a quick text to Marla to tell her he wouldn't be back until late. *Dream date?* was her quick response. He imagined the triumphant look on her face, but he didn't begrudge her the win—she and Rachel had accomplished what he'd been trying to do for weeks.

None of your business, he texted back. It was payback enough that she'd have to wait to hear about the date. He'd also give her the appropriate measure of grief to save face, but he'd end up thanking her for her nerve.

Waiting on the long line to get through immigration and customs at O'Hare was less trying than usual. Alex had no doubt it was due to the companionship. While Alex texted Marla, David called to let his housekeeper know there would be two for dinner that evening. They picked up their bags and headed out to the curb, where a car waited, door open, the driver ready to help them with their bags. "Maestro Somers, it's good to have you home."

"Thank you, Charles," David said. If the driver was surprised to see an additional passenger, he didn't mention it.

David's driver took them along the Kennedy Expressway and into the city. Less than an hour later, they arrived at David's penthouse apartment in one of the older buildings near the S-Curve. The brick building was by no means a skyscraper, but it had a beautiful view of the lake.

It wasn't until Alex realized David owned the entire top floor of the building that he began to wonder how wealthy the Somers really were. In Milan, Rachel had joked that David's grandfather had been "wealthier than God," but he'd assumed she'd exaggerated. Now he wasn't so sure.

The housekeeper greeted them at the door while Charles carried their bags inside. After a quick shower that felt like heaven, Alex wandered into the living room, opened the glass doors that led to the terrace, and stepped outside. The crisp breeze off the lake smelled wonderful after the stuffy airplane, though Alex soon retreated—as striking as it was, this was still Chicago in December.

He wandered around the living and dining areas, both beautifully decorated large rooms. Alex had expected the furnishings to mirror David's impeccable taste in clothing: classic and expensive. He hadn't been prepared for the ultramodern furniture or the modern art that adorned the walls. In retrospect, it wasn't so surprising that the man who adored contemporary music would also appreciate contemporary design.

There were a few personal photographs on display. The first was of Rachel, her arm around David's waist, both of them standing barefoot on a beach with the legs of their pants wet from the surf. The second was David and a beautiful young woman, she in a wedding dress and he in a tux. Helena, no doubt. There was also a black-and-white portrait of a formidable old man dressed in a suit that reminded Alex of the headshots he'd had made when he'd started performing—professionally done, revealing little about the subject. This, Alex guessed, was David's grandfather. The last was considerably older than the others, judging by the faded colors of the print. It was a formal portrait of a young couple and a small boy of three or four.

"My parents." David's voice jarred Alex back to reality. "It was taken about three months before they died."

"That must have been difficult, losing your parents when you were so young." Alex could see a great deal of David in his parents' faces.

"It was a long time ago."

Alex said nothing. Who was he to argue? David had already surprised him by offering the information. Still, he had to wonder. Even though his mother had been dead for more than twenty years, Alex still felt the loss. David had clearly loved his parents—their photograph was displayed as prominently as the others.

"The view is spectacular," Alex said, changing the topic. "Different from my apartment."

David handed Alex a glass of white wine, and for a few minutes, they gazed out at the lake.

"I love the shadows of the buildings and the color of the sun on the lake at sunset. I always dreamed of having a view of it when I was a kid."

"Sounds as though you got your wish."

"Yeah. I did, although it was really Marla's doing. It took her a while to convince me it was worth the extra money. She was right. It's worth every penny."

He had fought Marla for a year before he'd agreed to the move—he'd been worried about the cost. As he'd come from a home where there'd barely been enough money to buy food, the high-rise apartment with the killer view had seemed extravagant. Marla, who managed Alex's money as well as his schedule, spent an entire afternoon going over his finances with him. He'd been shocked to realize how much money she'd managed to make from investments. A year later, Alex couldn't imagine living anywhere that *didn't* have a view of the lake.

"Sometimes I wish I were home more often to see it," Alex added with a sigh.

"You don't like to travel?" David sounded surprised.

"I can take it or leave it. I never traveled much when I was a kid. Never really thought about it either. After my mother died, I just wanted a home. I found that with Rachel."

David said nothing but sipped his wine.

"Why didn't you tell me Rachel was your sister?" It surprised Alex that he wasn't angry David hadn't brought up the subject.

"I only learned a few weeks ago that you were the boy she'd shared an apartment with in high school. I intended to mention it, but the time just never seemed right." David paused for a moment, then added, "I didn't want to bring up difficult memories for you."

"Living on the street was hard, but it was also one of the happiest times of my life." David tipped his head to one side, clearly shocked to hear this. "I realize that sounds pretty strange," Alex continued, "but Rachel was my family. She saved my life the day she found me passed out in the cold. She kept me out of trouble and convinced me to keep playing."

"She told me you played for her every night before she went to sleep." David's expression was wistful.

He sounds almost envious. "Gounod's Ave Maria. Not a violin piece, but it was her favorite." He turned to face David. "So what about you, David? Do you enjoy traveling?"

"*Enjoy* would not be the word I would use to describe it." David's words seemed carefully chosen. "But it is necessary."

"Did you travel much as a child?"

"I often accompanied my grandfather on business trips. Later, when I was married, I traveled for pleasure. Helena enjoyed it."

"Rachel told me a little about her. Sounds like she was a wonderful woman."

"She was. Although I often wonder if she was happy." David paused, contemplated his wine, then added, "Perhaps there are people who can never truly find happiness."

Alex had the distinct impression David wasn't just referring to his late wife. How ironic, that David would have thought Alex's childhood too painful to discuss, and yet David's own life of privilege seemed to have left him empty and pained.

"Excuse me, sir." The housekeeper stood at the entrance to the living room. Alex was glad for the interruption. "Dinner is ready."

"Thank you, Sarah," said David. She nodded and left the room. "Shall we?" David motioned to the dining room, where the table was set for two. In the middle of the table was a short blown glass bowl filled with water in which several red flowers floated.

Sarah brought them two simple plates of salad and a crusty baguette. Alex's stomach rumbled—he hadn't realized until that moment how hungry he was. David refilled their wineglasses and they began to eat.

For the first time, Alex noted the sound of modern jazz in the background. "Thelonius Monk. I didn't realize you liked jazz."

"You could say it was my first love." David appeared uncharacteristically relaxed. "My grandfather detested it, but I would go to the West Village after school and buy used LPs. I hid the records under my mattress so the governess wouldn't find them."

"She would have told him?" Alex did his best to hide his shock. Even his foster parents hadn't been so intrusive—not that they had hesitated to beat him if he disagreed with their discipline. He wondered vaguely which was worse.

"Dorothy was something of a surrogate mother to me after my parents died," David explained. "She ran a tight ship—she was my grandfather's eyes and ears. She raised me."

"Your grandfather wasn't around much, then?"

"My grandfather didn't believe Somers Investments could run without him. He had little time for a child. I was—" David hesitated for an instant. "—a distraction."

"Rachel told me you went to LaGuardia Arts." Alex hoped that changing the subject might take some of the pressure off David, who again looked tense.

"Yes. I was a composition student."

"Composition? I didn't know you wrote your own music."

As David's expression grew tenser, Alex realized he had blundered once again into dangerous territory. He took another sip of his wine and sat back in his chair. There was no way he could have known it, but he resolved to be more careful when asking questions about David's past. He hoped to get to know the man better, not force him to reveal his deepest feelings. Not yet, at least.

"I am an adequate composer." David's words were practiced, self-effacing. "It's more of a hobby."

I'll bet he's far better than he'd ever admit.

"I'll be leaving now, sir." Sarah peered into the dining room. "The boeuf bourguignon is warming on the back burner, and dessert is on the counter."

"Thank you, Sarah." David nodded as she scurried out the door.

"Rachel tells me you're an accomplished poet, as well," Alex added, hoping to put David at ease again.

"My sister has been speaking out of turn. But I do enjoy writing."

It finally dawned on Alex that David was genuinely uncomfortable with praise. The entire conversation was proving far more treacherous than he'd anticipated. Alex took a long swallow of his wine, at a loss for words.

"What was Rachel like when you met her?" The question seemed to come from nowhere. Alex noticed the faint hint of color on David's cheeks, as if he'd realized the transition in their conversation had been abrupt.

"A lot like she is now. Smart. Independent. Honest."

"After Helena's death, I came to rely on Rachel." He didn't elaborate, though Alex knew it was Rachel who'd convinced David to leave Boston and sell the Beacon Hill apartment he and Helena had shared.

Alex took a deep breath, stood up, and walked behind David, then put his hands on his shoulders. David was tense, as if ready to do battle. Without thinking, Alex began to work his fingers into the tightness, pressing his thumbs into David's back.

David released a stuttered breath.

For a few minutes, Alex massaged David's shoulders in silence. Beneath his fingers, David's cashmere sweater was soft. Alex imagined what David's skin might feel like beneath the buttery yarn. "Are you always this tense?" he murmured.

"I'm afraid so." David's voice had a slightly throaty quality to it.

Alex trailed a finger over David's jaw, then offered his hand. "The couch would be more comfortable."

David followed Alex silently into the living room. A moment later they were seated on the couch and Alex began to knead David's shoulders once more.

"May I take off your sweater?" Alex asked. He had little doubt how he hoped the evening would end, but David still seemed hesitant, and the last thing he wanted was to push David away.

"Yes."

Alex ghosted his hands over David's back before finding the hem of his sweater and slowly lifting it over David's head. He had to remember to breathe as he took in the smooth skin. "Beautiful," he whispered as his palms made contact with David's bare arms. He wanted to bite and suck at that deliciously pale skin, but he fought the urge, instead returning to David's shoulders.

"I'm sorry," David said in a low voice. "I'm not very good at this."

David's words only served to renew Alex's determination to take things one step at a time. He found David's vulnerability both unexpected and attractive, responding to it by running his hands up David's arms and turning David's face toward him.

"Why don't you let me be the judge of that?" He met David's eyes.

Before David could reply, Alex brushed his lips over David's cheek. The skin there was freshly shaved and smelled faintly of sandalwood and soap. Alex breathed deeply, inhaling the scent and closing his eyes. He fought the urge to rush, instead slowing the contact, allowing himself a moment to let his physical need subside.

David found his mouth with a determination so fierce it took Alex by surprise. Alex opened his lips to David's slight pressure. David's mouth was warm and tasted of wine. He pulled Alex closer.

"God, David," Alex said, gasping for air as the kiss broke. "I've wanted to kiss you for so long."

"I should have done that in Paris." The corners of David's mouth edged upward at the admission. "I don't know why I hesitated."

"You weren't the only one," Alex reminded him, thinking David's hesitation seemed to have dissolved into quite the opposite.

"I'm glad to hear it. I had hoped that was the case."

David leaned forward, slipped his fingers through Alex's hair, and stole another kiss, rougher than the last, more demanding too. *Holy fuck!* When had David gone from hesitant to taking charge? Not that Alex was complaining, but the sudden shift in roles nearly took his breath away.

And that mouth! David had a wicked mouth, Alex decided as David's tongue danced around his own, teasing and exploring. The *man* was wicked—superbly controlled to the outside world, and yet here, when it was just the two of them, Alex sensed only uninhibited sexual energy.

David reached for Alex's shirt and made quick work of the buttons. No hesitation. Just raw need. Still, Alex was sure he hadn't imagined David's hands trembling with the effort, at least until Alex moaned his pleasure. David explored his chest with his fingers before he pushed the shirt off Alex's shoulders. What an incredible mass of contradictions this man was—but that just made Alex want David more.

"Smooth," David murmured appreciatively as he found the outer edge of Alex's tattoos with his hands and traced them from Alex's shoulders to his neck. He followed the pattern downward, pausing at a spot about an inch above Alex's heart. "But not here."

Alex considered for a moment how to respond. He hadn't lied when he'd explained the designs were meant as a rite of passage. He also hadn't been completely forthcoming about them.

"That's a scar," he finally said. "A little something I picked up at my last foster placement. Before I found Rachel." David leaned down and outlined the scar with his lips and tongue. Alex forgot to breathe, the contact was so unexpected.

"It's why you got the tattoo."

"Yes." Alex wasn't sure why he'd admitted it; he never told anyone else the truth. Maybe it was the dreamlike state in which he found himself as David continued to lave the scar, or maybe it was that sinful hand tweaking his nipple just shy of too hard.

"It's mesmerizing." David sat back, his expression almost serene, as if Alex's admission had given him the reassurance he had been seeking all evening. "I never thought a tattoo was a thing of art. But on you…." David pushed Alex down and bent over him, licking circles on the skin at Alex's neck and shoulders and working his way down the lines. David mouthed a pebbled nipple and nipped at it with his teeth as Alex arched his back in a silent plea for more. David slipped his hands beneath Alex, then supported his body as he sucked harder and flicked his tongue in insistent circles.

"Damn," Alex gasped. He opened his eyes long enough to see the closest thing to a grin he'd ever seen on David's face.

"Should I stop?"

"You better not." Having David take control was the hottest thing he could imagine. Unexpected. Then again, so much about David was unexpected.

David appeared to search Alex's face for a moment, then licked a line from one nipple to the other to give it equal attention, all the while pressing his thumbs along Alex's spine. David radiated the calm confidence Alex had seen when he conducted. David's hands no longer shook as they massaged Alex's back, and when their eyes met again, David's simmered with obvious lust.

"Oh, shit," Alex groaned as David pulled the peaked flesh with his teeth and released it, then repeated the gesture. A few minutes later, David withdrew, leaving Alex bereft and moaning the loss of that hot mouth on his skin. He needn't have worried—David now eased open the buckle on Alex's belt, unzipping his pants and pushing them down to his thighs. Another quick glance upward—perhaps to reassure himself that Alex wanted this too—and David had taken him in his mouth.

"God. David. Feels so good." Understatement of the century! Every inch of Alex's body vibrated with heat, like a violin string long after the bow had set it into motion.

Alex could swear David was grinning now, but before he could be sure, David swallowed him to the root, sucking and pulling, making him hiss with pleasure.

He'd need to thank Marla and Rachel, even if it meant admitting they'd been right all along. The thought made him chuckle. David responded by running the edge of his teeth underneath his cock. The chuckle became a throaty growl as his hands moved of their own accord to feel the silk of David's hair. David cupped Alex's ass and kneaded the muscle there.

"God. David. I'm gonna come if you keep this up."

David released Alex from his mouth. "Do you want to?"

Damn, but for just an instant, David looked like a little kid caught with his fingers in the cake batter. Devilish. A little playful, even.

"Not unless you're inside me."

This time, it was David whose breath stuttered as the weight of Alex's words sank in. "Bedroom, then," he said with a glint of mischief in his deep blue eyes. He got up off the couch and gestured to the hallway.

Alex smiled and stood up, allowing his pants to fall to his ankles before stepping out of them. David reached out and traced the tattoos again, this time following them down below Alex's waist. The horizontal lines ended there, but wisps of pattern trailed down his abdomen and the tops of his thighs like tiny rivulets of ink. David's touch made Alex shiver.

"It's cold here," David said in an undertone, his fingers still grazing Alex's skin as he spoke.

Alex exhaled softly, unwilling to break the spell. Then David dragged his fingertips up Alex's chest and cupped Alex's chin before whispering, "Come." Alex followed him silently down the hallway to the bedroom, his heart pounding.

CHAPTER 16

IT WAS hard not to look back at Alex as he led him to the bedroom, but David's willpower was absolute—he was terrified that if he looked, he'd lose his nerve. And oh, but he wanted Alex! He wanted to explore every inch of the tantalizing tattoos, taste the saltiness of his skin, take him in his mouth again. Make him beg for release.

Now that David's mind wasn't filled with Alex, the voice of insecurity reasserted itself. Why was it always like this? Why did he even have to think? In the living room, he'd been swept away by his physical need, unconcerned with rejection. Alex hadn't complained—in fact, he'd appeared pleased that David had taken the lead. Why was it always such a struggle to let himself be?

"David?" Alex turned his head with a gentle hand, as if he sensed David's hesitation.

Naked now, David made a conscious effort to relax into that hand, pressing against it greedily. Alex's skin felt cool against his own. He reached up and brought Alex's palm to his mouth, kissing it. "Do you want this?" he asked as he breathed in Alex's musky aroma.

"Hell yes." No uncertainty. Just reassurance.

David backed to the bed, sat down, and pulled Alex along with him. Alex laughed, tumbled onto his side and grabbed David's shoulders, capturing his mouth. As their bodies pressed together, David's hunger took over and he forgot his insecurity. David laughed too, pulled Alex's hair—not roughly, but enough to make him gasp—then rolled him onto his stomach.

David felt the powerful muscles of Alex's buttocks beneath the smooth expanse of skin. David was glad there was no ink here. Much as he found the tattoos powerfully appealing, he couldn't deny the perfect curve where back met ass was even more so.

He ran his palms hungrily over each cheek, following them with his mouth. He needed every sense filled with Alex, needed to taste him, smell him, possess him. He nipped, gently at first, then harder when he felt Alex's body rise to meet his lips. He watched the tiny marks blossom and fade, swept his thumbs over the pinked skin, then reached between Alex's legs to cup his balls with tender hands.

One moan and then another, each reassuring David, guiding him onward. Bolder now, he licked Alex's sac as he spread the globes of his ass. Tentatively, he traced a finger over Alex's opening. Just a light touch at first, but when Alex rumbled his approval, he licked a finger and pressed the tip of it inside.

"Want you inside me." Alex's voice was rough with arousal.

"You're impatient." David pressed farther inward to his knuckle, reveling in the knowledge that somehow he was the one making Alex beg.

"God, David, I've been waiting for this since the night I met you. Please."

David stilled, taking in the words, savoring them. No one had ever begged him before. Nobody had ever wanted him like this, or if they had, he hadn't recognized it.

"David. Fuck me. Please. I'm gonna lose my mind."

David laughed and reached for the bottle of lube and the condom he'd stashed under his pillow before dinner. He'd hoped…. He slicked up his fingers and went back to work, biting and licking, stretching Alex to contented murmurs of pleasure. In spite of Alex's pleas, or perhaps because of them, he took his time.

David heard Alex's music again. Not as clearly as in his dreams, but he could hear it nonetheless. One finger, then two, and the sound of the woodwinds danced through his thoughts as tiny slivers of light might illuminate a darkened room, revealing something long hidden. A third finger, and David heard the warmth of a cello as it echoed the melody. He didn't remember when he'd slipped on the condom. It was as if nothing mattered but Alex and the music. For a moment he waited, poised at Alex's entrance, savoring the sound and the anticipation.

"David. Damn. You're making me crazy."

David took his time, pushing through heat and pressure until he was fully seated inside. He fought back a curse, biting his tongue so hard he tasted the metallic tang of blood. In spite of his self-control, he whimpered, a sound low and pitiful to his own ears. *Unseemly.* The word echoed in his mind—his grandfather's voice, intruding on the moment.

No. He opened his eyes and focused on the hard body beneath his own, pressing his mouth to Alex's back, following the lines of the tattoos that rose and fell over his shoulder blades. The sound of the music from his dream replaced James Somers's voice.

"God, yes!" David wondered if the words had really come from his own lips.

He pulled Alex off the bed just a little, snaked his arms around Alex's waist, and reached for his cock, hard and waiting. He stroked in time with his own movements, following the tempo, faster now. It was all too intense—the music, the sensations, Alex's powerful body. David would come soon, but he was sure Alex was on the edge as well. He pressed his cheek to Alex's shoulder and heard Alex's panted breaths and moans vibrate against his ear. He increased the pressure and heard Alex's throaty cry as Alex spilled over his hand, hot and thick.

David's climax began like the distant rumble of the timpani and ended with a crescendo of sound—David's own voice, raw, unrestrained, and full of emotion. His vision exploded in white as Alex shuddered beneath him and gasped. Both of them struggled to catch their breath in the aftermath.

A minute, maybe two passed before the tension in Alex's body receded. David kissed the smooth skin of Alex's back, pausing to appreciate the inked lines once again, then groaned and rolled onto his side as his thighs seized with exhaustion. They lay there for the longest time, the only sounds their slowing breaths.

It was Alex who spoke first. "I don't think I can move."

David said nothing, instead leaning in for a kiss. Fighting his own battle with his exhausted body, he managed to roll out of bed to grab a washcloth, wet it, and walk back. Alex was already half-asleep, but his eyes fluttered open and he grinned as David wiped Alex, then himself.

Back in bed a minute later, David stifled a yawn and pulled the comforter and sheets over them. Alex was already asleep, judging by his soft rhythmic breaths. The sound was endearing and vulnerable. David shoved a pillow under his neck, which still ached from the flight. Alex rolled over and spooned David. "Feels good," he murmured into David's back.

"Glad you stayed?" David asked as they held each other in the deepening darkness.

"So glad." Alex worked his mouth into the crook of David's neck and nipped at the skin there, to David's soft moan. "So damn glad."

I could get used to this, David thought as he at last gave in to the urge to sleep.

DAVID awoke with the first light of morning and smiled to find Alex asleep beside him. As always, he had dreamed of Alex. He'd been afraid to open his eyes, afraid that he'd dreamed the night before as well. Alex's music replaced the thought—*what the hell am I doing?* The music was clearer than before. He had no doubts that Alex's presence made this possible.

Soundlessly, he slipped out of the bed, pulled on a pair of pajama bottoms, and draped an extra set over the chair by the bed for Alex. He smiled at the memory of the night before, venturing out of the bedroom and into the kitchen for a cup of coffee. A few minutes later, he headed down the hallway to his practice studio. Once inside, he pulled a few sheets of staff paper and a pencil out of the cabinet and sat down at the piano to write.

Almost immediately, thoughts of his grandfather intruded to distract him from the music.

"I don't understand why you insist on pursuing composition," James Somers said when David came home from the University of Michigan for Christmas. *"It's not as if you'd ever earn enough money composing to sustain a career."* As if David needed the money; he'd only wanted something that made him *feel*. But then again, James's views of success in life had never included happiness as a goal.

Twenty-One Years Before

As he did most evenings after the formal dinners James Somers insisted he attend, David sat at the piano in the music room, composing, pencil in his mouth, hands on the keys. Outside the tall french doors, snow fell in heavy flakes, illuminated only by the light from the interior of the room.

He'd had an idea—a wonderful idea that coalesced as he rode the train back from school that afternoon. A deceptively simple piece, he realized as he struggled to reduce to writing the music he'd imagined. It was late on a Friday night, and with no school the next day, he had worked far later than he'd intended, losing track of time.

It was nearly midnight when James Somers walked into the room, dressed for bed in his pajamas and robe, wearing a frown that made it immediately clear to David that he was displeased. "I can hardly sleep when you insist on making noise so late in the evening."

David set the pencil down on the piano stand. Hoping to assuage the old man's growing anger, he closed the cover of the piano and neatly stacked the composition paper. "I'm sorry."

"You should be," James snapped. David guessed it had been a long day at the office, or perhaps the stock market had taken a turn for the worse. To say that he was used to James's anger and frustration wasn't quite correct. He'd learned to tolerate it. Or perhaps he had learned it was best to take the blame for his grandfather's anger. He knew the consequences of failing to do so. James Somers had a temper that could reduce even the strongest man to a quivering lump of flesh.

"I'll go to bed." He didn't meet his grandfather's eyes but stood up and walked past him to the door.

"You're wasting your time." David had heard it before, usually followed by a lecture about how David had been neglecting his math studies. Not that he did poorly in them, but he had failed to receive the highest grade in his class last semester, something unacceptable for the grandson of the man who owned a good portion of Wall Street.

"Yes, sir."

"You should be focusing on your other studies. This"—James shot a disapproving look toward the piano—"can wait. I don't begrudge you a hobby. Lord knows the best of men need something to dabble in. Something to distract them from time to time. Like tennis. Or attending charity events. You don't need to finish the piece right now."

Charity balls? Tennis? David knew James despised those things. Composition was everything to David. It was a way to express the feelings he couldn't share with even his closest friends, let alone his grandfather. It was at times a puzzle to be solved, at others a means to forget that even now, he missed his parents. His mother's warmth, his father's strong yet loving arms.

"It… it's more than just that to me. It makes me happy. And I'm good at it." He shouldn't have said it, but he couldn't help himself. He'd heard his grandfather's disparaging words too many times, and *this* time, he felt strangely compelled to defend his love not only of composition but of music itself. How could he say that the music was nothing—the music he heard every waking hour of the day and even in his dreams? It was everything to David. Like breathing.

"You don't know anything, boy. It takes more than fanciful dreams to run a business. This family must have an heir, not a child who deludes himself into believing that a simple hobby will keep him fed and clothed."

"We have plenty of money. More than we could ever use. I don't think it—"

"This family has struggled to build a business," James nearly shouted. "It's clear you don't appreciate the effort that's gone into what we've achieved."

"That's not true," David protested. "I—"

"You're a dreamer. Lazy, like your mother. If it hadn't been for her dreams of travel and her fantasies, your father would still be alive to take over the business and see to the next generation of the Somers family."

The music he'd struggled to put down on paper was gone now, replaced by a cacophony of sound and pain. David fought back tears. He'd gotten good at hiding his emotions in the twelve years since his parents' deaths. He was strong. Strong enough that he wouldn't show his grandfather weakness. He also wouldn't raise his voice. He wouldn't become his grandfather.

"Good night, sir," David said as he retreated from the room.

He heard James's muttered "Waste of time, hardly worth bothering with. It's not as if you can't do it later."

The Present

DAVID closed his eyes and tried to focus on Alex's face. It took a few minutes, but the memory of the music from his dreams displaced the memory of his grandfather, the sound of a soaring violin drowning out James's voice. David took a deep breath and opened his eyes, his fingers moving over the piano keys, chasing the elusive melody.

I can do this.

It was nearly an hour later when he heard a knock on the studio door. "Come." He looked up from the piano to see Alex, wearing only the pajama bottoms, his hair disheveled. "Good morning." David slipped the composition beneath a stack of sheet music on the piano stand. Perhaps later, he'd tell Alex about it. For now, he decided he'd rather focus on Alex.

"Morning," Alex answered with a warm smile as he walked over to kiss David.

David had been about to suggest breakfast, but seeing Alex shirtless, his smooth skin catching the light from the window, David decided Alex would make a far more satisfying breakfast than anything he might find in the kitchen.

"What are you working on?"

"I've been reading through some of the submissions for the new music subscription," David lied.

"Sounded promising. Anything you might use?"

"I haven't heard anything that meets with my satisfaction." It was the truth. "At least, not yet. Are you hungry?"

Alex traced the outline of one of David's nipples with a finger. "I need to get going in about an hour," he answered before leaning in and kissing David again. "After yesterday, I swore to myself I'd actually check my calendar. I've got an interview scheduled for eleven at the television studio—something Marla set up."

"Unfortunate. I was hoping we might have some"—David brushed the stubble of Alex's beard with his fingers—"time for more than just breakfast."

"I eat fast. I think we can find the time." This time the kiss was longer, more demanding.

"Good," David said with a chuckle. "I was hoping you'd say that."

"SO?" MARLA waited for Alex in the studio green room, obviously impatient, her hands planted on her hips in mock irritation.

Alex raised an eyebrow. "So?" He matched her gaze.

"So what happened?"

"What do you *think* happened?" he parried.

"Damn you, Alex!" She strode over and faced him down. "Tell me what happened!"

"Your little scheme worked, that's what happened. But I really should strangle you both."

"You two needed a kick in the ass, if you ask me," she said with an indignant flick of her long hair.

"Yeah, I suppose we did." He knew he was grinning like an idiot, but he couldn't help it.

"Is he everything you expected him to be?"

Alex hesitated for a moment. "Yes and no," he replied at last, deciding on a little honesty. He figured he owed her at least that, since she'd done what he and David hadn't been able to manage. "He's a wonderful man, but he seems so... vulnerable."

"*Vulnerable*? David Somers?"

"He's wound so tight, I'm surprised he doesn't spontaneously combust."

"That could be fun," Marla noted with feigned lust. She wore her mother-hen expression now—the self-satisfied "I *so* know better than you" look that was uniquely hers. In spite of everything, he adored her for her meddling. "So are you going to see him again?"

"Of course. You know I enjoy a challenge."

"Good. From what I hear from Rachel, anyhow, he could use someone like you."

"Like me? In what way?"

"Someone with a little 'oomph'," she explained.

"'Oomph'? What the hell is that?" He shook his head and laughed outright.

"I don't know. *Joie de vivre*—something, *anything* to get him to start living his life again."

"That's a tall order for anyone," Alex said in all seriousness. "I'm not a shrink."

"No, but you're 'sunshine on a cloudy day'." She had often called him that, though usually when she was seated in front of the TV, pint of Ben and Jerry's in hand, and almost always with her face set in a deep scowl.

"And you're a die-hard romantic." Then, smiling at her, he added, "One day at a time, Mar. If it's meant to be...."

"Now who's being romantic?"

"I'm not being a romantic. I'm being a realist."

"Hah!" She shook her head and laughed.

"They're waiting for us," he said, changing the subject and opening the greenroom door. She shook her head, exhaled her best diva sigh, and followed him out.

Chapter *17*

FIDDLE firmly tucked under his chin, hair tied back in a short ponytail, Alex pulled the pencil from over his ear and scribbled a fingering above one of the notes on the sheet of music. He backtracked a few measures and repeated the phrase several times until he was sure he had it perfect.

He'd been practicing for nearly six hours now, watching the snow fall outside the window and hoping David would call him about getting together again. He went back to work. Better to focus on his music than on something he had no control over.

About thirty minutes later, there was a knock at the studio door. "Come in, Marla," he said without turning around. "And please don't tell me I missed some other interview or something. I actually checked my calendar for a change."

"Then perhaps you'd be able to find some time for dinner?" said the familiar baritone voice.

Alex turned around. "David! It's good to see you. When I didn't hear back from you, I figured you had plans." David's hair was slightly damp from the snow, and his cheeks were pink from the cold. *Positively edible.*

"Then you assumed incorrectly." David walked inside and closed the door behind him. "Or at least I hope you assumed incorrectly. I was stuck in a symphony association meeting all afternoon and I figured I'd just answer your invitation by showing up. I'm counting on my schedule getting a bit fuller." He leaned in to kiss Alex. His lips were slightly cold, but the effect the contact had on Alex was quite the opposite.

"Marla let you in?"

"She said she had a last-minute meeting and she wouldn't be joining us."

"Subtle as always. Not that I'm complaining." Alex snorted and went to put his violin away.

"Quitting so soon?" David asked with a challenge in his eyes, the edges of his mouth curled upward in a smile.

"Well, I…," Alex began, unsure of what to say.

"I was hoping to hear more of the Dvořák." The smile was broader now.

"Y-you want to play it with me?"

"I would be honored."

Alex swallowed hard. David really wanted to play with him? He wasn't sure why he was surprised; he hadn't even thought to ask. Sure, he'd coached with a few conductors over the years, but he'd never had someone of David's caliber simply volunteer to play with him.

Alex fought the urge to kiss David his thanks until he saw how incredibly uncomfortable David looked seated at the piano. Instead, he smiled back and told himself he'd thank David later, reassure him. *Baby steps.* "I'd love that."

David visibly relaxed at Alex's words. "Last movement, then?"

"Sure." He wondered if David had guessed it was his favorite, the bright and energetic *allegro giocoso*.

David depressed the A key and Alex tuned his violin. A moment later Alex nodded, and David began to play the short orchestral introduction. Entirely from memory.

Holy shit.

Alex wasn't sure what he'd expected—he hadn't had much time to expect anything, really—but David's lighthearted and romantic interpretation of the piece took him by surprise. Alex also hadn't anticipated David to be such a gifted pianist; he was far too used to conductors and teachers whose piano-playing abilities were limited to the hunt-and-peck-and-maybe-play-a-chord-or-two method.

The movement was over far too quickly. This time Alex didn't think twice. He shifted the violin into his right hand and walked over to the piano to kiss David, who appeared startled by Alex's spur-of-the-moment gesture. David's thoughts about the kiss, however, were obvious as he responded by pulling Alex closer and running his fingers through Alex's hair.

"Need to get rid of this." Alex laughed and pulled away, then set his violin in its case. A moment later he was seated next to David again on the piano bench. David moaned as Alex found his lips and began exploring David's mouth.

David pushed Alex backward against the keys, and a jumble of notes sounded as Alex sought to steady himself. As always, the raw intensity of David's physical need for Alex startled him. Unlike David's public persona, this part of David was visceral and uninhibited. Alex found that intensity mesmerizing.

David lifted Alex's T-shirt over his head and ran reverent fingers over Alex's ink, playing it much the way he had just played the music minutes before, each touch coaxing sounds from Alex. "Not fair." Alex took David's hand from his chest and kissed his palm, then began to unbutton David's shirt. Their roles now reversed, Alex pulled David off the bench, then unzipped David's jeans. He did not push them down but kissed the skin above the fabric of David's boxers, now visible through the open zipper. Alex felt the shudder that ran through David's body and smiled. He kissed on downward, mouthing David's erection through the soft silk.

"Alex." In their short time together, David had never spoken much during lovemaking, but it thrilled Alex that when he did speak, he spoke Alex's name.

Alex rid David of his last piece of clothing, then sat him back down on the edge of the piano bench. Alex kneeled between David's legs and kissed his way from one knee to another as he skated his fingers over the sensitive skin of David's inner thighs. David, in return, combed his hands through Alex's hair, raking his scalp with his fingernails.

"Condom?" Alex asked hopefully.

"None."

"We could go to my bedroom."

"We could stay here," David replied with a delicious grin. "I was hoping to find out how creative you really are."

"You doubt me?"

"No. It's my faith in you that keeps me go—" David's words were cut short as Alex began to nibble a slow circle around the tip of David's cock, dancing around the shaft with his tongue until David's response was an audible rumble. David smelled so good like this. Not that Alex minded the way David smelled after a shower, but he loved David's unique, musky scent.

Alex slipped his hand between David's legs and cupped David's sac as he pulled his hair free. He swallowed David as he rolled his balls, using his tongue to press David's cock against the roof of his mouth. All the while, he made sure to brush his hair against the sensitive skin of David's inner thighs and belly.

"God!" David's cry punctuated the silence of the room.

That's it. Alex grinned, but he kept up the pressure from hands and tongue, unwilling to leave David's surrender at a single word. With each new day they spent together, with each time they made love, Alex felt the wall around David's heart begin to crumble. He knew David felt it too. He sensed David's hunger to experience more than just the physical bond between them.

Alex wet a single finger and ran it back to tease David's opening. David leaned back to admit him, panting, moaning. But Alex just let his finger linger, not pushing inward.

Come on. Let me in, David. He circled and sucked. David's body shook with need, and Alex knew he was close. He withdrew his finger and sucked harder, hollowing his cheeks, humming against David's swollen width, pushing David to the edge and pulling back as he felt David's body tense.

"Please, Alex... I want... I need...."

Tell me what you need, David.

"Make me come. Please. I want to come in your mouth. I want to watch you swallow me down." David's voice was raw, husky. *Beautiful.* There was no missing the hint of a New England accent, but the words were rough, without pretense.

David's words were like music, wending their way into Alex's mind and sending heat down to his groin, causing him to moan. His mouth watered at the prospect of David shooting into him. Somehow it seemed even more intimate than intercourse. Alex pressed the tip of a finger inside of David. The piano keys sounded again as David leaned all the way back.

"Yes. God, yes!" David keened and shuddered as Alex ran the edges of his teeth along the underside of David's cock as he sucked. David drew up hard against Alex's forearm before spilling into Alex's waiting mouth. Alex was triumphant as he sucked and swallowed. What was it about the way David let himself go that made sex that much sweeter?

"Alex. So good. So fucking good. I've never...." David drew Alex up and ravished his mouth, his body still shuddering from release.

Alex sighed and lost himself in David's arms. It felt so good there. So right. So natural.

"DAMN," Alex said into David's chest as they lay together later on Alex's bed, bodies pressed against each other, hot and sweaty. "If that's what happens when you play for me, I may just have to lock us in here."

David understood what Alex meant, and although he'd have said it differently, the connection forged between them through the music was undeniable. He felt vulnerable. Shaky. And something else he couldn't name. Why was it so difficult to understand what he felt? Why did he need to understand? He was relieved Alex couldn't see his face—he was sure it revealed far more of what he felt than he was willing to concede.

"We should eat," David heard himself say. He pulled away from Alex, suddenly conscious of his nudity.

"Sure." His voice was bright, but David guessed that Alex had sensed his discomfort. "What did you have in mind?"

"The snow's pretty thick out there. Perhaps you'd let me cook for you tonight?"

"I... ah... sure. I'd like that." Alex looked embarrassed. "Marla and I aren't exactly great cooks. I'm not sure what we have in the kitch—"

"I'll make do."

"Sounds great. As long as you let me help. I'm sure there's something I can do."

"No doubt." The hint of pink on Alex's cheeks was charming, David decided. Realizing that if he didn't get dressed, dinner would be far later than he'd intended, David pulled on his jeans and sweater.

Alex stood up and stretched. It was difficult not to stare. David had seen Alex naked before, but it didn't matter. This time was like the first, and although he had traced the outlines of Alex's tattoos at least a dozen times now, he fought the urge to reach out and brush his fingers over them again. He wondered briefly about the scar on Alex's chest. Someday, he hoped he'd find the courage to ask Alex more about it.

THE kitchen was small but serviceable. As he rummaged through the cabinets and refrigerator for the makings of dinner, David decided Alex hadn't exaggerated when he said neither he nor Marla were cooks. By the time Alex joined him a few minutes later, David had already pulled out the ingredients for a simple meal.

"Do you have some white wine?" he asked as Alex lounged against the counter watching him. He was dressed in a pair of faded jeans and a gray T-shirt David supposed was a soft as it appeared.

Stop thinking about sex. Admittedly, he hadn't thought about much more since they'd played through the Dvořák. Even after the sex. He'd never had a partner as willing and responsive as Alex. Or as attractive.

"Sure. What are you thinking? French? Italian? Oregonian Pinot?"

What was he thinking? He repressed a lecherous grin—sharing his true thoughts at that moment would have been embarrassing—and considered the question in earnest. "Italian for the sauce," he told Alex. "Pinot for drinking, perhaps?"

"You got it." Alex sauntered out of the room, giving David an excellent view of that incredible ass and the makings of another hard-on.

A half hour later, Alex chopped an onion as tears streamed down his face. David handed him a damp paper towel. "At least I don't cut my fingers anymore," he told David with a healthy grin.

"That would be most unfortunate," David agreed as Alex mopped his face.

"So are you getting together with Rachel for Christmas?" Alex asked as he got back to work.

"No." David tried to relax the muscles in his jaw, with little success. "We spend Thanksgiving each year together. I have no plans for Christmas." He didn't add that he didn't celebrate the holiday, or at least hadn't since his grandfather's death. Not that he'd enjoyed the holidays at the estate either. He'd gone only because it had been expected of him.

"Would you like to come to midnight Mass? I've given up trying to get Marla to tag along."

David considered the offer. It wasn't as though Alex were asking him to a party or some other social engagement. It would be just the two of them. Comfortable. Or at least, more comfortable than the Christmas party at Doris's he'd been hoping for an excuse to miss.

"Yes," he said. "I'd like that." Well, perhaps not "like," but it wouldn't be torture to spend the evening at Alex's side.

"Great. I usually go to Assumption Church. If the weather's better, we can walk. Carols start around ten thirty, but to get a good seat, we need to be there by ten. Honestly, that's my favorite part."

"Are you assuming I'll stay the night, then?" David made a point of focusing his attention on pouring olive oil into the frying pan.

"I… well… I had hoped you might."

"I see," David said, turning to catch Alex's self-conscious expression. He waited until Alex was looking directly at him, then smiled outright. "And I hoped you might ask me to."

Alex's mouth dropped as he realized David had been teasing him. He laughed, then put down the knife and pinned David against the counter. "Maestro Somers," he said in feigned seriousness, "I do believe you are toying with me."

David inhaled a sharp breath—what was it about Alex that made him forget to breathe?—and met Alex's lips. And what could he do, really, but lose himself in Alex's mouth?

Something on the stove began to smoke, and he quickly pulled away to snag the frying pan from the flame. "Shit."

Alex burst out laughing.

"Don't even start with me," David warned as he began to laugh.

"Last time you said that y-y-you…."

"I have no idea what you are talking about, Mr. Bishop." David tried to keep a straight face but failed miserably. He knew Alex was imagining him sitting on his ass in the middle of the skating rink.

Alex laughed harder. "Off with you," David said as he struggled to stop from laughing again. "Dinner will be ready all too soon, and you have a table to set."

Alex bowed with a flourish. "As you wish, Lord Somers. We can't keep dinner waiting, can we?" He pulled out plates from one of the overhead cabinets, rummaged for silverware in the drawer, and was gone a moment later.

I could get used to this, David thought as he sautéed the onions and checked on the pasta. It would be far too easy.

CHAPTER 18

"WHAT do you think of this?" Alex held up a sleep shirt with a chocolate cow on it, half expecting David to roll his eyes. Not that David ever rolled his eyes—it seemed that in this, as in just about everything else, David Somers was not an average human. No, David's expression was more a combination of the over-the-reading-glasses disdain of a psychotherapist and a *Monty Python* I'm-too-serious-to-bother-with-this-nonsense deadpan.

In truth, Alex had invited the reaction and was enjoying it immensely. After the first or second time Alex had pointed it out to David, David had played along, clearly not too proud to admit to his snobbery when it came to gag gifts. And damn if David wasn't having *fun*. Alex was sure of it.

They'd been shopping since lunch, having stopped for sushi at a tiny restaurant David suggested where the owners knew him by name. It had been Alex's idea to go shopping, since he'd forgotten to buy Marla a Christmas present (he'd been distracted since he'd gotten back from Europe). David, who admitted he couldn't remember the last time he'd shopped for gifts (his personal assistant usually did that for him), had agreed to tag along.

"Not particularly funny," David said of the chocolate cow. "Regardless of her sense of humor, no woman appreciates being reminded of her chocolate tendencies. At least not coupled with a farm animal, and one with such broad hips." The twinkle in his eyes belied his utterly serious expression.

Alex chuckled and shook his head. Gone was the tight-lipped David Somers, replaced by a more relaxed, almost chatty David who liked to joke around. True, he was still awkward and at times stiff in public. But Alex found the awkwardness endearing, in part because it was something very few people ever noticed about David.

"Fine. I give up. I'll just get her a gift certificate to Starbucks. She likes those mocha latte thingies."

David raised an eyebrow. "Would you perhaps like some help?" he asked.

"Isn't that what you were doing by tagging along? Helping me?"

"No." David smiled. "I've been watching you pick things out and explaining what poor choices they are. That is not *help*."

"Okay, okay. But you could have said something earlier."

"And miss watching you flounder? I think not." David was grinning openly now.

"All right, Mr. Smooth. Why don't you show me how it's done?"

David put his hand lightly on Alex's elbow and led him out of the juniors department and toward the escalators in the center of the store. "On you go," he said. "Or do you need my help with that, as well?"

Alex smiled and walked onto the moving steps, knowing full well the jeans he was wearing were fitted in the ass. He slid one hand into his back pocket and hoped David would notice before he turned his head and asked, "So where are we going?"

"We... ah...," David began with uncharacteristic hesitation. "Just watch where you're going."

Bingo. Alex looked up at the top of the escalator and grinned.

As they reached the next floor, David added, "And don't think I didn't notice that."

"That?" Alex repeated.

"Turn right."

Alex complied. He figured he'd teased David about as much as he should for the afternoon. David had clearly enjoyed the ribbing, but Alex didn't want to find out where his patience ended.

"Stop here."

They were standing in front of a glass case filled with brightly colored silk scarves. The woman behind the counter smiled at them and asked, "How can I help you, gentlemen?"

"We'd like to see some of your Missoni scarves." David glanced in Alex's direction.

Alex thought the name was vaguely familiar, but he couldn't place it.

"Blues," David continued. "Turquoise, if you have it."

"Of course, sir." She bent down and retrieved three filmy bits of blue fabric, one with streaks of yellow throughout, another with hints of brown. David picked up the third, which mixed various shades of blue and tiny points of white.

"We'll take this one," he said. "And we'll need it wrapped."

"Not a problem," the saleswoman said. "I can take care of that for you."

Alex had to admit the colors were nice, although he had no idea whether Marla would like it or not. In fact, he felt pretty good about the gift until he handed the saleswoman his credit card and she confirmed the total on the register. He choked and coughed. David, smiling at his distress, tapped him on the back a few times, but Alex was sure he was trying hard not to laugh.

"Don't worry," David said as Alex got a hold of himself. "It's well worth the expense. She'll love it."

Alex was half tempted to remind his companion that unlike David, he wasn't as wealthy as God, but he bit back the retort. Marla was right when she said he had enough money that he should enjoy it once in a while. Why was it so hard to get used to that? It wasn't that much, really, in the grand scheme of things. And it was for Marla, not him. It was worth it. *If* she liked it.

THEY arrived back at Alex's apartment around six. It had begun to snow again, and the temperature was falling quickly. David's driver had dropped off some clothes in the morning, so Alex was surprised to find another package waiting with the concierge. This one smelled a lot like food.

"Chinese," David confirmed as he snagged the bags and pressed a bill into Mr. Carmichael's hand. The old man grinned and wished them both a merry Christmas. Alex couldn't help but marvel at how comfortable David was with staff. Not surprising, he guessed, given his upbringing. Alex always worried about when to tip and how much. Mostly, he relied on Marla to tell him what to do when they traveled.

"Nice. And when did you manage to order?"

"Last night." The elevator doors closed and David leaned over to kiss Alex.

Alex set the bags he was carrying down and wrapped his arms around David. "Who needs a butler with you around?"

"Is there anything else you need tonight, sir?" David asked with a straight face.

"I can think of something. After church."

"Excuse me for saying this, but that just seems a contradiction." David kissed Alex again as the doors opened. "Or a sin."

"Nah," Alex replied as he picked the bags back up. "No better way to celebrate the holiday."

DAVID closed his eyes as the organ sounded the first chords of the processional. Even from their seats near the front of the church, he could already smell the heady aroma of the incense. Frankincense, with overtones of rosemary and balsam. He'd seen one of the celebrants swinging the censer as they processed from the side entrance of the church just as the music began—his family wasn't Catholic, but he'd substituted often enough as an organist that he was familiar with the Mass. He hadn't needed the money, of course, but he'd enjoyed the work. He'd always enjoyed work, and it had given him an excuse to escape the dull holiday parties his grandfather held at the estate.

The choir was quite good. No doubt some of them were ringers—professional singers—perhaps from the symphony's chorus. As a child, he'd always wanted to sing. He'd heard the Vienna Boys Choir perform at Lincoln Center—Somers Investments had sponsored the performance—and he'd asked his grandfather if he could audition for an area boys choir he'd read about in the *New York Times*. James Somers had made it clear that he was already paying for David's piano and theory lessons, and that he couldn't be expected to pay for his grandson to *sing*. The old man hadn't even listened when David told him the only thing he needed was a ride to rehearsals.

As the celebrants processed down each of the aisles, Alex glanced over at him. David guessed he wanted to reassure himself that David was doing all right. He was. Surprisingly so. The familiar music was calming, and he found his mind drifting to Christmas, thirty-two years before.

"Come here, boy," James Somers told him as he played with a xylophone on the music room floor. "There is something you need to know."

David didn't like the enormous mansion much, but he loved this room with its thick oriental rugs and large windows that made it feel warm, in spite of the frost outside.

His grandfather looked ancient to four-year-old David. He'd been staying with the old man since his parents had left for a trip to Italy—a second honeymoon, his mother had called it. They would spend two weeks on the Somers's yacht in the Mediterranean before flying back home. They were coming back today, Christmas Day. David had been looking forward to it. He'd missed them both, and he missed their Manhattan brownstone and his room.

He gazed up at his grandfather, hoping he'd tell him his parents were coming back early and that he should ask Loretta to pack his things.

"There's been an accident," the old man said. David would always remember the expression on James Somers's face: hard, almost angry. Later, David understood the expression was one of pain. "Your parents are... your parents won't be coming home."

It took David nearly a week to understand that when his grandfather said his parents weren't coming home, he meant they weren't ever coming home.

"You okay?"

Alex's whispered question brought David back to himself. David realized with some embarrassment that he was the only one still standing.

"I'm fine. Thank you." He quickly sat down, resolving not to lose his focus again. He was here to listen to the music, wasn't he? This wasn't about revisiting Christmases past.

Alex touched David's arm, a reassuring gesture that made him smile. It had been only a week since they'd returned from Europe, and yet he was starting to think maybe this relationship would last longer than the others.

The Mass was over far too quickly, the choir singing "Adeste Fidelis" for the recessional. A few minutes later, David and Alex followed the rest of the congregants out of the nave and into the vestibule to wishes of "Merry Christmas." An elderly woman waved at Alex, who bent down and gave her a kiss on the cheek.

"Agnes! You look wonderful."

The old woman blushed to the roots of her white hair. "We've missed you," she cooed happily, allowing Alex to take her hand. "Been performing, I'd bet."

"Just got back from Italy. It's good to be home."

"I hear you're going to play for us on New Year's Day. Father Tom announced it."

"I always do," Alex answered with a grin, "don't I?" Then, perhaps realizing David was still standing at his side, he said, "I'm so sorry. Agnes, I'd like you to meet a good friend of mine, David Somers. David, this is Agnes Bonino."

"Good to meet you, Agnes." David held out his hand.

Agnes looked at David, then frowned and looked back at Alex for a moment in silent question. Alex smiled and Agnes cried happily, "David Somers? The maestro?" David nodded. "You don't know how long I've wanted to meet you!" She finally took his hand and shook it with a surprisingly powerful grip.

"My pleasure."

"You're both going to join us for a little refreshment downstairs, aren't you?" Agnes said with an expression of gleeful anticipation.

"I... ah... well, we—" Alex began.

"We would love to," David finished. Alex looked at him with obvious surprise.

"Oh, that's *wonderful*," Agnes said. "I'll go tell the girls. They'll be so pleased." She scurried off down the hallway.

"You didn't have to do that," Alex said. David was thinking the same thing himself. Why had he? He despised this sort of casual get-together.

"It's important to you." Another surprise, that he'd come to that conclusion without help. Usually someone had to prod him—his sister and, before her, his wife. But he'd sensed Alex's desire to join Agnes and her friends.

"Thank you." For a moment David wondered if Alex was going to kiss him here, where everyone could see them. Not that he cared, particularly, if anyone knew of his homosexuality, but he would have picked a better public place for that sort of demonstration of affection. Alex, however, smiled a bit more broadly and brushed the back of David's hand with his own.

Of course he wouldn't kiss you here, even if he felt comfortable doing it. He wouldn't want you to be uncomfortable. It suddenly occurred to David how much Alex must be going out of his way to accommodate his own awkward attempts at navigating Alex's universe. The knowledge did not give him great comfort. How long would it be before Alex tired of trying to appease him?

"Ready for some coffee cake?" Alex gestured to where Agnes had disappeared minutes before. David stifled a sigh and nodded, then followed Alex to the social hall.

ALEX did his best to stay focused on the conversation. Agnes and two of her friends had managed to corner him, quite literally, by the drink table. It wasn't the conversation that was a challenge, it was seeing David, himself surrounded by several women and one grumpy-looking old man, that was distracting. Although clearly holding his own, David was also obviously uncomfortable. Out of his element.

"Excuse me," he told Agnes as he gently made himself a path between the women. "I need to take care of something." *I need to rescue David.*

"I don't know," one of the women was saying as she leaned too close to David. "Just listen to the radio. You'll hear it. No more singing. Auto-Tune this, cut that. If it was up to me, I'd ban all the rock stations. Hop-hop—"

"Hip-hop, Martha," the old man corrected in a disinterested monotone.

"—rap. Get rid of it all. Jazz too."

Alex was just about to interrupt when David said, "That would be a pity."

The old man looked up with interest, and the three other women appeared pleased with David's response.

"Music is artistic expression. Each of us appreciates different foods. It's the same with music. Who am I to say that if you don't enjoy listening to Beethoven, for example, you are somehow wrong?"

Martha, who appeared to be in utter shock to hear David speak these words, huffed loudly and walked away. David immediately looked uncomfortable, but he relaxed as the old man said, "I absolutely agree with you. And more power to you for telling Martha where to take it."

David blinked his surprise. Alex guessed David hadn't realized he'd told anyone to take anything anywhere.

"David," he said as he stifled a feigned yawn, "we really should be going. It's almost one thirty."

"Of course." David turned and nodded at the group still crowded around him. "It's been a pleasure."

They walked out of the room, stopping on the way so Alex could kiss Agnes good-bye. He thanked her for the homemade cookies she pressed into his hands, and promised to see her again soon. A few minutes later, they were out on the chilly street, pulling up their collars and flagging down a taxi.

"I apologize," David said as they settled into the cab. "I didn't mean to offend your friends."

Alex chuckled. "Martha needed a good kick in the ass," he said. "None of the others want to challenge her. I'm guessing after your little lecture, she'll be quiet for a while. Nothing like having the CSO's music director tell you how it is."

"I hadn't intended to be so harsh."

"You were just being honest," Alex countered.

"I'm afraid I'm generally too honest and too willing to give my opinion."

"I like that about you." Alex put his hand to David's jaw and swept a thumb over the hint of stubble there.

"I…," David began. Then, perhaps thinking better of it, he said simply, "Thank you. I felt remarkably comfortable tonight. Thank you for asking me to come."

"You're welcome." Alex squeezed David's hand. He had sensed it too, how David had seemed more relaxed than usual, even at the gathering after the Mass. "Spend tomorrow with me?" He didn't want David to leave after breakfast. "We don't do much on Christmas," he continued when David didn't immediately answer. "Marla makes killer pancakes, and we usually just hang out and watch a game."

"Game?"

"Basketball. But you don't watch basketball, do you?"

"No."

Of course he doesn't watch basketball. What the hell were you thinking?

David smiled. "But I'd like to."

"IT'S gorgeous!" Marla shouted, throwing her arms around Alex before picking up the scarf and modeling it in her pajamas. He and David were only slightly better dressed in sweatpants and T-shirts—Alex's. David had finally admitted to Alex that he didn't own "sweats." Alex had laughed and tossed him a pair—a bit too long in the legs, but passable, David decided—after which Alex told him he looked "cute" in them. David wasn't sure it was a compliment, but he decided he liked the feel of the fleece. He also liked the way it smelled of Alex.

"I'm glad you like it," Alex said with a quick glance in David's direction and a mouthed "thank you."

David exhaled a long, slow breath as he contemplated the gift he'd picked out for Alex. He hoped he wasn't entirely obvious in his discomfort. *Steady. You can do this. One foot in front of the other.*

Marla had already given Alex his gift, a hand-knit sweater she had undoubtedly picked up in Milan and which he now wore over his T-shirt. David recognized the label; he shopped at that store on occasion. Alex had joked that Marla made all his wardrobe choices, and David didn't doubt it, judging from Alex's predilection for ragged jeans and sweatpants.

"I'm going back to bed," Marla announced with an all-too-obvious yawn. "Lunch at noon, boys."

"Or whenever she wakes up," Alex said after she'd left.

David once again thought of the gift he'd picked out for Alex and debated whether he should just forget about it. David had bought it, thinking it was perfect but unsure whether a gift was even appropriate at this juncture in their relationship. They had dated less than two weeks, and he feared it was premature. In an effort to hide his discomfort, he picked up the half-empty coffee cup from the side table and brought it to his lips. The coffee was cold. Bitter. He forced a smile and managed to swallow.

Alex rubbed his chin and returned the smile. David wondered if Alex could read his mind, then brushed the thought away. *"You overanalyze,"* Helena had always told him. *"Just be."*

David hesitated a moment longer, but before he could make up his mind, Alex stood up. "More coffee?" he asked.

"Thank you." David's voice sounded stiff to his own ears.

"Back in a minute."

He watched Alex leave and blew a gentle stream of air from between his lips to calm his anxiety. Outside, snow had begun to fall. He got up and walked over to the window. Lake Michigan appeared gray on the horizon and David heard a mournful and haunting adagio. He loved this city. Here, away from his grandfather's watchful eye, he had found a measure of happiness with his music. Only his Italian villa came close to giving him that sense of well-being, and the peace it offered was a different one entirely: a haven, a place to hide when the world became too overwhelming. It was there he had retreated after Helena's death, amidst the vineyards of the Po Valley.

He started at Alex's warm hand on his shoulder. "Here," Alex said, handing him the coffee. "Fresh pot."

"Thank you." David fought the urge to lean back into Alex's body. He didn't want to appear too eager, too needy.

"I hope you don't mind," Alex said, the words spoken far too close to David's ear, "but I have a gift for you."

Mind? "I...," he began as he stared down at his coffee.

"I realize it's a bit soon," Alex said, "but I wanted you to have it."

The words surprised David—his own thoughts of a short time ago, voiced. Why was it so difficult for him to express his feelings with the same honesty? It was something he admired in Alex: his open heart. "You are too kind." He cringed inwardly as he spoke the words. They were so practiced. And yet when he felt vulnerable, he relied upon such social niceties.

Alex's response was entirely unexpected and at odds with David's own: he wrapped his arms around David's chest and pressed his head to the back of David's neck, then kissed him tenderly. David's body tensed of its own accord, but Alex kissed him again, this time below his ear. David shuddered and pulled away, his heart beating wildly.

You're afraid. He was surprised he recognized the emotion—a scant two weeks ago, he'd have ignored it entirely and retreated to the safety of his own thoughts. Now, however, he forced himself to turn around and meet Alex's questioning gaze.

Another moment's hesitation. *What are you waiting for?* He wanted to kiss Alex. Why was it so hard to give in to his need? "You really shouldn't have gotten me anything" was all he said.

He could see disappointment in Alex's eyes. Or at least, he thought he saw it there, but it was gone before he could be sure. For the first time since he'd met Alex, regret blossomed into something more: guilt. Still, he stood there, rooted to the spot, unable to express himself, even though he knew he wanted to—that he *needed* to thank Alex for his patience.

As always, Alex rose to the occasion. "Honestly, I didn't know who I was buying it for," he offered before wrapping his arms around David and drawing him into a warm embrace. He laughed, tense laughter that only served to remind David of how woefully inadequate he was to put Alex at ease. "Back in a minute."

Alex returned with a large package wrapped in simple brown paper with a green raffia ribbon. He handed it to David and said, "Merry Christmas, David."

Silently, David took the package and pulled open the tie, then unfolded the paper and turned the canvas around. It was the painting from the gallery. The one he'd hoped to purchase at the fundraiser but which had already been sold. "You… you were the patron who purchased it?"

"Yeah." Alex combed his fingers through his tousled hair. "I wasn't sure what I'd do with it. But when I realized you wanted it, I hoped…."

"I don't know what to say." David was surprised by his own honesty. "It's lovely. I thought of the lake when I saw it. I imagined it hanging in my studio. But really," he added, uneasy once more, "it's far too generous a gift."

Alex shifted on his feet and David noticed his jaw tighten. *Damn!* He'd ruined things with Alex again. This time, however, he didn't just sit and hope Alex would step in as he had done before. He stood up and kissed Alex—a passionate kiss he hoped would communicate all of the things he couldn't bring himself to admit. The tension in Alex's body abated with the contact, and David, too, felt himself relax.

"Thank you," he murmured against Alex's ear after the kiss broke.

"You're welcome."

"I have something for you as well, Alex." He walked over to the front hallway where he'd left his portfolio, pulled out a small package, and walked back to the living room. "Merry Christmas."

Alex unwrapped the gift and stared silently at it for a moment, clearly moved. He ran his fingers reverently over the slick paper—a program from a 1962 performance of the Sibelius Violin Concerto—pausing at the autograph to eye it with wonder. "I listened to an old recording of David Oistrakh when I was little. My mother loved his playing," he said.

"When I heard you play," David explained, "I thought of him. I never heard him play in person, of course, since he died before I was born. Still, I hear much of his passion in your playing."

"Where did you find the program?"

"I have a friend in Philadelphia. A collector." David smiled. "I hope you like—"

"It's wonderful, David." Alex set the program down on the coffee table and gathered David in his arms. "Better than wonderful. Perfect."

David swallowed hard, fighting a wave of emotion so powerful it left him nearly breathless. Was he falling in love with Alex? *Nonsense. You've barely known him a month.*

"Come back to bed?" Alex asked, his voice rough. "We've got a few hours before Marla wakes up again."

CHAPTER *19*

THE symphony did not perform on New Year's Eve, so Doris Pinchley-Bates took full advantage of the gap in the CSO's schedule by throwing a party for the musicians and staff. This year, however, the party also served another purpose. For the past few months, the symphony association had been in talks with the musicians' union over the musicians' contracts. And although Doris assured David things had been progressing well in the negotiations—David was relieved not to be involved—Doris said she hoped the party might help to ease the way for an agreement between the two sides. The musicians' union had been playing under the old contract since the season had begun, but things had grown tense over the past few months, and an agreement between the sides was ever elusive. In spite of her reassurances, David could tell Doris was far more concerned than she let on.

Labor concerns aside, Doris's New Year's party was one of the few parties David found he enjoyed, mostly because it had become a tradition for the musicians to give impromptu performances throughout the evening. Never one to be embarrassed to take part in the musical celebration, David generally accompanied the players on the lovely Steinway grand Doris had purchased for just such an occasion. Impeccably tuned and regulated to David's own preferences, of course.

Having finished accompanying a flautist on a Bach sonata, David now retreated to the edge of the large ballroom and nursed a glass of champagne. A string quartet played Mozart for the guests, and David watched the violinist with longing. Alex had left two nights before for a gig in New York City and was not due back in town until early the next morning. David had gotten used to having Alex by his side—they had spent nearly every night together since Christmas, mostly at the penthouse.

"Pining away, are we?"

Doris's voice startled David; he hadn't realized she'd been standing behind him.

"Excuse me?"

"I may not be young anymore," Doris said with a particularly flirtatious swing of her long hair, "but I'm not blind."

"I don't know what you're talking about." But he knew *exactly* what she was talking about.

"Don't play coy with me, David." She sipped her champagne but held his gaze. "If my star conductor is spotted out and about town on the arm of one of the symphony's guest soloists and no rehearsals are involved, I notice."

"And if only rehearsals were involved?" he countered with a raised eyebrow.

She laughed and gesticulated with her champagne flute. "I wouldn't mind either way. Although it would be more interesting if there *was* more than just music involved."

Interesting. She clearly knew more about his personal life than he realized. He wasn't sure if this disturbed him or set his mind at ease. Not that he'd deny his sexual orientation if asked—his reputation in the music world was too well established to suffer—but it might make it easier for him to handle the symphony association if he was up-front with her.

"More than just music is involved."

Her response surprised him. "Then why isn't he here? And why aren't you showing him off?" When he said nothing but just drank his own champagne, she laughed again and added, "You thought I would be scandalized, didn't you?"

"Perhaps not scandalized, but—"

"We knew you were gay when we hired you, David," she said without missing a beat. This time he stared at her and hoped he wasn't gaping. "Not that I'd have minded, you know, if you'd swung both ways." She gave him one of her usual ravenous looks, although he could tell it was just for his benefit. "We had no problem with John before you either. Although," she added with a coy smile, "some of his public antics were a bit scandalous." It was evident from her expression that she had enjoyed his predecessor's penchant for excess.

David felt the smile spread across his face. "I should have learned by now never to underestimate you," he said with a chuckle and a shake of his head.

"And well you should." She finished her champagne and touched the back of his hand genially. "But seriously, it's nice to see a real smile on your face. I haven't seen you this happy in years. Helena would be pleased."

"Thank you." She was right. He *was* happy. And although he would not have shared it with her, or anyone else for that matter, he was composing again. That, too, made him happy.

She smiled, then glanced over his shoulder and said matter-of-factly, "I really must be circulating. I do hope you'll enjoy the rest of your evening. I have a feeling it will be a good one." She was gone before he could ask her what she'd meant.

He set his glass down on the tray of a passing server before turning his attention once more to the music. He felt someone touch the small of his back—a soft, sensual touch. "What—?" he began.

"Missed me?"

"Alex?"

"Damn well better be," Alex said in an undertone, "or I might get jealous."

David took a deep breath to steady himself. Why did this man always affect him so? "You don't seem the jealous type," he said as he turned around and took Alex's hand in his.

"You'd be surprised, Maestro. But you didn't answer my question." Alex's eyes were full of mischief.

"I missed you."

"Good."

David pursed his lips to stifle the grin that threatened to spread over his face. "I didn't think you'd be back until tomorrow."

"I came directly from the airport." Alex glanced at his watch. "Made it with an hour to spare too."

David leaned in and kissed Alex—not an overly passionate kiss but a heartfelt one. They'd held hands before in public, but this was much more. David hadn't meant to kiss Alex. He hadn't thought about it at all—it had felt so natural. The look of unadulterated pleasure on Alex's face at the gesture told David he hadn't overstepped the boundaries of their private and professional lives.

From the corner, David realized Doris was watching them. She smiled her approval, then went back to chatting with some of the other guests. "She knew you were coming tonight, didn't she?"

"Doris?"

"Taking a cue from Marla and my sister?" He tried to keep a straight face, but he knew he was failing miserably.

Alex laughed. "Did you know Doris has a private plane?"

"I seem to recall her mentioning it. Probably when she was trying to get me to join her on her private island in the Caribbean." Alex raised an eyebrow. "I declined. Politely, of course. It's nice to know that she finally got the message."

"And what message would that be?" Alex spoke these words so close to David's ear that David shivered involuntarily.

"That it's our turn to play a bit," David said. "Any other messages will have to wait until later."

"Later?" Alex's voice was a husky whisper.

"Hmm. You didn't think you'd be going home alone tonight, did you?"

"I was hoping I wouldn't be." Alex squeezed David's hand again.

"Where's your violin?"

"In the foyer. The maid is protecting it with her life."

A few minutes later, David sat at the piano looking up at Alex. "What's your pleasure, Mr. Bishop?" he asked loudly enough for the gathering crowd to hear. "Beethoven? Dvořák? Mendelssohn?"

"Grappelli, I think."

David sat up a bit straighter, momentarily unsure what to make of Alex's request. Stéphane Grappelli had been one of the greatest jazz violinists of the twentieth century. David knew every one of his recordings, something he'd mentioned to Alex over dinner a few nights before. It wasn't what David had expected, hadn't been what David had ever thought of playing with Alex, but it was not an unwelcome request.

"Blue Moon?" David asked. If Alex could challenge him, he could certainly return the favor. Not that he had any doubts as to Alex's ability to play any of Grappelli's work.

"Perfect." Alex tucked his fiddle under his chin.

As Alex tuned, David glanced around the audience, noting the looks of pleasant surprise on the guests' faces. It wasn't as though the musicians played only classical music at Doris's gatherings; many played jazz and rock selections. But it was the first time *he* had played anything but the classical repertoire at such a gathering. He found the idea surprisingly appealing. Doris was nearly beside herself.

David closed his eyes and drew a long breath, then brushed his fingers over the keys, the crisp technique of the classical piece he'd played less than an hour before now replaced by a more comfortable, almost sensual approach to the instrument. He looked up and met Alex's gaze, familiar, smoldering with intensity. There was something else there too, though David was hard-pressed to place the expression. Sexual attraction, certainly. But more than that. The thought faded with the sound of Alex's violin, and David lost himself in the music.

Later, back at David's apartment in the early hours of the morning, David held Alex against him as they lay in bed after making love. "Happy New Year," he murmured before kissing Alex's hair.

"Definitely happy." Alex tightened his arms around David's waist.

Two Weeks Later

DAVID stood at the ship's bow, looking out over the water at the sunrise. He took a slow, deep breath and stretched his arms above his head. The weekend trip to the Bahamas had been unexpected and the break from his work at the symphony unwelcome. Still, if he was going to be forced not to work, there were few better ways to spend the time than on the water.

"It's beautiful." Alex pressed his lips against David's neck and wrapped his arms around David's chest.

"It is."

"Couldn't sleep?"

"Mmm." David leaned into Alex's embrace.

"Worried about the symphony?"

"Yes." There was little use in hiding his anxiety. Alex could see through him. "Rachel's right when she says I'm not very good at letting things run their course."

"The symphony association will work something out with the musicians' union. I can't imagine Doris letting the strike go on more than a few weeks."

David inhaled sharply as Alex kissed his neck again. It didn't matter that they'd made love just hours before; being near Alex always made him feel like this. "No. I doubt she will, if she has any say in it."

"Doesn't she?" Another kiss, a nip.

David shuddered. "It's difficult to concentrate when you do that."

"Good." Alex's voice was warm and throaty by David's ear. "Then I'm doing my job."

Three days before, David showed up backstage at Alex's Miami concert. David was supposed to have been conducting the first of the

CSO's modern series that same night, but the phone call he'd received from Doris the morning of the concert had changed everything. The musicians' union had rejected the latest contract proposal from the symphony association. Things had apparently gone from bad to worse.

"I have instructions from our attorney that you are not to be involved in this fiasco," Doris warned when she called to give him the news. "Besides, you need to remain neutral here. We can't have you alienating either side."

He hadn't liked to hear it, but he knew she was right. He'd always walked the fine line between the symphony association and the musicians. It was his place. Funny, how that always seemed to be his place—the neutral third party. Liked by everyone, and still alone.

He sighed and took a deep breath of the ocean air, willing himself to relax. What good did it do to rehash the entire sordid affair over and over? Alex was right. He needed to let it go.

"You're a thousand miles away." Alex turned him around and kissed him soundly on the lips.

"I don't want to be that far away." It frightened him to realize how much he wanted to be here with Alex. They hadn't even been together two months, and he already wanted to believe Alex would always be there. He knew better, though. Alex wanted him now. Soon, he'd realize his mistake.

"Good." David closed his eyes and sighed as Alex traced the line of his jaw with his fingers. "That's much better." Alex now began to feather kisses at David's throat.

"We'll make Bimini this morning. I was thinking maybe some snorkeling and then lunch on the beach."

"Mmm." Alex licked David's ear and lingered there. "How much time do we have until we get to the Bahamas?"

"Time enough." David grabbed Alex around the waist and slipped a hand down Alex's pants to cup his ass.

Please, David thought as he led Alex back to the stateroom, *don't let this end too soon.*

THREE days later they were back in Miami, having cleared customs at the docks. With a few hours before the flight to Chicago, David suggested lunch at a small deli in Boynton Beach. They grabbed sandwiches and walked to the beach, where they tossed down a blanket and ate as they watched the surf.

"When do you leave for LA?" David asked as he looked out over the water.

"Wednesday night."

"Looked at your schedule for a change?" David's lighthearted tone belied the admonition.

"Nah." Alex wiped his mouth with a napkin and grinned. "Marla texted to remind me."

David laughed, and for the first time in days, Alex thought he looked relaxed. "God forbid the woman finds another job. What will you do?"

"Rely on the kindness of strangers?" Alex set his sandwich down on the wax paper wrap and leaned over to kiss David. He tasted like pastrami and rye.

"You should be so lucky." David's eyes twinkled in the bright sunshine. "Pickle?"

"Thanks." Alex took the wedge from David, and their fingers brushed. He popped the pickle in his mouth, then pushed David onto the sand and claimed a kiss. "I never thought sandwiches could be so hot."

"If you're trying to get me to say it's 'hot pastrami'," David replied with a warm chuckle, "you're dreaming, Bishop."

"I guess I'll survive." Alex sighed theatrically, then kissed David again. David wrapped his arms around Alex and pulled him closer. "But only if you keep doing that."

"My pleasure." David's lips had barely touched his when David's cell phone rang.

Shit. "Back to reality so soon?"

"I should take this," David said as he pulled the phone from his pocket. "It's Doris. Maybe she'll have some good news for a change."

Alex sincerely hoped so.

"Doris, so good to hear from you." David winked at Alex and brushed a stray lock of hair from Alex's eyes. Alex sighed and rolled onto his side. "No, Doris. I told you I'd be unavailable for a few days. You could always have called my assistant. He'd have been able to reach me."

There was a pause in the conversation as Doris responded. Alex took the opportunity to kiss David's neck and slip his arm around David's waist. David shivered.

"No, Doris. You've given me orders not to get involved. Either you allow me to participate in bringing the two sides together, or I'm staying out of this." David's body tensed as he spoke these words.

"No. I am not going to take the association's side in these negotiations. You yourself understand how foolhardy it would be for me—"

Alex took a deep breath. Just hearing the strain in David's voice made him anxious too. *Damn.* This was exactly what he didn't want for David and what he knew was David's worst nightmare—being forced to stand between the parties but unable to take any action to draw them back together.

"I do *not* think the musicians are asking for something unreasonable, nor do I think the symphony association's financial concerns are out of line. I'm simply trying to say—" David sat up, his jaw visibly tense, his shoulders tight. "Doris... Doris, I don't see that this conversation will improve the situation. If you want my help, then you must permit me to help. But until I have your permission to intervene, we have nothing to discuss. Good-bye, Doris."

David tapped the phone to disconnect the call and shook his head. "Doris can be quite exasperating at times."

Alex sat up and drew David against him, kissing his shoulder and trying hard not to sigh. "I can imagine. Anything I can do to help?"

"Nothing. Thank you." David's tone was formal, distant.

So much for relaxing.

"We should be going," David said after a moment.

Alex knew they had several hours before they needed to get to the airport, but he didn't argue. If it would make David more comfortable for them to spend the last few hours of the trip waiting at the departure gate, he was fine with it. "Sure." He stood up and offered David his hand. David, distracted, ignored it as he picked up the remains of their lunch.

Alex shook the sand from the towels, and they were back in the car a few minutes later, headed for Miami International.

THEY arrived at O'Hare two hours behind schedule. The weather suited David's dark mood—icy rain fell steadily from a gray sky. Alex had slept nearly the entire flight. David couldn't blame him. After the call from Doris on the beach, he hadn't wanted to talk. As always, Alex seemed to sense this and gave David his space.

David ignored the messages on his cell phone and the texts from Doris telling him to "call right away when you land." Whatever she wanted, it could wait until he got home.

They retrieved their bags and headed out to the curb, where his driver would meet them.

"Maestro Somers!" The voice from behind them startled David. "Mr. Somers!" David turned around to face a television camera and a reporter from one of the local news outlets.

"I'm Sharon Kleves," the reporter said. "Your office told me I might find you here."

My office?

"I was hoping you might give us a statement regarding the latest impasse in contract negotiations with the symphony."

"I hope that both sides will reach a resolution as quickly as possible." It wasn't the statement he *wanted* to give, but he wasn't naïve enough to think defying the symphony association's strict orders to stay out of the melee would help anything.

"But Maestro, surely you want the strike to end?"

David stared into the red light of the camera and said, "Of course. We all do."

"But the symphony association is threatening to cancel the entire season if the musicians don't come back to the bargaining table. How can you just sit back and allow this to happen?" The reporter shoved the microphone back in his face.

"I'm sorry. I have nothing more to say about the matter." He spoke the words through clenched teeth.

"David?" Alex's voice brought David back to reality. "The driver's here."

Thank heavens! "Excuse me, Ms. Kleves. I must be going." He turned on his heel and headed outside.

Once settled into the car, Alex asked, "How are you doing?"

"I'm perfectly fine." David realized his tone had been harsh. "Thank you for asking," he added, hoping Alex would forgive his sharp response.

"I'm sorry you had to deal with that." Alex took his hand and rubbed his thumb against his palm.

"Nothing I haven't dealt with before." The press had been hounding him for weeks now, ever since news of the strike had broken. And for weeks, he'd been telling them the only thing he was allowed to tell them: no comment.

"How did they know to find you here?"

"Good question." He gritted his teeth. "Given the number of messages Doris left while we were airborne, I'm quite sure this was her doing. She'd have called my assistant and gotten the flight information from him."

"But wasn't she the one who told you not to get involved in this?"

"That was the symphony association's decision."

Alex shook his head and blew air from between his lips. "And she doesn't agree with the association's decision." David nodded. "So she hoped you'd just ignore them?"

"Exactly."

"I wouldn't want to be in your shoes." Alex's expression was sympathetic. "I'd be pissed as hell."

David said nothing but gazed out the window of the car at the darkening sky.

Nineteen Years Before

"YOU'RE doing *what*?" James Somers bellowed from across the room. He held a letter in his hand and waved it around as if he were trying to get David's attention. David had been expecting this particular confrontation for the past two months, ever since he'd sent his college acceptance letter back.

"I plan to enter the University of Michigan in the fall to study composition and conducting." There. He'd said it. He steeled himself for the tirade.

"A *state* school? And why the hell would you be majoring in music? We've been through this before. You'll study business at Duke like your father, complete your MBA—"

"I won't." David's heart raced. A trickle of perspiration ran down the back of his neck, between his shoulder blades, and to his waist.

"You *what*?" His grandfather now stood only a few feet away from him. The old man's face was red, his brow furrowed, and his upper lip curled in anger. David wasn't sure he'd ever seen James so angry.

"You heard me." David made sure his voice was even. Whatever happened, he would *not* raise his voice. "I don't want to go to business school."

"But your grades in math have been outstanding. You're at the top of your class."

"I want to be a musician. I don't enjoy—"

"Who the hell cares what you enjoy? This isn't about enjoyment. It's a career. It's about the family business."

"The family business will survive without me. I don't need—"

James slapped David hard across the cheek. David fought back tears of anger and shame as he cupped his stinging face. "How *dare* you! After all you've been given. You owe your parents better than this."

David's gut roiled with guilt as his grandfather's words hit home. Momentarily speechless, he backed up a few feet and stood, openmouthed, staring at his grandfather.

"Nothing to say to that, boy?" James's voice resonated with triumph.

David felt panic spread through his body, cold and clawing. He felt this way any time he thought about majoring in business. Until now, he'd been able to push the feeling away. He'd told himself he would stand up to his grandfather, explain that he would make a terrible businessman, plead with him to understand that he was a good musician—outstanding, even. But faced with the reality of James's hard expression, David couldn't immediately form the words to respond.

"I thought not." His grandfather's face softened a bit. He knew his words had resonated with David. "I've indulged your little hobby long enough. I let you go to that music school in the city. I've permitted you to take piano lessons instead of spending more time at my side learning the business. But now you need to be a man and take responsibility. You need to carry on the Somers name."

Hot tears spilled over David's cheeks. Tears of despair. Heartache. He thought of his parents, of his mother's warmth, of his father's sense of humor. Of the love he'd felt when they'd been alive.

Would they want this for me? He already knew the answer. In that instant, he realized he'd known it all along.

"No," he whispered.

"What?" The old man was obviously stunned.

"I said no. You're wrong. They didn't want that for me. They wanted—they expected me to make my own choices."

James laughed. "You were a child. How could you know what they wanted?"

"I know." He took a deep breath, then continued, "But it doesn't really matter. It's what *I* want. It's what I *need*." He braced himself for another blow, but it didn't come. "So you can disown me, if that makes you feel any better. I don't need your money. I've been given a full scholarship. They want me." *Someone wants me.*

He and his grandfather didn't speak about his studies again before he left for school. And although David had been prepared to be kicked out of the house, he knew that James would never do it. David was, after all, the last of the Somerses. And even if David would always be a disappointment, blood was everything.

CHAPTER 20

Chicago

Six Weeks Later

ALEX stood at the glass doors to the penthouse patio and watched the sun illuminate Lake Michigan. David was still sound asleep.

The symphony strike was now well into its third month, and for the past month, Alex had done his best to keep David as busy as possible. He was pretty sure David knew exactly what he'd been up to, but he hadn't complained. Even with their active schedules—David was still working on programming for next year's season and Alex would be leaving in less than a week for a gig in Japan—Alex could sense David's restlessness. It wasn't as if David could schedule anything to fill the time either. Unless the symphony association cancelled the entire symphony season, which was looking more and more likely as time went by, David's contract didn't allow for any substitute work.

This past week, things had gotten worse. David had taken to pacing the apartment, telephone in hand, trying to convince the symphony association to make another settlement offer. "You'll lose far more of your precious revenue if the entire season is cancelled," he'd heard David snap at Doris.

It hadn't helped that the reporters called David regularly to press him about the heightening tension between the musicians and the symphony association. He knew that each time David repeated the words "no comment," it took a little bit out of him. David's mood had worsened. His frustration at being powerless to do anything about the strike was obvious.

Alex tried to get David out of the apartment as much as he could. He coaxed David to take long walks on the beach, hoping he might get David to open up a bit more about how he was feeling. And although David humored him and never resisted Alex's suggestions, he said little when they walked, instead gazing out at the water as if his mind were somewhere else entirely.

They'd been out late the night before to hear a new jazz ensemble, and had tumbled into bed at nearly three in the morning. And that hadn't been for sleep. They'd finally dozed off in each other's arms around four. But even when they made love, Alex sensed the growing distance between them, a distance of David's making. Alex had been half-tempted to contact Doris and persuade her to allow David to take work elsewhere during the strike. His suggestion that David speak to the symphony association about it had been met with a curt "perhaps." Alex knew better than to press the issue.

Alex sighed and padded off to the kitchen to make some coffee. He'd practice a bit. There was no better way to clear his fuzzy brain. Ten minutes later, armed with a mug full of David's dark French brew, Alex grabbed his violin and headed down the hallway.

Early morning sunlight flooded David's studio, and the ancient oriental rug felt soft and warm beneath his bare feet. Alex tucked the violin under his chin, pulled his favorite bow from the case, then headed over to the piano to plunk out an A and tune. Tuning required little thought, and he glanced over the piano stand, noting an orchestral score and several sheets of composition paper behind it. He gripped the violin tighter beneath his chin and reached out to push the score aside, revealing what he recognized as David's immaculate script.

For a moment, he wondered if the composition was the jazz piece he and David had worked on when they'd been passing time. It only took a second for him to realize this was something on a completely different scale: a symphonic work, scored for full orchestra and solo instrument.

Alex hummed the first few bars of the melodic line. The music was instantly recognizable; he had heard bits and snatches of it before, coming from the studio. The music David said he was considering for his modern series.

David had told him it was someone else's work. And yet the calligraphy was definitely his.

Alex read through the rest of the piece—what looked to be the first movement of a modern concerto. There was no title, and other than his certainty that the piece was written in David's hand, nothing to identify its author.

Without thinking, Alex fingered the notes. The score was written for violin—Alex was sure of that as well. There was no mistaking the range or the phrasing. No other instrument Alex knew of looked like this on a page. But why hadn't David mentioned it?

It's not your business. He'll tell you when he's ready.

He forced himself to focus on the task at hand and finished tuning his instrument. He didn't mean to look again, but the manuscript drew his gaze once more. He hesitated another moment, then pulled a music stand out from the corner and placed the music on it.

DAVID rubbed his eyes. It didn't seem to matter that the man from his dreams had slept by his side; he had still dreamed of the music and of Alex. Over the months they'd spent together, he had toyed with the idea of telling Alex about the music. He wanted to share it, to ask his opinion. More than anything, he wanted to hear Alex play the piece. But each time he got up the nerve to mention the composition to Alex, he stopped himself.

It's not good enough yet. You'll share it with him when it's ready.

He sat up in bed and stretched. Even now, he could hear the music. But as his head began to clear of its usual morning fog, he realized that he was no longer dreaming: the music drifted into the room from somewhere in the apartment. From the practice studio.

Alex was playing the music.

My music.

Unnerved and unsure if he should be thankful or mortified, David tossed on his bathrobe and headed for the studio.

ALEX had just finished reading through the piece when David opened the studio door. "So this is what you've been hiding," Alex said with casual innocence.

David's expression darkened and his jaw tensed visibly. "This is my studio. I have no need to hide things here."

Shit. Alex pulled his violin from under his chin and rested it on his hip. "No, of course not." He was keenly uncomfortable with the implication that he had been snooping around in David's private affairs. "I didn't mean to pry."

Damn. I could have handled that a bit more tactfully.

David studied him for a moment, and Alex thought he saw the makings of an internal struggle in those dark eyes. "I apologize. I didn't mean to imply that you were prying."

"Maybe we should get some breakfast." Alex hoped the offer would defuse the situation and give David a way out if he was ill at ease discussing the piece. "I feel a caffeine headache coming on."

"In a minute." David's tone was less harsh this time, as if he were contemplating something.

Alex hadn't expected David's response. Then again, David had already begun to open up to him about his past and his insecurities, so Alex supposed it wasn't all that surprising. Buoyed by David's reaction, Alex began to put his violin away. Whatever David had to say, he'd say it in his own time.

David walked into the room and over to the window without looking directly at Alex. "I've been working on it for several months now." His gaze was focused on the city beyond. "I haven't composed in years. I... I simply couldn't bring myself to do it."

"And now?"

"And now... I feel almost compelled to do so."

Alex said nothing but finished dusting the rosin off his violin and loosened his bow before putting it into the case and locking it into place. When he looked up, he noticed David studying him intently.

"What did you think of it?" David finally asked. Alex had the distinct impression David was afraid to hear the answer.

"It's very good." Alex offered David a reassuring smile. "You have a real knack for scoring the violin. It's technically challenging, but not so much so that the beauty of the instrument is lost."

"Thank you." David appeared more than relieved as he settled down on the couch. "I've agonized over it. There is more, of course—several movements—but the first movement has been the most challenging."

Alex set his violin on the table and joined David. He took David's right hand in his own and squeezed, then kissed it.

"Still," David continued as if he were unaware of the physical contact, "there's something missing."

Alex struggled to find the right thing to say. Although David was hardly the enigma he'd been when they first met, this was one side of him Alex knew little about. From Rachel's description of David's relationship with his grandfather, Alex guessed the old man hadn't approved of David's composition. Hell, he'd barely tolerated David's conducting. Alex would approach this carefully. "It sounded quite beautiful to me."

"No. There's something missing. Something I can't put into words. A feeling that's lacking. You felt it too, didn't you?"

Alex swallowed hard. Of course he'd felt it, just as he'd felt David's emotional hesitation in everything he did. The music was controlled, although it skirted the edge of glorious revelation. Alex sensed that just as keenly. But how to express that kind of criticism to a man who allowed himself no faults?

"I... I don't know." *Brilliant. Just brilliant.*

David stood up and stalked back over to the window. The tension in his body was palpable, powerful. "You do know. You simply won't say what you think."

Of course David was right. But Alex was wedged so tightly between a rock and a hard place that he wasn't sure he could squeeze his way out.

"We've known each other long enough that I expect your honesty." David turned and glared at Alex.

"I've always been honest with you, David."

David's laugh was both harsh and full of pain. "But not always forthcoming."

"Look, I know the strike's been stressful. I know you want to be working. That you *need* to be work—"

"I *need* your answer. I need to know what you think. Or do you believe I can't handle the unvarnished truth?"

"I don't want to hurt you." Again, the truth, for what it was worth. Alex had the sense that he was riding a tidal wave of anger, grief, and pain—David's grief, buried years before, and the pain of never being good enough in the eyes of the only father he'd ever known. Anger had been the only reaction David had received when what he needed was encouragement and understanding.

Alex stood up and reached for David's cheek. "I love you."

David pushed his hand away. "I asked you for the truth. For your opinion. Not for your sympathy or your pity."

"Pity? I meant what I said. I love you, David. I know how much you've wanted to compose again." Alex froze, stunned by the realization of what he'd said.

David, however, didn't seem to have heard it. "You have no idea. How could you?" A muscle in David's cheek twitched, though his expression was like stone.

"It's a wonderful piece. I can hear where you're going with it. The emotion you want to express. Take your time with it. You've got other things on your mind. You don't need to finish the piece right now."

"Finally." David shook his head in obvious disgust. "It's clear you feel it's lacking."

"Not lacking. Just not quite there yet." Why the hell had he said that? Looking at David, he knew he'd just crossed the line, that David would not take the criticism well.

"At last." Alex heard the tension in David's voice. It was as if David were fighting to control himself.

"What do you mean?" For the first time since David had entered the room, Alex felt edgy. Nervous.

"Only that you dance around the truth. You think I'm too fragile."

Alex silently kicked himself. David was right. Alex had been trying to protect him. "I know this is difficult for you. I only wanted to—"

"But it's all so easy for *you*, isn't it?" David's eyes were like ice. "There's nothing you can't do, nothing you can't fathom. You see the music on the page and it speaks to you. And when you play, it's just as easy. Every note, every expression is perfect. The rest of us mortals—" He shook his head and laughed, his laughter making Alex feel suddenly cold. "—are relegated to watching you in awe. You can't even understand what it's like to fail, can you?"

The words stung. They *hurt*. But that wasn't the worst of the emotions that wormed their way to Alex's heart and began to tear it to pieces. No, the worst thing was the realization that he'd just told David he loved him—something he'd never told anyone before, even Yoshi—and David was pushing him away as surely as when they'd first met.

Alex fought to maintain his composure. "I didn't lie to you when I said the piece was beautiful. I also didn't lie when I told you what I feel about you. Please don't push me away."

David inhaled an audible breath, and for a moment, Alex thought David might realize that there was nothing to fight about. But then David's expression grew even more forbidding. "It's not just the music. It's your naïve approach to life."

Alex felt as though he'd been slapped. "What are you talking about?" He didn't even try to disguise his shock at David's words. Or his anger. "You're angry, David. I get that. But taking it out on me... that's not fair. I've never—"

"Everything is good for you, isn't it?" David snapped. "You're blissfully ignorant. Pollyannaish. Maybe you just don't care that people die and things go wrong."

Alex's gut clenched at the accusation. He'd never withheld anything of his past from David. He'd told David things he'd never shared with another soul. How his mother had died and how they hadn't let him see her. How he'd waited outside her room. How he'd begged them....

"Dammit, David. You know that's not true." He struggled to hide the hurt and push back his growing anger.

"I don't know anything." David stalked over to the window. "I know what you've been trying to do these past few weeks... how you thought you could get me to forget about things."

"I only wanted to help."

"I don't need your help." David's face was flushed, his gaze hard. "Do you think I'm a child? That I need you to hold my hand? Show me the way?"

"You're angry, David."

"That's the second time you've made that observation. Have you just realized it? Bravo, then. Another amazing performance by Alex Bishop!" David laughed, and the bitter edge wounded Alex. "But perhaps *you're* the one who needs the help if it's taken you so long to figure that out. Then again, I suppose it's not terribly surprising that you might need some guidance, given where you've come from."

"What are you saying, David?" Alex knew he should just let it go, that it was just David's insecurity speaking, but he couldn't help himself. He could take a lot of shit—hell, he'd lived through more shit than most—but this sounded too much like some of the taunts he'd heard in school. "That just because my family was poor—"

David's cell rang and he pulled it out of his robe.

"Don't answer that. We need to talk about this. I can't—"

David looked directly at Alex and tapped the phone, his face set in a hard frown. "Hello?" David's voice simmered with residual anger. "Yes, Doris. Where else would I be on a Sunday morning?"

"David—"

"Excuse me, Doris." David looked back at Alex. "I need to take this call. We can speak about this later."

"No. Tell her you'll call her back." He didn't mean to raise his voice again.

David ignored him. "Sorry about that, Doris." He paused, then added, "No, no. Really, it's fine. It's not important. It can wait."

Alex clenched his jaw. Not important? How the hell was this not important? David had dismissed him. There were no two ways around it.

David had already turned away, his gaze intently focused on the window once again. Alex knew if he stayed here a moment longer, he'd scream.

The painting of Lake Michigan he'd given David for Christmas caught his eye. The lake. He needed to clear his head. Take a walk. Maybe if he took a break, spent some time alone, he'd have a clue of how to approach David, what to say. *If there's anything you* can *say.*

He grabbed his violin, walked back to the bedroom, and threw on jeans and a sweatshirt. He was shaking, he was so angry. More than that, he was entirely at a loss to understand what had just happened.

David was pushing him away, and at that moment, Alex was just fine with that. *Fuck this.*

"DORIS, if you want me to intervene, I'm more than happy to do so, but if all you want to do is tell me how unreasonable the union is being, I'd prefer you leave me out of it." He was half-tempted to tell her he'd call her back, but Alex had already walked out, and he wasn't going to chase after him.

"You don't need to finish it now. You're wasting your time." David tried to ignore the memory of his grandfather's words as it wove tendrils of anger and shame through his gut.

"David, you're not listening to me."

Doris was right. He was still staring at the door to the studio, hoping Alex would come back.

"You don't need to finish it now." How dare Alex tell him what he should or should not do?

"I'm really not interested, Doris," he snapped. "I'm at the end of my patience with the symphony association and the musicians." He'd raised his voice to the woman who was, for all intents and purposes, his boss. More surprisingly, he didn't care. If he had to hear one more of the symphony association's complaints about the union negotiators, he would explode.

"But David—"

"I don't think the union will appreciate an ultimatum." David fought to keep his voice level this time.

He heard the front door open and close. *Of course he's leaving. What did you expect?*

"David?" Doris's voice brought him back to himself.

No. It's better this way. Better to let him go and move on. You're fine on your own. You've always been.

"No, Doris. Until you and the symphony association realize that you can't resolve this without reaching a compromise, I want nothing to do with it. I've made my opinion quite clear."

"But—"

"Good-bye, Doris." He disconnected the call before she could protest.

Suddenly overcome with a wave of anger he could not contain, he slammed the phone down onto the table, but it skidded off and clattered onto the floor, cracking the protective case into several pieces. He stared at the bits, stunned at what he'd just done.

He shouldn't have pried into your personal documents.

He hadn't been ready for Alex to see his composition. He hadn't *wanted* Alex to see the piece. Not yet. Maybe not ever.

He walked over to the music stand and pulled the score off, then moved it back to the piano and settled onto the bench. He played a few chords, trying to focus on the music. But every time he tried to get beyond what he'd already written, his mind brought him back to Alex.

What the devil had gotten into him? He never lost his temper. God knew he'd been on the receiving end of far too many of his grandfather's tirades over the years. He knew he should go after Alex, apologize.

For what? For him to tell you it's over? What else could he say after the way you just treated him?

He forced himself to focus on the music again. A few more chords. Still nothing.

"Dammit!" He slammed the cover down over the keys with such force that the strings vibrated in response.

CHAPTER 21

MIDNIGHT. Alex sat on the couch, drinking a beer and listening to Mahler's Symphony No. 9. Stewing. Trying to forget David's words. *"I suppose it's not terribly surprising that you might need some guidance, given where you've come from."*

He didn't mean it. Alex had been telling himself that for the better part of four hours. And yet David's words had wounded. How many times had he gotten into fights in school because someone had called him poor, worthless—or worse, called his mother that?

"Where's David tonight?" Marla stood in the entryway to the kitchen, her face set in a frown.

"Busy." Alex did his best to look as though it didn't matter. He also tried to forget the three phone calls he'd made to David. He'd finally left a message. *"I know you're angry, David, and you have a right to be. I shouldn't have pried. But please call me. Let's talk things over."*

"Can't fool me, you know." She sat down beside him so their shoulders touched. "Dark, brooding music, a beer… what happened?"

"Nothing. He's busy."

She narrowed her eyes and glared at him. "I'm visualizing lots of fire. David, surrounded in flames."

"That's not how he works." He didn't want to talk about any of this with her, but he knew she wouldn't let it drop until he answered.

"So tell me how he works."

"He shuts down." *Well, after he lashes out, that is.*

"Ah… okay, I get it. You did something to tick him off."

Alex said nothing.

"So what did you do? Track mud into the apartment and on the oriental rugs? Leave your underwear on the floor?"

"Stop," Alex said as he shook his head. "You know he's not like that."

"Tell me what happened and I'll leave you alone." She put her arm around his shoulder and squeezed.

He leaned his head against her and exhaled through tight lips. Until that moment, he thought he could handle David's rejection. Now he wasn't so sure. "Honestly, I don't know. Not really." He took a deep breath, then continued, "I found a score. Handwritten."

"His composition?"

Alex nodded. "It was really good, but…."

"But he wanted to know what you thought." When Alex didn't respond, she said, "The old 'does this dress make me look fat?'."

In spite of himself, Alex laughed. "Yes," he replied with resignation. "He's a little sensitive about his composing."

"A little?" She shook her head. "You mean he's insecure."

"Pretty much."

"So the ice man has a weak spot."

"Not funny." Alex scowled at her, finished his beer, and set it on the coffee table.

"Nah, I guess it's not." She hugged him and gave him a sympathetic smile. "So what are you going to do about it?"

"I tried calling a few times. I told him we should talk it through, but I think he needs to work this one out on his own." God, he wished it weren't that way, but he was also pretty sure David *did* need time.

"You're in love with the guy, aren't you?"

"Could be." He wouldn't tell her he'd confessed his love to David—that was too painful. Instead, he pointed the remote at the stereo, and the room fell silent.

She raised her eyebrows.

"What?" He glared at her. "You expect me to go knocking on his door? Not gonna happen."

"I wasn't suggesting that."

"Look, if he figures things out, I'll be here waiting. If not...." He didn't want to think about the alternative. He didn't want to think about anything. It hurt a hell of a lot more than he was willing to admit to her or even himself. "I'm going to bed."

"Alex?"

"Hmm?"

"I'm sorry," she said. "I didn't mean to make light of it."

"No offense taken. I'll be fine. You know I will." He usually was, right? *Only you've never fallen so hard before.*

She stood up and kissed his cheek. "I'm here if you want to talk, you know."

"Yeah, I know. Thanks." He forced a smile, then turned and walked out of the room. He knew she'd let him mope—as much as he'd ever moped. At least for now.

DAVID gazed out the living room window at the darkening sky. The cognac in his hand was his second that night, and the tension in his body had abated somewhat. He set the nearly empty glass down on a table and pulled his cell phone from his pants pocket. The screen was cracked from when he'd thrown it, but it still worked. His jaw clenched at the memory.

There were three messages, all from Alex. David had avoided playing them, but now he did, forcing himself to listen as if it were penance. The messages were simple and heartfelt, each in essence the same: "Call me and we can talk." Not that he'd expected histrionics from Alex.

He didn't call back, in part because he was still angry, although not as keenly toward Alex as that morning. He was angrier with himself. He'd treated Alex terribly, yelled at him, called Alex things he didn't believe himself. He'd acted just like his grandfather. He'd lost control. He'd sworn he'd never act like the old man.

A lot of good that did you!

Besides, what *was* there to talk to Alex about? It wasn't as though he'd forgotten what he said to Alex. Alex certainly wouldn't have forgotten either. No one deserved to be treated the way he'd treated Alex. It just proved what he'd known all along: he was better off alone.

CHAPTER 22

Two Months Later

HE STUDIED the music on the piano as if it might fly off the page. He wished it would; he was getting nowhere trying to capture it on paper. It was elusive—ever on the brink of discovery. Incomprehensible.

"You still don't hear it, do you?

He knew Alex stood behind him, as he often did in dreams, but he didn't turn around. The music was clearer; it always was when Alex was close. "You're torturing me."

The skin of David's neck muffled Alex's response. "You torture yourself. You just won't admit it." Alex traced the outline of David's cheeks with his fingertips.

"I'm afraid," David whispered.

"Loneliness is a far more frightening thing." Alex brushed his lips against David's neck, sending tiny shockwaves of pleasure throughout his body.

David turned around to kiss Alex, but Alex was gone.

AS HE had most mornings since Alex left, David sat at his piano, having no incentive to remain in his bed longer than necessary. He had made slow and steady progress on his composition, although he was still not pleased with it.

He imagined Alex standing in the studio, playing the music he had written. Echoes of Alex's violin still swirled about the place and in David's mind. He got up, opened a drawer of an old file cabinet, and pulled a yellowed folder labeled "Reviews" from the back. He sat on the comfortable armchair in the corner, his feet on the ottoman. As he opened the folder, bits of dust rose into the air, visible in the bright light that filtered through the window.

Out of the corner of his eye, he saw the painting Alex had given him. His gut clenched. Why hadn't he taken the blasted thing down? Every time he saw the painting, he thought of Alex. Torture. Nothing less. And yet it was still there as a reminder.

Of what? Of your stupid ego? Of what you knew would happen but didn't want to face?

He forced his eyes down to the papers in his hands. He didn't want to read them, but he figured it was penance of a sort. Better that he embrace reality in all things than continue to dream like an overgrown child.

March 4, 2007

The New York Times

The opening performance of the modern music festival at the Brooklyn Academy of Music featured compositions from several young composers, including a piece by the newly appointed musical director of the Chicago Symphony Orchestra, David Somers. Maestro Somers, a strong advocate for new music, will feature works by modern composers of various styles in his inaugural season with the CSO. Somers conducted his own orchestral fantasy entitled Spirit's Rest. A strong entry in the festival, Somers's piece nonetheless fell short of the mark, sacrificing expressivity for a more technically powerful approach....

David took a deep breath, replaced the yellowed newsprint in the folder, and picked up another.

January 22, 2009

The San Francisco Chronicle

A veritable potpourri of modern classicism filled the Davies Symphony Hall in a salute to the best and brightest new composers. Led by guest artist David Somers, the San Francisco Symphony played to a capacity audience which included the governor of California and other dignitaries in town for trade talks. The symphony, under Maestro Somers's solid baton, made easy work of the challenging repertoire. Among others, Somers's own composition, Verity, was well received by the crowd. Although technically competent, Somers's writing lacks the depth of feeling of a more experienced composer. Perhaps with a little more seasoning, Somers will achieve the depth that one senses lurks behind his intense and brooding presence.

He replaced the folder and closed the filing cabinet. How long had he sat at the piano today? He'd lost track of time. The growing darkness outside was the only indication he'd been working nearly the entire day. Sarah had come and gone with food he'd hardly touched. Without the day-to-day routine of his work for the CSO, the days and nights had begun to run into each other. He slept when he was tired, he ate when he was hungry. He showered and dressed because he'd been taught at a young age that one's appearance was paramount.

Appearances. For all the good they do me.

The piano keys stretched out before him, and he settled his fingers lightly upon them, touching but not depressing them. The pattern of black and white repeated itself from left to right, reflected in the highly polished wood of the instrument. For a moment, he could almost imagine Alex was there, nodding to indicate his readiness, fiddle tucked under his chin.

Without thinking, David began to play. Not his music, but the second movement of the Sibelius Violin Concerto. The one Alex had played the night they'd met. As he often did when playing through the accompaniment to a piece without the soloist, he filled in the melodic line. The result was unsatisfying—the piano could not sustain the breath of the soaring melody like the violin—and yet he couldn't help but play as he imagined Alex. He could have played a hundred different pieces, each perfectly suited for solo piano. Why had he chosen this one? Slow, plaintive, utterly romantic, and full of angst. So entirely unlike himself.

The movement ended. But when the next movement, a brighter, more playful composition, would have begun, David just sat there and let the final notes fade into nothingness. That's when he realized his face was wet.

He couldn't remember the last time he'd cried. The silence in the room was overwhelming. He heard nothing but his own breathing.

He lifted his hands from the keys and brought them to his lips. The slight pressure of his forefingers against his skin called to mind the feel of Alex's mouth. More tears. Silent still, but this time his chest ached and his gut clenched. It hurt. Not exactly a physical pain, and yet not an entirely emotional one. The silence clawed at him.

Silence, like pain. The words were unspoken, but he heard them as clearly as if he'd uttered them. *Silence.*

He looked up at the music on the piano stand, blurry through his tears. He didn't need to see it, though. The notes were burnished into his brain, so much a part of himself that he didn't need to play them to hear the music now. And yet this time, when he looked, he saw only himself in the notes.

His heart beat wildly against his ribs as the realization struck him: the music had always been *his*. His thoughts—inspired by Alex—but his thoughts alone. He had always looked beyond himself to hear the music, and his compositions had been as flat and unfulfilling as the Sibelius without the violin. All along, he'd believed that the music hadn't just been inspired by Alex but that it was *Alex's*.

David had been wrong. The music was his alone.

He'd tried to write Alex's music—to capture Alex in the notes. He'd tried to imagine Alex, to remember the melody of his voice, the cadence of his breathing, the harmony of his soul. What David hadn't realized was that Alex had already made a place for himself in David's heart and that the music existed there. All David needed to hear the music was to let go of the wall he'd built around his heart.

"I don't understand." The words he had spoken in his dreams. *"Please. I have to know. What must I do to hear it?"*

"Surrender...."

The musical connection he'd longed for had been there all along for him to claim. He just hadn't understood how to find it. With a trembling hand, he picked up the pencil from atop the piano and began to write.

THE knock on the studio door startled David awake. Judging by the angle of the sunlight through the window, he guessed it was midmorning.

"Come." He shuffled the manuscript beneath the stack of music and stood up.

Rachel peered inside, then ran over to him and gave him a warm hug. As always, he reciprocated with slight hesitation.

"Rachel. I didn't expect you until tonight."

"I caught an earlier flight from LaGuardia. Your assistant told me you were still home, so I thought I'd just come directly from the airport." She released him and he saw the look of shock on her face. "You look terrible. Is everything all right?"

He had no doubt he looked a mess. He brushed his chin with his hand and felt the stubble there. His neck and shoulders hurt from bending over the keyboard and writing. Still, he felt surprisingly good.

"I'm fine. Just working late. I must have fallen asleep at the piano." He offered her what he hoped was a reassuring smile. "I'm glad you were able to make it earlier."

"I was so glad to hear that the musicians' union approved the contract offer. You must have been out of your mind in the middle of that fiasco."

"Unfortunate that it took the cancellation of the entire season to resolve the issue." He was still furious with the symphony association for taking so long to come to a compromise with the musicians. At least the summer series at Ravinia and the Summer Outdoor series at the Pritzker Pavilion in Millennium Park would go forward as planned, though it was little consolation. He had missed out on the modern music series he'd been looking forward to for several years now.

Rachel squeezed his hand, then stepped back and looked him over again. Her gaze traveled to the untouched breakfast. He hadn't even heard Sarah set it down. "How about we get some hot breakfast? Sarah says you haven't been eating much."

"You needn't worry about me."

"Will you at least join me? The Nutri-Grain bar they served on the airplane was pretty sad."

"They serve breakfast bars in first class?"

"You know I won't fly first class for such a short flight. It's a waste of money."

"You have plenty of money."

"I won't use James's money."

He sighed, though he hadn't intended to. He was too tired to engage her on the subject of his grandfather.

Perhaps sensing she'd pushed him too hard, she added, "I'm happy to share the Somers name, David. Truly, I am. But I won't take a penny of the old man's money. I know it's unkind to speak ill of the dead, but—"

"You don't need to explain. I understand." Of course he understood her conflicted feelings—the only difference between them was that he had grown up in the Somers household and she had been adopted into it. He'd never told her, but he admired her need for independence. Still, that hadn't stopped him from ensuring she would want for nothing when they settled his grandfather's estate.

SARAH had set a second breakfast out on the counter in the kitchen.

"I took the liberty of asking Sarah to make us something to eat." Rachel smiled at David. "I hope you don't mind. Besides, you look like you could use some food."

"Thank you." David sat down on a stool facing hers at the kitchen counter. "But I'm far from wasting away."

Her frown told him she was unconvinced, but he didn't argue as she poured them both some coffee. "What have you been up to in the meantime?" She pulled apart a croissant and dipped it in her coffee.

"I've been quite busy." No doubt she knew he and Alex were no longer seeing each other. He had no interest in engaging her on the topic.

"So are you going to tell me what happened with Alex?" she asked as she set her coffee down. "Last I heard you two were a couple, but then Marla told me you haven't seen each other for months."

"We parted ways. We just weren't suited for each other." It's what he'd been telling himself since Alex had left. He'd almost come to believe it too.

She eyed him with obvious suspicion. "When we last spoke, you seemed so happy—happier than I can remember. I don't understand."

"Happiness is not the sole measure of compatibility."

She stuffed a piece of cheese in her mouth without looking at him. She took her time to chew, sipped her coffee, then put the cup back down on the table with a clatter.

"Is something wrong?" His mind had wandered back to the elusive composition, and the noise brought him back to himself.

She opened her mouth, then paused as if she'd thought better of it. "No, nothing," she said after a moment. "I'm just clumsy. So what are your plans today?"

He saw something in her expression that gave him pause, but he was too distracted to consider it in depth. "There's a donors' party tonight at Doris's home. I'm sure she'd love for you to come."

"That'd be great. What's the occasion?"

"I'm pretty sure she's trying to mend fences with the musicians. Knowing Doris, she figures that plying them with alcohol will make them more likely to forgive the symphony association's behavior during the strike."

"Sounds like Doris. What's the dress?"

"It's a pool party." The thought irked him. No doubt Doris believed a more casual atmosphere might also make the symphony association more receptive to her peacemaking overture. But parties were difficult enough for him. Pool parties were well beyond his comfort zone.

"Sounds like fun. I actually remembered to bring a bathing suit."

David envied her enthusiasm. It was one of the things he loved about her. "My driver will be by around five to pick us up. I have a bit of work to do, so feel free to make yourself at home."

"Thanks," she answered cheerfully. "I will."

"DO WE really have to do this? You know how I hate these things." Alex glanced at Logan as they walked up to the entryway of the large home with its imposing brick façade, perfectly manicured lawn, and bushes trimmed within an inch of their lives. The expensive cars in the driveway looked like an ad for a high-end European auto dealership. Audis, Porsches, Mercedes, and even a few Maseratis lined the street past the corner, not to mention a half dozen stretch limos with drivers waiting inside.

Alex suggested taking in some jazz at a downtown club, but Logan insisted they at least make an appearance at the party first. "I told Yoshi I'd be hanging out with you. I think he's worried I might get into trouble if left to my own devices."

"Yoshi's jealous?" That was a surprise. Alex had never known Yoshi to be the jealous type. He wondered vaguely how he'd handle it if he saw David with someone else. *Not well.* He forced a smile and pushed the thought away. "Fine," he said with mock resignation. "I'll do it for Yoshi. But if you think I'm going to swim, you're dreamin'."

"And I was looking forward to seeing *all* of those sexy tattoos, for once." Logan bit his lower lip.

"You wouldn't see all of them even if I *was* wearing a bathing suit." Alex watched the blush spread over Logan's cheeks.

The housekeeper met them at the front door and led them through the residence and into an enormous backyard. Doris's home featured a large pool set toward the back of the property, lovely flowering trees and beds, and a freestanding cabana building. Guests had begun to congregate, and several people splashed in the pool while they floated about with drinks adorned with paper umbrellas and fruit.

"Logan!" Doris buzzed over like a hungry insect.

Logan kissed her on both cheeks, then looked down at her dress. "Gorgeous, if I may say so myself." He looked over at Alex and grinned outright. "Doris commissioned me to make her a gown for the CSO opening in the fall, and I thought I'd bring along a few confections from my new store in Paris. It suits you, Doris."

"You are *such* a little devil, Lo." Doris flicked a lock of her hair, then fixed her hungry gaze on Alex. "And you, Alexander Bishop," she said as she planted kisses on his cheeks, "what *have* you been up to?"

"It's good to see you, Doris." He hadn't seen her since New Year's Eve. His chest ached at the memory.

"You and my handsome conductor were all over the gossip pages. And then nothing. What happened?"

Alex managed a stiff smile. "Busy schedules." Doris glanced at Logan, who shrugged.

She didn't press the issue. "Please, boys, enjoy yourselves. The pool is open if you'd like to take a dip." Her eyes sparkled at this suggestion. "The bar is fully stocked."

"We may take you up on that." Logan laughed as he pulled Alex over to the makeshift bar on the terrace.

Alex was relieved he didn't have to explain anything to Doris. "You can't be seriously considering swimming…?"

"And why *not*? I have nothing to be ashamed of." Logan made a pouty little face and waved his hand dismissively. "And if the little old ladies want to gawk… let them!" This statement was immediately followed by "Two martinis, dry."

Alex opened his mouth to protest, then shut it again, deciding that a martini suited him fine. He needed something strong to make it through this.

Drink in hand, Alex followed Logan over to a group of people by the pool. Alex politely greeted each one, none of whom he had met before (although they all seemed to know him). They asked him about his summer concert schedule and when he would be back at the CSO. They spoke about golf and sailing, the summer season at Ravinia, the upcoming outdoor concert series at Millennium Park, and Taste of Chicago.

Nearly a half hour later, he managed to escape the conversation using the excuse that he needed a refill on his drink. He arrived at the bar just as the man in front of him picked up his drinks, then turned around and nearly bumped into him.

"David." He should have realized David would be at the party. It was a CSO gathering, after all. How long had it been since they'd seen each other? Two months? David hadn't returned any of his calls, and Alex had finally given up trying to speak to him.

"Alex." David was dressed in a short-sleeved shirt and pressed jeans. He held a drink in each of his hands. Alex noticed dark shadows under his eyes and a few more tiny lines around his mouth. David looked tired. Older.

"How have you been?" God, it hurt more than he realized to see David again.

"I've been busy." David's response was terse, and Alex thought he heard a hint of anger in his voice.

"I know." Alex smiled, hoping to put David at ease. "I was glad to hear the strike was over. I'm sure you're relieved."

"Yes."

Shit. This conversation was far more difficult than Alex had anticipated. "I heard you play at Ravinia last week. I've always loved *Harold in Italy*. It's so full of joy and promise."

David's eyes widened almost imperceptibly. Was he surprised Alex had gone to hear him play? "*Harold in Italy* was a breakthrough for orchestral scoring." He spoke in the scholarly tone Alex knew he used when he felt ill at ease.

"Berlioz was a true master." Alex tried to think of what to say. His stomach felt full of lead weights and his face felt hot. He wished he'd refilled his drink sooner—a little extra fortitude to soothe his jangling nerves. "Makes me wish I played viola better."

"I'm sure you're a far better violist than you suggest," David said.

The praise perplexed Alex. Why was this man so difficult to fathom?

"Have you made any progress on your violin composition?" Alex didn't care that it was a sensitive topic; he was tired of tiptoeing around the issue. What did he have to lose, anyhow, since David was acting as though they barely knew each other? It couldn't get any worse.

David's response was measured. "Some progress." At least he didn't seem angry this time.

"That's great news, David. I hope that someday you'll consider letting me perform it with you."

"You certainly are more than capable of doing it justice." David's cool mask made it difficult to read his true feelings about Alex's offer. "But I don't believe that would be a good idea under the circumstances."

"Circumstances?"

"You're a talented man," David explained. "I couldn't hope to have a more accomplished violinist perform the work. Still, given the current state of affairs, it would be unwise."

"The 'current state of affairs' doesn't need to be the status quo." Alex realized he was now speaking in the same circuitous and stilted way as David.

Why is it so hard to be myself around him?

"Let me rephrase that," Alex said. *Here goes nothing.* "My feelings haven't changed. I still want to be with you, David."

A muscle in David's jaw twitched visibly, and Alex knew his words had achieved their intended effect. "I... I need time."

David's hesitation was far better than a brush-off. It left open the possibility of *something*. Or at least Alex hoped that was why David had hesitated.

Alex offered David a patient smile. "You've got it. I hope when you're ready, you'll come find me. Either way, though, I wish you well."

"Thank you." The pain in David's eyes took Alex off guard.

"Good-bye, David." And with another warm smile, Alex disappeared into the growing crowd.

AFTER Alex left, David stood, holding the untouched drinks, watching the place where Alex had been. He felt a wave of barely distinguishable emotions at seeing Alex again. Anger was the easiest to comprehend. But there was something else—something far more disturbing that lurked beneath the surface. David's arms ached and his chest felt tight.

Was it grief? No. Of course not. He'd been the one who'd chosen to end things with Alex, after all.

"David!" Rachel appeared wearing a very tiny bathing suit. To David's great consternation, he noticed a tattoo on her shoulder blade: a hummingbird hovering over a flower. It took all his focus to keep from spilling the drinks at the shock of seeing her nearly naked. Not to mention the tattoo, which did nothing to keep his thoughts off of his encounter with Alex.

"I'm sorry to keep you waiting." He kept his eyes focused on her face.

"It's all right." She giggled, then added, "Logan kept trying to dunk me, so I escaped the pool."

"Pool?" For some reason, the word simply didn't resonate with him at the moment.

"Yes, the pool." Rachel frowned at him.

"Right. Of course. The pool." His brain unfroze and he did his best to school his expression.

"Is something wrong?" She took her drink from his hand and sipped it. "You look like you've seen a ghost."

"No. Not a ghost."

Rachel said nothing.

"I hope you don't mind," he began, finally making up his mind. His head was beginning to pound and he felt ill. "I'm leaving."

"Leaving?"

"I'll send my driver back to take you home when you're ready."

"I.... But...," Rachel stammered. "Of course. I have his number—I'll call him when I'm ready to leave." She looked up at him with obvious concern. "Are you sure you're all right? If you're feeling ill, I can leave with—"

"I'm fine," he interrupted. "I'll see you later."

"Sure. I'll see you back at the apartment."

DAVID had done nothing but pace the living room since he'd arrived home from the party more than an hour before. For years he'd been able to control his anxiety, suppress it. And yet five minutes alone with Alex and he was completely lost.

The photographs on the long side table caught his eye. They'd been there for years. Why was he so drawn to them now? He gave in to the urge to touch them, picked up the photograph of his parents, yellowed with age, and ran his fingers reverently over the surface of the glass.

A memory, long forgotten, resurfaced with the touch. His grandfather was seated in his study not long after David's parents had died. A month, maybe two. David peered in through the slightly open doorway, his curiosity getting the better of him. He'd heard something. A sound. Sad. Pained. Someone crying?

His grandfather turned to meet his gaze. His eyes were red, his face wet with tears. Silently, David made his way into the room. He almost never went inside the study, with its floor-to-ceiling shelves of books and its austere furniture covered in dark-green leather. He reached out and touched his grandfather's face, wanting to understand and afraid of what he might discover.

"Are you all right, Grandfather?"

For a long moment, James Somers did not respond, as if his words had left him as surely as David's parents had left them both. But then a remarkable thing happened. The old man gathered David into his arms and held him.

David felt his grandfather's body tremble, though James said nothing. All David knew was the warmth of that embrace and his grandfather's slow, steady breaths. He wasn't sure how much time passed, but James at last released him from his arms.

"Get ready for bed." James's voice was once more as David remembered: powerful and resonant.

"Yes, sir." David scurried out of the room without looking back.

It was the only time David ever saw his grandfather cry. Funny, how he'd forgotten about that. Why had he only now remembered? But of course he knew the answer. He'd wanted to forget the old man's pain as surely as he'd wanted to forget the grief he'd felt when he finally understood he would never see his parents again.

Alex. Forgive me. I don't know how to love you.

He set the photograph back down, then headed for his studio. The manuscript still sat upon the piano stand, where it had been since he'd finished it. He picked it up and walked over to the small desk in the corner of the room, then pulled out an ancient fountain pen that had once belonged to his father. He sat down and laid the first page on the smooth surface of the blotter. He'd been trying to think of a name for the concerto since he'd completed it, but until tonight, he'd come up empty. He touched the pen to the paper and began to write.

CHAPTER 23

DAVID strode off the outdoor stage at Tanglewood, the Boston Symphony Orchestra's summer home. It was unusually hot and muggy, and his starched tuxedo shirt chafed angrily against his neck. Once safely inside his dressing room, he tugged at one end of his tie and unbuttoned the top of his shirt, at last freeing himself from the constricting fabric. He was in a foul temper, and his usually cool manner had worn so thin that he snapped at his assistant. He'd been doing a lot of that. "I don't *care* if the audience wants me to return for another bow, I have *finished*."

His assistant meekly ducked out of the dressing room as David peeled off his jacket and tossed it onto the couch. The air-conditioning felt cold against his damp skin, causing gooseflesh to rise on his arms. He unbuttoned his shirt and tossed it on top of the jacket, kicked off his shoes and socks, and threw his pants on the pile for good measure. He opened the glass door to the shower, turned on the water as cold as he could stand it, then stepped inside.

Perfectly awful performance.

How could he forget the french horn section's late entrance in the first movement of the Mahler Fourth and the out-of-tune oboe in the last? He knew the heat and humidity were to blame for the orchestra's less than stellar performance, but he didn't care. It was simply inexcusable.

Ten minutes later, feeling some semblance of his former self, he stepped out of the shower and grabbed a towel from the hook next to the stall.

"Nice."

"Who the hell let you in here?" David demanded.

"Your assistant." John Fuchs laughed and watched him with keen interest. David quickly tied the towel around his waist and made a mental note to give his assistant a thorough dressing-down in the morning. "I thought you'd be happier to see me, David."

"You didn't tell me you were coming." David's face felt suddenly warm. There were few people who could embarrass him more thoroughly than his former mentor.

"I tried. As a matter of fact, I left several messages for you, none of which you returned."

"It was an oversight." David glanced at the phone he'd deposited on a nearby table. He was afraid both that Alex would call and that he wouldn't. In the end, he'd just avoided answering. It was easier that way. If someone really needed to contact him, his assistant would field the call.

"Bullshit." John chuckled. "Not given the temper you're in. I haven't seen you like this since—"

"Why are you here?" David interrupted.

"—since Helena died," John finished.

David remained silent this time.

"Rachel tells me you aren't seeing the violinist anymore." One side of John's mouth quirked upward provocatively.

"Which violinist would that be?" David reached for his bathrobe and tossed it on, not caring that he'd just flashed John more skin than he'd intended.

"What's the rush? The view was quite nice." John bit his lower lip and grinned.

David scowled and proceeded to run a comb through his wet hair. He knew John only meant to rattle him, and he was damned if he'd let the man know he'd succeeded.

"Where's Roger?" David pulled his change of clothes from the closet and set them out over the nearest chair.

"Chicago. Visiting his mother in the nursing home. She's not exactly my biggest fan, you know. I don't want to be responsible for a cardiac event. Or a stroke. She's still convinced her son is going to remarry. And a woman at that." When David didn't respond, John added, "You really are moping. I've never known you not to laugh at my jokes."

"I never laugh at your jokes." In spite of his mood, David was half-tempted to smile this time.

"Touché. So the David Somers I know and love is still in there."

David ignored this.

"What did he do to offend you?"

"How do you know *he* offended *me*?" David found himself enjoying the banter, if not the subject matter.

"I doubt you could offend Alex. And let's be honest here, you do have a knack for pushing the good ones away." John sat down on the couch and crossed one long leg over the other, draping his arms over the pillows to either side of him.

"Alex did nothing," David lied as he took his robe off and made sure the towel about his waist was well secured. The mild amusement he'd felt at John's teasing was now gone, replaced by the usual tension in his gut at the thought of Alex.

"Interesting."

"*What's* interesting?" David struggled with his shirt, which stuck to his damp forearms as he pulled it on. He'd have toweled off more, but he had no intention of giving John any more of a show.

"That he didn't do anything and you still let him go."

"We weren't suited for each other." David finished buttoning his shirt and realized he'd missed a button. He bit back a surge of anger and a curse, then began to undo the buttons and start over.

John raised a pale eyebrow and shook his head. David wasn't sure if he was more amused about the situation with Alex or the shirt. Probably both. "Was he kind?"

"Yes," David answered, "of course." Well he wasn't going to lie about Alex, was he?

"Talented?"

"Definitely. But you already knew that." David managed to button the shirt properly this time. He dropped the towel around his waist and grabbed a pair of silk boxers. The shirttails left most of his legs uncovered but covered the important parts. *Let him gawk.*

"Intelligent?"

"Of course."

"A good lover?"

"I don't think that's an appropriate—"

"Answer the question," John interrupted as he leaned back further into the couch and crossed his arms over his chest in open challenge.

David pulled on his pants but said nothing.

"I'll take that as a definite 'yes'."

David let out a long breath. "I assume you're expecting dinner." Best to change the subject. It would only be temporary, but at least it'd give him some time to think about how to handle John's questions. *Thank God Roger isn't with him.* He couldn't imagine how he'd have managed with *both* of them prodding him.

THREE hours later they sat on the terrace of the Somers's Connecticut estate, their late dinner now finished. The air was much cooler here, and after several glasses of wine and some food, David felt much more like himself. For the past hour, at least, John had avoided any mention of Alex.

"Are you going to come clean now?" John refilled their glasses.

"How's Roger?" David countered.

"He's fine. Now answer my question."

"I have nothing to say on the subject."

"Rachel says you're in love with him." John swirled the wine around the cut crystal glass.

David schooled his expression—how many times had he done that tonight?—and looked past John to the stars visible between the tall oaks.

"She also says you've been composing again," John continued.

Why had Rachel spoken to John about his personal life? He made a mental note to speak with her about what he considered a flagrant breach of etiquette. "I don't see how that is at all related to the first statement."

John laughed. "You know I don't give up easily. Although I was hoping this would take less time than it did to get you to consider returning to Chicago. Perhaps if I prance around in my underwear—"

"I fail to see the humor in this." David lifted his wineglass to his lips and took a deep swallow of the crisp Vinho Verde.

"No, I suppose you wouldn't. But you're doing a lousy job of pretending you don't care about him."

"Hmm."

John stood up and stretched. "Mind if I spend the night in the guest room?"

"As if there were ever any question."

"Good." John smiled kindly. "I'm heading back to Chicago in the morning to pick up Roger. The flight to Costa Rica leaves in the evening."

"Tomorrow? You came all this way just to see me?" For the first time that evening, David was surprised.

"Seemed like a pretty good reason to me." John finished his wine and headed into the house.

David watched John leave, then got up and walked over to the railing and rested his elbows on the smooth wood, looking out over the dark estate. The moon had risen high in the sky, and ribbons of silver shimmered on the lake. The cicadas buzzed in the trees, and the faint scent of lavender and jasmine from the formal gardens mixed with the smell of freshly cut grass. He wondered if Alex would like it here, surrounded by the vast lawn, the water, and the forest. He pictured Alex's hair blowing in the wind, hearing his carefree laugh and feeling Alex's hands on his skin.

He has done nothing to hurt you and he has done everything to love you. And still you pushed him away.

David thought of Helena. It had become more difficult to picture her face in his mind, to remember the way she had felt in his arms and the sound of her voice. He had tried to be everything for her—the father she never had, the friend she so desperately needed, and the faithful husband she so deserved. He had tried to make her happy, to show her that he had enough love for them both.

Just as Alex has done for you. And still you pushed him away.

He took a deep breath, pulled his phone from his pocket, and tapped the icon marked "Alex." Alex's phone rang several times, and then David heard "Sorry I missed you. Leave me a message and I'll call you back."

There was a soft beep, and David looked at the phone. He tapped it, disconnecting the call, then closed his eyes and took another deep breath. He knew he should leave Alex a message, at least to tell him that they should talk. But he couldn't do it. He put the phone back in his pocket and refilled his glass of wine.

CHAPTER 24

ALEX greeted symphony benefactors and local dignitaries in the green room after the Blossom Music Center concert. Marla, who had traveled with him for the appearance, stood in the corner watching him with an expression of motherly concern. She had been wearing the same expression on and off since he and David had ended their relationship, and it irritated Alex to no end.

Since they'd left Chicago, she had been doing her utmost to make sure he was aware of David's performances by dropping not-so-subtle hints (and the occasional brochure) about the conductor's whereabouts. He tolerated her interference—although he had, cursing, tossed nearly a dozen press releases and newspaper articles in hotel wastebaskets— because he felt more at ease when she traveled with him.

An hour later they sat in a limousine headed to Cleveland, where they would spend the night before flying back to Chicago the next afternoon.

"I was hoping to check out the Rock and Roll Hall of Fame in the morning," Alex told her as he pulled out his cell phone to check his messages. "The last few times we've been here, we didn't have enough time."

"Sounds good." She stretched her feet out onto his lap and looked at him longingly.

"If you'd drop the four-inch Manolos, you wouldn't need me to rub your feet." No risk of that happening.

"But you're sooooo good with your hands." She winked at him and wiggled her toes.

"Okay. Messages first, then a foot rub." He tapped his phone a few times, then stared at the screen.

"What?" She looked at him with eager interest.

"It's nothing." He did his best to regain his composure. The last thing he wanted was for her to start pestering him again about contacting David.

"Come on, Alex," she prodded. "You don't expect me to—"

"David called." It wasn't worth fighting her; she'd have wheedled it out of him anyhow.

"Finally." Her grin was triumphant.

"He didn't leave a message."

"Oh." She looked disappointed. Then, brightening, she added, "But he called you. That's progress. Call him back."

He looked at her, eyes narrowed. "He didn't leave a message."

"But he—" she began.

"No. I said I was going to give him time to think about things. When he's ready, he'll get ahold of me."

She made a noise somewhere between a groan and a sigh. "One of these days, I'm going to—"

"Oh, shut up and let me rub your feet."

A WEEK later Alex was aboard a plane bound for Portland to play two summer concerts—one with the Portland Symphony, a repeat of the Sibelius he had performed with the CSO, the other a rock concert, a favor for a friend. Although it was a long flight, Alex decided to forgo his usual "plane nap," as Marla liked to call them. Instead, he ordered a drink from the flight attendant.

Marla pulled a large envelope out of her carry-on. "This came by courier for you right before we left. No return address. I figured it was probably music, so I brought it along."

"Thanks."

She yawned, kicked off her shoes, and stretched out like a lioness for her nap. "Night."

He smiled as she leaned her head against his shoulder and closed her eyes. The flight attendant set a drink on the tray table, and Alex sipped it as he looked out the window. He glanced back down at the envelope and slid a finger under the seal, then pulled out a sheaf of papers. Marla had been right—it was music. But not the music he'd expected to see.

For a moment Alex stared at the papers. Handwritten. The notes achingly familiar. But there was something new this time. A title. *Tattoos*. His mouth felt dry, but his eyes burned. At the bottom, in David's script, was a dedication: *For Alex.*

CHAPTER 25

DAVID and Rachel sipped their wine on the terrace of David's Chicago apartment, watching the sun slowly descend over the city. The sound of traffic from Lakeshore Drive was barely audible over the breeze from the lake. Rachel had arrived from New York only a few hours after David had returned from yet another guest conducting gig. David was more than relieved to be home and, for once, happy for the company. His grueling summer schedule had, for the most part, kept his mind off of Alex, but when he was home, he found it more difficult to put Alex out of his thoughts.

How many weeks—months?—had it been since he he'd last seen Alex? Since he'd finished the violin concerto, he hadn't dreamed of Alex, or at least he hadn't remembered his dreams when he awoke. But he still had the note Alex sent him, thanking him for the concerto. *I'll be here waiting, David*, Alex had written. David wondered how long anyone could wait.

"You look tired." He saw concern on his sister's face, and it disturbed him. The last thing he wanted or needed was her pity.

He breathed in the scent of the lake and the city and replied, "My schedule was more demanding than I had anticipated."

"What are you up to tonight?"

"A hot shower and a good night's sleep. I have to meet with the symphony association to discuss next year's subscription series first thing in the morning." He took another sip of his wine, then added, "Why do you ask?"

"I'm going to the House of Blues tonight to hear an old friend play. Care to join me?"

"I'll have to pass. I need to be prepared to defend the financial viability of my modern music series, and I haven't yet reviewed the numbers." Truth be told, he just wasn't interested in going out, and it had little to do with getting anything to the symphony association.

"I understand. Maybe we can catch some jazz downtown later this week."

"I'd like that." They sat in companionable silence until Sarah came out onto the balcony to let them know dinner was ready.

AFTER dinner, Rachel left to take a shower and get dressed for the concert. David wandered back over to the living room, grabbed a handful of papers to review for the meeting, and noticed what looked like a ticket envelope sitting on the coffee table next to Rachel's purse. Curious, he picked up the envelope. The yellow sticky note on the front read, *For the Collective Soul concert—Alex.*

Strange, that Alex was playing at the House of Blues and Rachel had neglected to mention it. No doubt the old friend she'd mentioned was Alex. David knew Alex sometimes did studio work with rock bands, but he also knew Alex occasionally played live concerts.

He opened the envelope and contemplated the tickets.

You could go to the concert. He came to see you conduct at Ravinia, after all. What harm would there be in just hearing him play?

Whatever he thought of his relationship with Alex, he couldn't deny the man was supremely talented. It was a large venue. No one would need to know that he was there, not even Rachel. He would slip inside and get lost in the crowd instead of going to the balcony box, where she would see him. He would leave unnoticed afterward.

About an hour later, as David sat in his studio playing through some of the music for the upcoming CSO season, someone knocked on the door.

"Come."

"I'm leaving," Rachel told him. "I'll be back late. Sure you don't want to come?"

"I'm sure." He barely glanced up from the piano, afraid he might betray his growing excitement at seeing Alex again. "Enjoy yourself."

"Thanks." As she turned to leave, she reached for the door and dropped her purse, sending its contents flying everywhere. David stopped playing, stood up, and helped her retrieve the scattered items. A few minutes later, the contents of her purse back where they belonged, she gave David a quick hug, said her good-byes, then left.

David stood and stared at the studio door for several minutes, thinking. He knew the concert was sold-out, but with a little luck—and a few phone calls—he guessed he'd be able to scare up a ticket. Promoters always held on to a few extra tickets for VIPs. For once, he would use his position to his advantage.

He walked over to the table where he'd set down his phone when he heard a shuffle of paper underfoot. He bent down and picked up a ticket with the House of Blues logo prominently printed on it. He smiled. Subtlety had never been Rachel's strong suit.

AN HOUR later, dressed in jeans and a casual shirt, David walked into the foyer of the House of Blues. The band had already begun to play, the music filtering in through the closed doors. After showing the security guard his ID—really, did he *look* like a teenager?—and getting his hand stamped with the word *over*, he climbed the stairs to the main floor of the venue.

"Hey!" shouted the doorman over the din of the music. "Your ticket is for the premium box in the balcony. You can take the elevator up."

"I'd like to go to the main floor first."

"Yeah, I guess you can do that." The bouncer looked at David as if he'd lost his mind. Then he shrugged. "Just letting you know your seat is upstairs, that's all."

David nodded and continued up the steps. He already regretted his decision to come—he felt uncomfortable here. Surprisingly, he was not overdressed, and he was hardly the oldest audience member. Still, he felt utterly out of his element.

He made his way through the throng of people and to the back bar, where he ordered a Guinness. He took a long swallow from the plastic cup, then turned to look up at the stage.

The crowd was on its feet, clapping hands and whistling. Used to the more intimate jazz venues, David found the amplified music overwhelming. He inwardly chastised himself for being such a "stiff," as Rachel had loved to call him when he turned down the volume on the car stereo or, worse, changed the station from rock to classical. Secretly, though he loved classic rock and had, much to his grandfather's chagrin, listened to groups like the Stones, the Beatles, and The Who when he was in college.

The band played a few more songs before the lead singer introduced Alex, who joined them on the next song. David was surprised to hear another violinist, as well as two viola players, accompany the band—he wasn't sure what he had expected, but he certainly hadn't expected to hear other string instruments added to the mix.

David leaned against the back railing as Alex entered to renewed applause. Alex wore his usual jeans and black T-shirt, his hair falling over his shoulders. As always, Alex's stage presence was palpable. The crowd responded to his easy, comfortable manner much as they had in Paris. Rock and roll became Alex, and David couldn't help but marvel at the incredible versatility of Alex's musicianship.

David's shoulders relaxed as he sipped his beer and took in the sound of the music. The mixture of strings, electric guitar, and the pulsing drumbeat was hypnotic. It was difficult not to get caught up in the energy of the music, powerful and driving. For a time, the music displaced the sound of Alex's melody in his mind, and he forgot his conflicted feelings.

David's thoughts strayed to the last time he'd seen Alex. Alex had so clearly wanted to engage him. And he, in turn, had wanted Alex.

Then why did you run?

He thought about John's visit. John was right, of course. Alex was all of those things: kind, talented, intelligent. And there was no denying he was an attentive and experienced lover. So why did David still hesitate?

You're afraid. It pained David to admit his fear. He'd spent too many years steeling himself against his grandfather's criticism. Leaving himself vulnerable to anyone, let alone someone for whom he cared deeply, was something he had learned to avoid. He knew he held Rachel at arm's length, allowing her to get close to him in controlled situations, and then only for short periods of time. He knew he could share even a tiny bit of himself with John because he saw him so rarely.

The set finished and the crowd cheered so loudly that the room rumbled and shook, bringing David back to himself. Alex bowed after joining the other band members on stage.

Time to leave. It wouldn't do to run into his sister or, worse, Alex himself. David set his empty glass down on the bar and turned to leave with just a quick glance back at the stage. For an instant, he saw Alex look directly at him. Then, without hesitation, David hurried out of the room and down the stairs, out into the late-summer night.

ALEX smiled and bowed to the audience. He hadn't had this much fun in months. Performing like this, without the pressure of the technically challenging classical repertoire to stand in his way, was pure heaven. One of the other string players turned to him and grinned. He bowed once again before wiping the sweat from his face with his shirt.

As he came up from his bow, he looked toward the back of the room. His breath caught in his throat as his eyes met David's.

Turnabout is fair play. He willed his heart to stop pounding against his ribs and did his best to ignore the dull ache in his chest that accompanied seeing David again.

The crowd roared louder, and he bowed for a third time. But when he looked back to the bar, David was gone.

What will it take, David, for you to admit the truth? How long do you need? He thought of the composition and of the dedication, and he smiled.

A FEW days later, during a rare period in which David was not working, Rachel convinced David to accompany her to the new modern wing at the Art Institute. She'd be leaving in two days, and David had resolved to spend more time with her this visit. The sun shone brightly, but the breeze coming off of Lake Michigan was refreshingly cool for late summer, so they decided to walk from their end of Michigan Avenue to the museum. From time to time, they stopped to do a little window-shopping, finally making their way to Millennium Park to watch the changing faces on the Crown Fountain.

As always, David said little. Rachel kept up a pleasant banter, telling him about her work and her newly renovated SoHo apartment. "I have three bedrooms now," she told him. "You have no excuse but to stay with me when you're in New York."

"I'd like that." He meant it too.

Rachel stopped and stared at him. "Who are you and what have you done with my brother?" she demanded with a broad grin.

"I haven't been very good about visiting you, have I?" To his surprise, he grinned back at her. The grin belied his discomfort, but the expression was genuine. "I'd really love to spend some time with you there."

She threw her arms around him and hugged him, nearly knocking him off-balance. His body tensed at the touch, and he forced himself to relax, finally putting his arms around her in a tentative embrace. "I do love you, you know," she said as she released him and headed off down the street.

He said nothing, truly at a loss for words. That he couldn't tell her the same, although he *felt* the same, shamed him into silence.

"I meant what I said. I love you, David." Alex's words reverberated in his mind.

"There's a wonderful Thai-French fusion restaurant that opened a few blocks away," Rachel said as they reached the corner. "I think you'll like it."

He watched her for a moment, then offered her a heartfelt smile and followed.

AFTER lunch, they stopped at the Art Institute. David told Rachel about the upcoming CSO schedule and about the new subscription series he was planning. Rachel, for her part, carefully avoided the topic of Alex, and David was grateful for it. Still, judging by the way she danced around the topic, he got the definite impression that his sister *wanted* to raise the subject but was biding her time or waiting for an opportune moment to do so.

Later, they took the bridge from the new modern wing over to Millennium Park. They ambled about the park, enjoying the summer flowers and watching the sailboats on Lake Michigan—something David rarely got to do, since he usually took the limousine from his apartment to Orchestra Hall. Rachel suggested they take the BP Bridge from Millennium Park to the cancer survivors' garden. The winding modern steel structure, designed as both a pedestrian bridge and sound barrier between Columbus Drive and the park, shone in the afternoon sun. As they strolled along the bridge, David glanced at the tall black high-rise in the near distance. Harbor Point. Alex's home.

Alex. Would he ever be able to wander the city and not think about him? Even now that he had finished the composition, David still heard the music when he thought of Alex.

It didn't seem to matter that the piece was finished—David still heard it everywhere, just as he saw Alex everywhere he looked. He shook his head as if to clear his thoughts, and he heard Rachel ask, "Is that the Pritzker Pavilion?"

He nodded, then paused, hearing the music once more.

I must be losing my mind.

"Do you hear something?"

"There must be a rehearsal at the Pritzker this afternoon," she said offhandedly. "I hadn't even noticed it until you asked."

David frowned before heading toward the open-air pavilion, only vaguely aware that Rachel was still following him. The music grew louder as they drew closer. Stopping at the edge of the raised structure, he looked up at the stage and blinked, as if he might wake up at any moment to discover he'd been dreaming.

"What...?" David fell silent as the enormity of what he was witnessing—what he was *hearing*—struck him. The chamber orchestra on stage was not just playing music, they were playing *his* music. He approached the stage, walking underneath the modern latticework and onto the grass.

The conductor stood, his back to the empty audience seating area, long white hair blowing about in the wind: John Fuchs. To John's left was Alex, dressed in jeans and a black T-shirt, fingers flying over the fingerboard of his instrument, bow moving in long, determined strokes.

"Why don't we sit down," Rachel said from behind him. "You look a little unsteady on your feet." Her voice sounded far away, and he realized he felt dizzy.

He followed her in silence and took a seat in the fifth row, still staring up at the stage in shock. He wasn't sure what surprised him more—the fact that he was sitting, listening to a piece of music he had never expected to hear performed, or that the music itself sounded as good as it did.

He felt a soft hand on his shoulder. "It's such a beautiful piece. We wanted you to hear it. To really *hear* it."

"We?"

"The people who love you."

He swallowed hard and clenched his jaw in an effort to control his emotions. He couldn't look at her. If he did, he knew he'd lose whatever was left of his resolve. He wanted to be angry, to stop the rehearsal. But he was the one who'd sent the piece to Alex. It had been more than just an expression of his gratitude and his love: he had *wanted* Alex to play it.

The soaring, glorious sound of Alex's fiddle rang out through the pavilion and mingled with the scent of fresh grass and the slightly tangy smell of the air off the lake. Dreamlike. Undeniably beautiful.

It wasn't until nearly halfway through the final movement that David understood the difference between this piece and the others he had composed before. He could hear it now as clearly as he heard the soaring line of the violin above the orchestra—the depth of his own emotions, transformed into sound. All these years, he'd heard the music the way it was meant to be, but when he wrote it down, he had filtered it through his fear. He'd stripped it of emotion. He'd made it *safe* to share, but he'd lost the essence of it. The recognition that *this* had been the missing element in this composition was at once revelatory and painful.

"WONDERFUL reading, everyone!" John Fuchs lowered his baton and offered Alex his hand in obvious gratitude. "Alex, words can't even begin to describe the joy I hear in your playing. It's as though the piece were written just for you."

Alex smiled awkwardly, happy that he'd had the presence of mind to remove the very personal dedication from the copy David had given him. Still, at John's words, he looked out into the audience. Rachel had obviously succeeded in bringing David here.

He may be angry with you. He felt almost sick, as if it were his first audition and his entire career was riding on its outcome. Regardless of David's reaction, it was worth the risk. David needed to understand that his music shouldn't be hidden away in the studio—that he'd created something that deserved to be shared with the world. Maybe David *had* understood it after all. Why else would he have shared something so personal?

Alex took a deep breath and looked back at John. "I should go. See what you can do to convince him to let us perform it next week."

"But certainly *you* would be the best man to do that, Alex." John gave him a knowing smile.

"I don't think so." Even from this distance, he could see David's face. As always, David's expression was unreadable. Distant. Alex figured David was angry, but he could live with that. Today had never been about him. It had always been about David. He doubted David would ever look at his own composition in the same way again.

It's a gift to you from all of us.

CHAPTER 26

DAVID watched Alex walk off stage, then saw John wave as he exited the stage to the wings. He appeared a moment later from behind the wall and walked up to the seating area.

"Rachel! David!" John wore a broad grin as he met them halfway up the aisle. "It's so good to see you both."

Rachel smiled and kissed John on both cheeks. "Thank you so much for playing through the piece. It sounded magnificent. You had me in tears."

"Maestro." David inclined his head and reached out to shake John's hand. John bypassed David's hand and put his arm around David's shoulders like an old friend. Together, they walked out of the formal seating area and onto the grass behind it.

"I really can't tell you how thrilled I was to hear your work," John said without missing a beat. The read-through so completely disarmed David that he did not voice his displeasure with his old mentor and made no effort to protest. "The piece is simply stunning."

"Thank you." Overwhelmed, David couldn't think of anything better to say.

"Sheer brilliance, if you ask me. It's almost as if the piece were written for Alex—"

"I didn't know you had planned a read-through today." The last thing David wanted at that moment was to rehash the discussion he and John had about Alex.

"Really?" Fuchs glanced at Rachel and winked. "But certainly you'll allow us to perform it at the upcoming festival."

"No." *And why not? You heard it for yourself. It's everything you hoped it would be, perhaps more.*

Fuchs raised his eyebrows and smiled. "Well, of course you *will* agree, David. The piece is too exceptional to gather dust on a shelf somewhere. Surely you must—"

"I do not wish it performed."

John stopped and looked at David carefully. "Why not?"

Because it hurts. Because it reminds me of what I've lost.

"My compositions are quite personal to me."

"You can't sell yourself short and hide your talent from the world. You must know what a breakthrough this is."

"No," David lied. "I do *not* know."

John frowned, then shook his head in obvious frustration. "This isn't about the music at all, is it?"

David said nothing as he struggled to school his expression.

"Go after him. Tell him you love him."

"I don't—"

"David." John sighed audibly. "I've known you too long. I know you love him. What are you waiting for? He's obviously in love with you. Couldn't you hear it? It was in every note he played."

"I…." He needed to get out of here, to go somewhere and think. He felt lightheaded, unfocused, as if he were about to… to what? To yell? To laugh? To *cry?*

"I'm very sorry, John," David managed to say. "I really need to be going." David didn't wait for John's reply before turning and heading out of the pavilion.

"David?"

David turned around. "Yes?"

"I could hear your soul in this music." John was smiling. "That is nothing to be ashamed of."

THE walk back to the apartment did David a world of good. The sun was setting as he reached the building, and David felt a bit more clearheaded, although he did not feel entirely focused. He skipped the elevator, opting instead for the stairs as he sometimes did when he needed time to think.

He took a deep breath as he reached the top of the stairs to his apartment. He still hadn't decided whether to allow John to perform the piece, but he knew that if there was to be a performance, no one but Alex would play the solo. No one else *could* play it the way David had intended it to be performed.

Alex. David felt warmth spread over his body at the realization that it had to have been Alex who'd asked John to conduct the piece. Had John come all the way from Central America just for this? What had Rachel said? *"We wanted you to hear it. The people who love you."*

His eyes burned. He gritted his teeth and willed away the tears that threatened. As he put his key in the lock, he heard music from inside. A violin. He wondered vaguely if Sarah had left the classical station on while she was straightening up and making dinner. He recognized the piece with its simple, straightforward melodic lines. Bach, Partita No. 3.

When he opened the door, the warm tone and unbridled enthusiasm of the performance enveloped him; he'd have recognized the style anywhere.

"Alex."

Alex turned away from the window as he finished the last few bars of the piece. "David. I hadn't intended to come, but John was right. He said I should be the one to ask you about performing the piece at the festival. Sarah said I could wait in the living room." He shifted on his feet and grinned at David like a child who had gotten caught with his hand in the cookie jar. "I got a little bored waiting. I hope you don't mind."

Mind? Why would I mind, if seeing you here makes me feel... something?

"There's no need to apologize." David tried to avoid looking Alex directly in the eyes, afraid Alex would see the barely contained emotions there.

Alex laughed and ran his fingers over the violin strings. "I have to admit that John's not the only reason I came today." He loosened the hair of his bow and began to pack his violin away. "I also wanted to tell you how incredible your composition is and apologize if my performing it disturbed you."

"It didn't disturb me." David hesitated a moment, then added, "I wrote it for you." *Hearing you play it moved me, made me want....*

Alex clicked the latches on the case closed and walked over to David, who had not moved since he had entered the room. Despite Alex's smile, his eyes reflected pain and longing.

He has done nothing to deserve the pain you have inflicted upon him. He has done his best to take away your own.

"Alex," David began, "I...."

"It's okay. I told you I would give you time. It was wrong of me to come here like this. I guess I just couldn't stay away."

"I am glad you came."

"You're glad I came, but...?"

David thought for a moment, then said, "There is no 'but'. I missed you. More than you know."

"It's good to hear that. Sometimes I don't know what to think about you... about us."

"Nor do I," David replied. It was the truth.

Alex nodded and smiled again. Then, picking up his violin case, he headed past David to the door. "I said I'd give you time." Alex repeated it as if he were trying to convince himself.

"I'm still glad you came." David rested his hand on Alex's shoulder. Just the feel of Alex's body beneath his fingers made him long to take him in his arms. "Alex." David turned Alex slowly around.

Alex stared at him.

"I want...." David pulled Alex toward him, compelled by a force greater than himself. The barest touch of their lips set his heart racing in his chest.

I love you.

Their kiss deepened, the months of hunger for the intimate and loving touch driving David to a depth of emotion he had never felt before. He ran his hands through Alex's hair, inhaled the scent of him, felt Alex's body respond as well as his own. His heart hurt, his body screamed for the contact, his soul moaned in agony, wanting more.

I can't do this. I'll lose myself in him.

He backed away from Alex in shock, his body still thrumming with need. "Please leave," David whispered, his voice sounding pathetic to his own ears. "I'm so sorry. I just can't...." David knew how much his words must have wounded Alex.

"I love you, David." David thought he heard a tremor in Alex's husky voice. "But it was wrong of me to come here. You told me you needed time. I should have respected that. I won't bother you again."

Alex turned and closed the front door without looking back. David stood, staring at the door, hoping it would open again and Alex would still be standing there.

IN THE hallway outside of the apartment, Alex leaned against the wall and exhaled. The elevator opened and Rachel stepped out.

"Alex?"

"Hey." He didn't attempt to force a smile.

"You look terrible. Is something wrong?"

"I…," he began. Then, thinking better of it, he said, "No. Nothing. My mistake."

Before she could answer, he stepped into the elevator. He hoped she'd forgive him.

"DAVID?"

David was still standing in the hallway when Rachel walked inside. It was as if he could still hear Alex's music ring throughout the apartment, and although he knew she was there, he said nothing. He wasn't sure he could speak even if he tried.

"Are you all right?"

"Perfectly." Of course he wasn't.

"Listen," she began, "I'm really sorry if the read-through today upset you."

"It didn't." The truth this time, but he had only just understood that it hadn't been the music that had rattled him. No, it was the realization that he didn't know how to move forward, that he'd been rationalizing his solitude for years. That even when he and Helena had been together, he'd been alone. He'd *chosen* to be alone. And now, faced with the prospect of change, he was lost. He'd never known anything but being alone.

"But then why—?"

"I'm going for a walk. Please don't wait up for me." He didn't look at her as he left a moment later.

CHAPTER 27

DAVID barely noticed the slight breeze off the lake. He walked for nearly an hour without paying attention to where he was headed—he only knew that he needed to think, to calm the storm of emotions that raged within him.

People were out and about, enjoying the last gasp of summer. The leaves on the trees in the park rustled with the late summer breeze as he made his way through the underpass to the sandy Lake Michigan shore. He noticed many couples on Oak Street Beach, some on blankets, others on benches, holding hands and talking in hushed tones under the faint glow of the pathway lights.

When he could walk no more, David sat in the sand and drew his knees to his chest, much like he had done as a child on the edge of the lake at the Connecticut mansion as he'd listened to the sounds of water lapping against the rocks. He glanced to his right and saw a young couple seated there, the woman's head on her lover's shoulder, their fingers intertwined. He closed his eyes and recalled an image of himself on just such a night, Helena in his arms.

"Do you ever wonder what we'll be like thirty years from now?" Helena asked.

"I'll be gray and even more foul-tempered. You, I have little doubt, will be even more beautiful than you are right now."

He couldn't imagine her ever growing old—he hadn't wanted to break the magic of a rare moment alone with her to think about their future. He lived for these fleeting moments; they were a welcome escape from the cold reality of his life, filled with commitments, duty, and conflict with his grandfather at home. Not to mention his guilt at not being a proper husband to her.

"You will not be foul-tempered. Not if I have anything to say about it." She kissed him on the cheek and held him tighter. "Are you happy, David?"

He closed his eyes at her touch. "As happy as I've ever been. To be here, with you...."

The sound of voices stirred David out of his reverie. An older couple wandered across the beach in their bare feet. Like the younger pair, they held hands. The woman caught his eye and smiled at him as they passed. Seeing the woman smile, David wondered if the reason he had never envisioned himself growing old with Helena was that he knew instinctively that it couldn't last.

Perhaps there are people who can never truly find happiness. The words echoed hollow this time. He had believed it once, or rather, he'd believed the words described him.

He saw Helena's face, pale and wan. Her skin was nearly translucent, her tiny body nothing more than a whisper of its former self. He had been sitting at her bedside for days. She was dying. And yet in his heart, he still held out hope—it was far better than imagining the pain of living without her.

She drifted in and out of consciousness, and his own existence didn't feel much more solid. He ate the food put in front of him— tasteless and dull, much like how he felt. He truly loved her, loved her spirit, loved the warmth and security her friendship gave him. But his love alone was not enough to sustain her.

"You really must sleep, David." Her voice was less than a whisper. Had she been awake and watching him?

"I'm fine." He had repeated those words a hundred times before to friends, family, and to her. He would not burden her with his suffering.

"No, you're not."

"Rachel will be here soon." He had waited longer than he should have to tell her to come. Some part of him had reasoned that if Rachel weren't here, Helena wouldn't die.

Helena's eyes lit up at his words. "You'll take care of her, won't you?"

"She'll have enough money that she'll never want for anything."

Helena smiled sadly, and David took her hands in his. "The only thing she needs is your love."

Helena passed away less than a day later. She would have celebrated her twenty-seventh birthday in three months. James Somers never accepted Rachel's adoption, although he never cut David out of his will as he'd once threatened to do in retaliation. James died only a few months later—at work and alone. Despite the fact that his grandfather had shown him little more than disapproval and scorn over the years, David had cried when the old man died.

Had he been as distant with Rachel as his grandfather had been with him? *No, you've shown her affection.* Still, he knew he had never fully given of himself to her. He hesitated every time he saw her, every time he hugged her. And in spite of this, she accepted him with all her heart and loved him as he would always want a sister to love him.

Now he had pushed Alex away. Alex, who had lost so much in his life yet did not fear to lose again. Alex, who had done nothing but show him kindness—who loved him despite his cold heart.

David's eyes filled with tears. In the darkness, he knew no one would see him cry, but he didn't care if they could. In the darkness, his heart broke for the little boy who barely knew the love of a mother and father, for the man who had lost his best friend far too young, for the disappointment of reading reviews of his work and knowing they only told the truth, for the times he pushed his sister away, for the man who loved him despite his fear and made no excuses for it.

Alex. So different from Helena. They'd both loved him; he knew that. But where Helena had held his hand and led him through the difficult times, Alex expected him to stand on his own two feet. And what had he done? He'd run away like a fearful child. He'd run from nearly every relationship he'd had. Loneliness was easier than pain. Had he learned that from his grandfather?

He sat in the sand, his face wet. He lost track of time. He cried until he had no more tears to shed, then took a deep breath, pulled his phone from his pocket, and tapped it as he walked over to the water's edge.

The voice on the other end of the line sounded sleepy.

"I'm sorry to be calling so late, John."

"Please don't apologize, David, I was just about to turn in," John Fuchs replied. "I'm happy to hear from you anytime. What can I do for you?"

"You have my permission to perform my work." David inhaled the sweet scent of the water. "There is, however, one condition I must insist upon."

"Of course," John replied. "Anything."

"Alex Bishop must play the solo."

CHAPTER 28

"ALEX?"

Alex cradled the phone between his shoulder and chin. "What's up, Mar?"

"Rachel and I are heading over to the Velvet Lounge to hear some jazz. You interested?"

"Nah." Alex sat on the couch wearing only his pajama bottoms, listening to Mahler and drinking a beer, his bare feet on the coffee table. "You guys have fun."

"You sure?" She had that motherly, overly concerned tone of voice that irritated him to no end.

"Look," he snapped, "would you please stop worrying about me?"

"Not possible." He figured she'd say that.

"Have fun." He also figured ignoring her was the best approach. "I'll see you later." He hung up before she could speak again, then went into the living room and lit the gas fireplace.

Fifteen minutes later, there was a knock on the apartment door. "Damn." Of course she'd come and try to coerce him into going out with them. He shook his head and padded over to the door. "Look, Marla, I really don't want to—"

It wasn't Marla standing at the door.

"David? I'm sorry, I thought...." *Fuck. Handled, as always, so tactfully!*

"May I come in?" David looked a bit windblown, his pale skin flushed, his hair disheveled. It was the hottest thing Alex could imagine, and he hoped the twitch of his jaw muscle hadn't betrayed his body's reaction to seeing David like this.

"Of course." Alex motioned David in and closed the door behind him.

David strode into the living room. He still exuded the same controlled confidence, and yet this time, Alex sensed something different about him. He seemed determined. As if he needed to say something and it couldn't wait a moment longer.

Before Alex could even ask why David had come, David said, "I have agreed to let John conduct *Tattoos* at the festival."

Alex grinned.

"This pleases you?"

"Of course. Why wouldn't it? Do you have that little faith in your talent?"

"I… yes." David's blunt and honest response took Alex aback. He'd known all along that David constantly doubted himself, but he hadn't expected to hear such a proud man admit his weakness.

"I've always doubted my abilities." In spite of David's composure, Alex saw something raw and vulnerable in David's eyes. "Does that surprise you?"

"No." Alex had no reason to be anything but honest in his response. "I just didn't expect you to admit it."

David smiled. "I gave John my blessing to perform the piece under one condition." Alex raised an eyebrow but remained silent. "I want you to play the solo." Alex thought he saw a brief flash of fear in David's eyes.

He's worried I'll say no.

"It would be an honor."

At these words, David's face relaxed and he released an audible breath. "Thank you." David ran a hand through his hair and attempted another smile. This one looked far less convincing, and Alex guessed he had something difficult he wanted to say. Alex tried to ignore the butterflies in his gut and schooled his expression, expecting the worst.

David shifted his weight from one foot to the other and rubbed the bridge of his nose. "Alex," he said, "it's true that I wanted to tell you about the piece." He took a deep, audible breath, then continued, "But I really didn't come here to tell you about the concert. I came here to apologize."

Alex wasn't sure what he'd expected, but he certainly hadn't expected this. "Apologize? For what?"

"For being an ass." This time David met Alex's gaze unflinchingly. The determination Alex had seen before was back. "I treated you poorly." David seemed almost compelled to speak, as though if he stopped now, he would forget how to form the words. "You've been nothing but kind to me. You don't deserve to be treated that way." David stood straighter and raised his chin, the tiny lines around his mouth more visible.

"What do you want, David?" Alex reminded himself that he could handle David's rejection, though he was having a hard time believing it.

David reached out and touched Alex's face with his right hand, running his fingertips over Alex's cheekbone and jaw. "I want *this*." David's voice was barely a whisper. "I want *you.*"

Alex repressed a shudder at the words. "David," he said as he fought his body's visceral response to David's gentle touch, "you don't have to do this. I meant it when I said I would wait for you."

"I don't need to wait. I'm tired of being alone. I'm tired of wishing I was with you, tired of seeing you in everything I do, in everywhere I go, in the notes I put to paper." He paused for a moment, his fingers brushing Alex's lips. "I'm tired of being afraid of losing you while pushing you away at the same time. I—"

Alex kissed David with a deep, reassuring kiss that made Alex feel as though he was floating.

"You still want me, even after I've been so cold to you?"

"You haven't always been cold." Alex took David's face in his hands and offered him a reassuring smile. "I've felt warmth and passion from you. I hear it in your music. But I admit I almost gave up hope about us—until you sent me the music and I read the dedication."

"When I heard you play the piece, months ago, I wanted so much for you to like it." Alex knew the words were difficult for David.

"I *did* like it. But I never should have—"

"Yes. You *should* have told me the truth. But you knew I wasn't ready to hear it, so you hesitated. You knew I was afraid. And I knew it too. I pressed you until you had no choice. I wanted an excuse to push you away, like I've pushed everyone else in my life away."

Alex nodded. He had no idea what to say.

"After you left, I tried to work on the music again." David shook his head and let out a bitter laugh. "Then one day, weeks after you had gone…. The pain of losing you…. It was like a revelation. I finally heard what I'd been trying to hear for months." He looked at Alex, clearly at a loss for words.

"Earlier tonight, you asked me to leave. And now? What's changed?"

"I don't want to spend the rest of my life alone. It's not an easy thing for me to admit, that I might *need* someone. That I need *you*."

"Thank God." Alex pulled David to him and claimed his lips, reveling in the feel of David's body against his own. David's face was slightly rough, the hint of shadow on his cheeks only serving to intensify Alex's hunger.

"I love you." David spoke the words in an undertone against Alex's cheek.

"David." Alex's voice sounded hoarse to his own ears. He forced his eyes open, wanting to take in every aspect of the chiseled face, the slate-gray eyes with the hint of blue, the way David's dark hair fell onto his shoulders like silk.

"When you told me you loved me," David said, sounding breathless, "I didn't want to hear it. Do you still feel the same? Because—"

"I love you, David. That never changed. It's why I couldn't stay away. It's why I waited." Alex chuckled. "It's why I've nearly worn out my recording of the Mahler *Resurrection*."

"Mahler?"

"Marla has her Ben and Jerry's. I have Mahler."

David laughed, a genuine, uninhibited laugh that lit up his entire face. "You both have good taste." His laughter still rang about the room as he pushed Alex onto the couch and pinned Alex's wrists against the leather. He ran his tongue along Alex's forearms, sucked on each finger, exploring every inch of skin. "Or should I say, you taste good?"

"Works for me."

"Good." David pulled off Alex's shirt, taking his time to reveal the skin beneath, then stopped for a moment and gazed down at him with obvious hunger.

"Something wrong?"

"No." David's voice was low and full of emotion. "I just wanted to look at you."

"What do you see?"

"My future." David's smile faded and his lips tightened at the admission.

Alex drew David's face to his and kissed him. David's body was like an overtensioned violin bow, almost but not quite resisting Alex's kiss. Alex understood how much trust David placed in him, that he was willing to admit the depth of his feelings. "Good," he said, echoing David's reply of a moment before. "Because I see you in mine."

At those words, David's entire demeanor changed. He melted into Alex just as Alex melted into him. They held each other like that, the only sounds their breathing and the beating of their hearts. Alex would have been content to stay like that forever. "You're much more of a romantic than you're willing to admit, you know."

"That's between you and me," David said. "A secret. God forbid Doris learns the truth. I'll never hear the end of it."

Alex laughed and pulled David off the couch.

"Where are we going?"

"Stay right there." Alex ducked into his bedroom and grabbed a comforter. A moment later he set it in front of the fireplace and grinned at David. "What good is a rug in front of a fireplace if it's just to look at?"

"Marla?"

"Out late." Alex opened his arms, and this time David didn't hesitate.

"I like this. Holding you."

"Me too." Alex carded his hands through David's soft hair. It had grown longer since they'd been apart, and Alex decided he liked it that way. "Kiss me, Maestro. And tell me you love me."

"I love you, Alex." David took Alex's face in his hands and kissed his nose, his chin, then his lips, the kiss deepening as they both kneeled on the quilt. The fire hissed, but the only thing Alex noticed was the hushed exhale of David's breath against his cheek. "Lie down. Let me show you."

IN THE early hours of the morning, the telephone rang. Alex grabbed the receiver without opening his eyes.

"Hmm?"

"Is it safe to come home now?"

Alex laughed. "Marla, have you been spying?"

"Rachel gave me a heads-up when David didn't come back. She was pretty worried about him, so I told her I'd check if he was with you."

David opened his eyes and smiled. Alex's heart nearly burst—he looked so happy. So peaceful.

"And?" Alex winked at David.

"You tell me."

"He's here."

"Good." He heard the satisfaction in her voice. "I'm on my way home. I'll see you both later."

CHAPTER 29

One year later

ALEX glared at his cell phone as he made his way through Charles de Gaulle Airport. "Look, Tiffany," he growled, "I know Maestro Guest was expecting me tomorrow. All I'm asking is that you tell him I'll be there a day later than I promised. It's not like there's a rehearsal tomorrow anyhow."

He listened for a moment, holding the phone away from his ear and shaking his head. "No, I can't get Marla to call him. She's on a cruise in the Mediterranean. Yes, I understand you're not my secretary, but—"

"Look, Tiffany," he began again, with the most patience he could muster. "I'm in Paris. They have the most amazing chocolate here. If I promise you I'll bring back a pound—all right, a kilo or two—will you do me a favor and let Guest's people know I'll be a day later than planned? I'll FedEx the candy tomorrow morning, okay?"

He grabbed his bag off the carousel, juggling his violin in the other hand, phone held against his ear by his shoulder. "Thank you so much, Tiffany. I owe you one—" He laughed. "—okay, *two*."

He touched the phone and popped it back into his pocket, then caught his suitcase before it toppled to the ground. He glanced at his watch.

Shit. I'm going to be late. Damn Italian flights!

He dashed outside the terminal and hailed a taxi. *"Le Zénith, s'il vous plaît,"* he told the driver as he settled into the back seat.

Forty-five minutes later, he hopped out of the cab and dashed into the front lobby of the theatre. *"Complète"* read the sign on the placard in the lobby.

"Damn." *I should have known it would have sold out.*

He'd never missed a performance of David's original works, despite his hectic schedule. He walked up to the ticket booth and, donning his most charming smile, said to the attendant in perfect French, "Excuse me, miss, but I really must get inside to hear the concert."

"I'm so sorry," she answered, barely glancing up from her papers, "but the show is sold out and it's already started...." She finally looked up at him and Alex saw recognition in her expression. "Monsieur Bishop? I... I had no idea.... Please, let me help you." Alex breathed a sigh of relief.

Five minutes later, he was seated high in the balcony, in one of the only remaining seats. He took a deep breath, closed his eyes, and smiled.

Happy birthday, Maestro. You've outdone yourself again.

IT WAS nearing midnight when David walked into his hotel room. He'd tried to escape the party afterward with little success. He'd been on the road too long—he'd been ready to go home to Chicago for weeks now. There was a light on in the bedroom, and he wondered vaguely if the maid had been in to turn down the bed. As he walked into the sitting area, however, he saw a small table set with china, lightly fragrant flowers, lit candles, and a bottle of wine chilling in a bucket stand.

"Happy birthday, David." Alex stood in the doorway of the bedroom wearing David's black silk robe.

"I hadn't expected to see you." David walked over to Alex, wrapped his arms around Alex's waist, then brushed his lips over

Alex's. Denial for now. Later, he would thoroughly ravish those lips. "I thought you were flying to Vienna tonight."

"Was. I had to promise Tiffany a few pounds of French chocolate to make it here."

David shook his head. Far be it from him to question the ways of Hollywood agents or their employees.

"Don't even try to understand it. It's too surreal. Consider it my birthday present to you. Or one of them, that is."

David kissed Alex, plundering his mouth. As if Alex would complain. "I missed you." David allowed himself a single contented sigh.

"The chamber piece is gorgeous." Alex's lips were now a tantalizing inch from David's ear.

"You were there?" He didn't attempt to disguise his pleasure at the knowledge that Alex had come to the performance.

"Nosebleed section. I figured I'd surprise you here rather than fight the crowds backstage."

David stepped back and pulled a newspaper out of his coat pocket. He'd almost forgotten he was still wearing his coat. "*The International Herald Tribune* review, from last night's preview concert."

"I'm sorry I couldn't be there." Alex took the paper, which was open to the arts section. "*David Somers's newest composition,* The Muse, *will have its premiere tomorrow night at Paris's Le Zénith. The preview audience reveled in the unparalleled blend of romantic modernism and technically challenging scoring of Maestro Somers's composition. Maestro Somers, music director of the Chicago Symphony Orchestra, conducted his own work before a standing-room-only crowd.... This writer sincerely hopes that Maestro Somers's 'muse' continues to delight the classical music world with more masterpieces in years to come. 'The Muse' is truly a triumph.*"

"An adequate review." David watched Alex for his reaction.

"You're joking, right?"

"Yes." David laughed and pulled his coat off, then tossed it onto the sofa. "I'm surprised at your lack of faith in me. I've proven to you over and over again that I'm quite capable of making a joke, and yet you still doubt me." He leaned in and kissed Alex.

"But what's this next bit? *Maestro Somers will also premiere a work featuring piano and violin next month at Le Club Jazz in Paris?*" Alex frowned and raised an eyebrow. "I certainly hope no one else is premiering that work with you, *Maestro*. I've been waiting forever to hear you compose something a bit more 'out of the box'."

"That long? If I'd known, I'd have written it sooner." He chuckled and walked over to the table to pour them both some wine. "But to answer your question—no, I have *you* booked for the premiere. I wouldn't think of performing it with anyone else. Of course if you intend to renege on your contract, I'll be sure to contact your agent."

"I don't know. I'm thinking I'll renege just so I can see your face when Tiffany answers the phone." David ignored this and handed Alex his glass of wine. "But seriously, I don't remem—"

"That's because you still never check your calendar."

Alex pulled his phone out of the pocket of the robe, tapped one of the icons, and gave David a sheepish look. "My bad.... How can I make it up to you?" He tossed the phone onto the couch, then sidled up to David and began to nip at his neck.

"I'll consider the proper punishment. In the meantime, I'm sure you can manage something to satisfy me. Two weeks is far too long. Besides, as you so thoughtfully pointed out, it *is* my birthday." He kissed Alex's lips and released a slow breath.

DAVID set his empty glass on the table by the remains of their dinner. He stood up and held out his hand.

"I love you, David."

"Am I so obvious?"

"No." Alex squeezed his hand, then kissed it, his lips lingering over David's skin. "Not obvious. Human."

"I love you too."

The corners of Alex's mouth edged upward. "You're not the only one who needs to hear it."

David reached down and untied the sash of Alex's robe before pushing it off his shoulders. He took a moment just to steal a look at Alex's naked body. In the semidarkness of the candlelight, the wild tattoos that covered Alex's body resembled dancing notes on a page.

"Turn around." David whispered the words. He didn't want to interrupt the sound of the music that still accompanied Alex's presence. Not the same music as before—it never was the same—but it was just as beautiful. More so, perhaps. He reached out and gently touched the black markings on Alex's back.

When had it happened? When had the intricate patterns become the music from his dreams? David followed the trail of markings on Alex's body with his lips, and Alex's breath hitched in reply.

"David." Alex gasped as David reached the slight indentation at the base of his neck.

"Shhhh…." David nibbled his way across a wavy line of ink. "I can only hear the music this way."

"Music?"

"Why do you think I called the piece *The Muse*?" David led Alex to the bed and pushed him down, then straddled him. Slowly, deliberately, David began to map out every inch of Alex's exposed skin, tasting it, feeling it—seeing the music in his mind's eye, hearing the rhythm synchronized with Alex's breathing. He reached the place on Alex's chest where Alex's heart beat; he felt the vibration in his lips as he lingered there.

"What do you hear?" Alex asked.

David closed his eyes and listened. "I hear *you*, Alex. My love, my muse, my teacher, my partner, my desire, my inspiration. I hear the music in your soul, and it becomes my own."

Alex sighed, then dropped his arms to his sides and arched his back, his body determined to meet his lover's. David ghosted his fingers over the rough skin of the scar, then bent down to kiss it. He often wondered why that scar held so much interest for him. He'd come to believe that it served as a connection between them—the shared experience of pain.

"Did you get the tattoos to cover the scar?" he asked Alex before kissing it tenderly.

"No. I wanted to feel the pain." Alex's face was peaceful, and he appeared genuinely pleased that David had asked.

"I don't understand." David kissed the scar again.

"Tattooing hurts more over scar tissue."

"But then why...? Why hurt yourself where you've already been hurt?"

"The tatau—the process for creating the Pe'a—is meant to be painful. It's something you endure. It makes you stronger. It's a symbol of courage." Alex carded his hand through David's hair, a reassuring gesture that let David know not only that his questions were welcome but that Alex wanted to share this with him.

"When I was knifed," Alex continued, "I had no choice. I defended myself, and I nearly died. But the tattoos"—he took David's hand and covered the scar with it—"they were *my* choice. I chose to experience the pain. To make it my own."

"You covered the pain. Just like you covered the scar."

Alex nodded and smiled. "The pain became my strength."

"It's beautiful." David's eyes burned as he too smiled. David skimmed his hand over the taut skin of Alex's abdomen, playing the sensitive skin like an instrument.

"Feels so good. Please.... More...."

David continued to explore Alex's torso with his gossamer touch, drawn once more to the firm lines of the black ink, hearing the music in his mind, seeing it taking shape on Alex's skin. He heard the violins in the shimmer of Alex's hair, and he lingered there, the soft strands between his fingertips. The powerful muscles in Alex's arms evoked the distant thunder of the timpani. The smooth line of Alex's jaw became the sound of the woodwinds, the slight hollow of his cheeks the violas, the arch of his brow the cellos. David heard the orchestra as if it resonated from Alex's soul.

"Alex," he whispered, overcome by the beauty of the music and the man.

In her last incarnation, SHIRA ANTHONY was a professional opera singer, performing roles in such operas as *Tosca*, *Pagliacci*, and *La Traviata*, among others. She's given up TV for evenings spent with her laptop, and she never goes anywhere without a pile of unread M/M romance on her Kindle.

Shira is married with two children and two insane dogs, and when she's not writing, she is usually in a courtroom trying to make the world safer for children. When she's not working, she can be found aboard a thirty-foot catamaran at the Carolina coast with her favorite sexy captain at the wheel.

Shira can be found on Facebook, Goodreads, or on her website, http://www.shiraanthony.com. You can also contact her at shiraanthony @hotmail.com.

VENONA KEYES is a modern woman who believes in doing it all; if doing it all is only in her head. She amazes people that she can be wholly unorganized yet pack a perfect carryon suitcase for a ten-day trip to Paris. Ms. Keyes is a believer in the just in time theory, and can be seen sprinting in airports to the gate before the plane door closes.

Venona has experienced love and loss at the deepest level, and is thankful for writing and daydreaming, for it kept, and still keeps her sane. Writing also introduced her to some of the most supportive and wonderful people, to which she will always be grateful.

Venona is a voracious reader, loves her two feline boys, volunteers at an animal shelter, is an accomplished speaker, enjoys swimming, biking, skipping, and her beloved over-grown garden.

You can find Venona Keyes on Facebook and can email her at VenonaKeyes@yahoo.com.

The BLUE NOTES series

BLUE NOTES

SHIRA ANTHONY

http://www.dreamspinnerpress.com

Also in the BLUE NOTES series

THE MELODY THIEF

SHIRA ANTHONY

A BLUE NOTES NOVEL

http://www.dreamspinnerpress.com

Also in the BLUE NOTES series

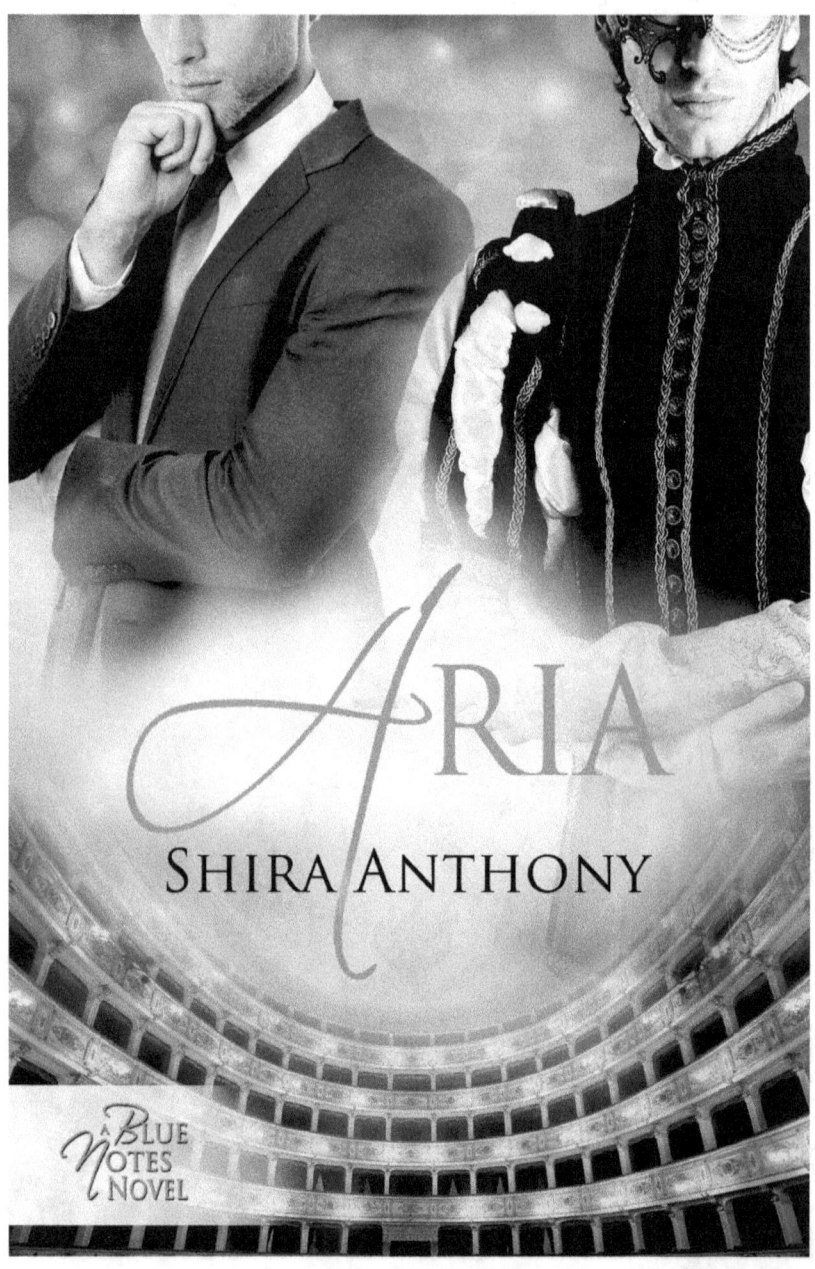

ARIA

SHIRA ANTHONY

A BLUE NOTES NOVEL

http://www.dreamspinnerpress.com

Also from SHIRA ANTHONY & VENONA KEYES

http://www.dreamspinnerpress.com

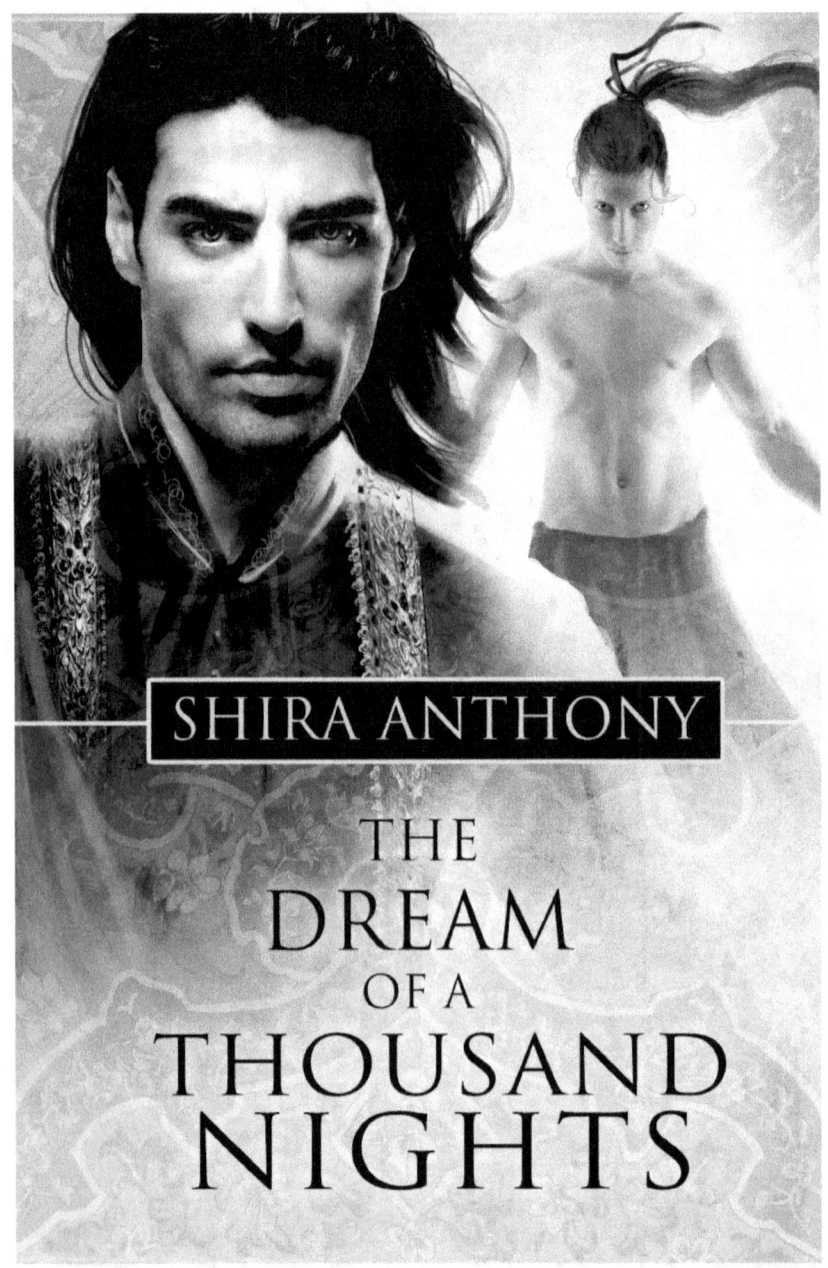

Read more from VENONA KEYES in